CIRCLES IN HELL SERIES

Beelzebub: A Memoir

A Circles in Hell Novel

by

Mark Cain

ISBN-13: 9781089881025

'Beelzebub: A Memoir' is published by Perdition Press, which can be contacted at:

MarkCainWrites.com

Cover art by Dan Wolfe (www.doodledojo.co.uk)

To Michael. Counselor, collaborator, cheerleader, friend.

Beelzebub: A Memoir

As told to

Mark Cain

Foreword

I live close to Austin, on the edge of the Texas Hill Country, an arid though affable region of the state that has been described by many as not dissimilar to Tuscany. That seems a bit generous to me. Maybe Tuscany after a thousand-year drought. Still, this portion of the Lone Star State has its own subtle beauty.

Northerners, familiar with the picture-perfect landscapes of the Hudson Highlands or the Berkshires, or perhaps the lush, verdant rain forest that is the Pacific Northwest, would probably disagree. They might offer up the old joke that if the Devil owned Texas, he'd rent it out and live in Hell.

Ha.

My house is on slightly less than two acres of heavily wooded land, surrounded by other houses on lots that are also slightly less than two acres of heavily wooded land. The result is that I am afforded a fair measure of privacy.

It suits me. I'm a loner who never married, has little family and fewer friends. It's not that I dislike people. I just like the absence of them better.

By profession I am a writer. What do I write? Anything, really. Magazine articles, an occasional book of non-fiction, novels. I have never, until the present volume, however, written a biography. Or, rather, ghost-written an autobiography.

But I'm getting ahead of myself. How I found myself to be the writer, or at least transcriber, of this tale is a story in itself that I shall relate here in brief.

My back yard has a pool and a spa, both completely hidden from the outside world by the house itself and the surrounding trees. My home, as well as these two giant bathtubs, one cold, one hot, are luxuries I afforded myself out of the royalties of a book I wrote a few years back on social networking. Why that particular effort of mine sold a million copies is beyond me. I don't even understand the topic, but give me a blank page and I can blather out anything, and the blathering almost always makes me money. It's a gift, and my mother told me never to look a gift horse in the mouth. This expression has always seemed strange to me, though, if I'm honest, so has my mother. But never mind.

To continue, I have these two bodies of water just outside my back door. I am fond of floating in my pool in the heat of the summer and parboiling myself in the hot tub during the winter. Out here, in the Hill Country, we still have a little bit of night sky left, and I enjoy seeing the faint blur of the Milky Way as I immerse myself in water.

I don't know how much longer I'll be able to do that. (See our galaxy, that is. I suspect I'll be able to get wet for many years to come.) The light of encroaching civilization makes the Milky Way fainter each year.

But back to my two ponds. Last January, on the twentieth, I believe, I was sitting in my hot tub, sipping on an IPA from a plastic tumbler, and soaking up the water's 103-degree heat, while breathing air chilled to below thirty, unusually cold for my part of the world. The hour was late, nearly midnight, and I was staring up, where the overcast skies had suddenly parted to reveal a full moon, a Supermoon, and it seemed to fill half the sky. Because it was the first full moon of the year, it was also dubbed a "wolf moon." The satellite was an unusual color, a rusty red. This was a rare event, a super blood wolf moon. More significantly, I was watching a total lunar eclipse.

Only later did I learn that such an event has been viewed throughout history as an ill omen.

As I was gazing upward, there was a loud, "Kerplop!" beside me. Half the water of the hot tub was displaced, flowing over the lip of the tub into the swimming pool beneath. In an instant, the temperature of the remaining water hopped up at least twenty degrees.

At the same moment, there was a noise like thunder, accompanied by the sulfurous smell of rotten eggs.

"Yikes!" I yelled, jumping by instinct into the pool, which, like most Texas cement ponds, is kept full of water year-round.

That hop was not well-conceived. The sudden temperature change between the heated spa water and the cool of the pool knocked the wind from my lungs, shriveling up the old gonads and damn near stopping my heart. My survival instinct kicked into overdrive, and I scrambled out of the pool almost as quickly as I got in.

"Why the hell did you do that?" said a deep, raspy voice from the hot tub.

Leaning back against the limestone rim of the spa, as he took full occupancy of the tub, was a giant. He must have been at least seven feet tall and over seven hundred pounds, maybe more. The superheated water didn't seem to bother him, though maybe it did, because his skin was ruddy to the point of being red. He had a forked beard. On his head, he wore a black fez.

And he had horns, like a bull's, growing from his temples.

"Who ... who are you?" I gasped, backing away.

The giant grabbed my terry cloth robe from where it lay draped across one side of the tub and tossed it to me. "Put that on. Your teeth are chattering. Besides, I don't want to stare at your dinky while we talk. You know, people shouldn't skinny dip, not even in their own backyards. It isn't dignified." As he spoke, I heard a strange buzzing whenever he landed on a zee sound. Perhaps it was a speech impediment, but it made him sound like a swarm of mosquitos.

The horned creature stood in the tub, and I could see he was wearing a black Speedo. "Observe," he said, again buzzing a zee. "Dignity, man. Always dignity."

I don't know how a seven-hundred-pound giant wearing a Speedo could consider himself dignified. He looked like a Russian oligarch fresh from a swim near his dacha in the Crimea. Pretty grotesque. Not that I said that out loud. Terror held my tongue. With an effort, though, I again asked, "Who are you?"

"I'm Beelzebub."

As if his name summoned them, a hundred insects flew out of nowhere and began orbiting his head. In irritation, he waved them away.

"The ... the Lord of the Flies?" I managed to croak. I think it's perfectly reasonable that I was terrified. This was, after all, my first supernatural encounter.

He scratched his crotch. "The very same. Also, one of the princes of Hell." He looked at me, eyebrows arched. "Impressed? And close your mouth before a fly flies in it."

Under the circumstances, that seemed like wise counsel. I shut my trap and fell backward into a nearby deck chair. "I thought you were a myth."

"Yes and no." Then he grinned at me, revealing a long black canine. A tooth, that is. Not a dog. For some reason, the sight set me to shivering again. Well, that and the frigid air. Along with still being wet, icicles were beginning to form in my nostrils.

"Cold?" he asked, mildly amused. He pointed at me, and from his finger came a blast of heat that struck my robe. Now I felt as if I'd just come out of the steam room at the gym. Despite my panic, I was grateful to be warm.

"Thank ... thank you."

"No problem." Beelzebub sat down on the ledge of the hot tub, regarding me intently.

We sat there for a minute, sizing each other up. At last I ventured, "Why are you here? Are you going to drag me down to the fires of Hell?" I thought, ruefully, that he'd be within his rights. I wasn't much of a believer, and my body of good works, beyond the occasional check to the World Wildlife Fund, was pretty meager.

"Maybe later," he said, grinning again. "No, I want to hire you."

"Hire me?" I said in surprise.

"You *are* a writer, aren't you?"

"Well, yes, that's how I make my living."

He nodded. "A pretty successful one, too. I've read your stuff. You're competent, if not particularly talented."

"Hey!" I protested, offended. "I may not be Shakespeare, but I get the job done."

Beelzebub rolled his eyes when I mentioned the Bard. "That blowhard. Why say anything in seven words when you can do it in seventy? He's almost as bad as Melville. No, that's why I came to you, because you *do* get the job done, quickly, efficiently. I like efficiency."

"Oh," I said, mollified. "And what do you want me to write?"

"My autobiography."

"You mean your biography, don't you? You have to write your own for it to be an autobiography."

The Lord of the Flies snorted. "Come on. All those Hollywood types coming out with autobiographies. You know most of them can't write worth a crap. They wouldn't know subject and predicate from shit and pee. They hire ..."

"Ghost writers," I said, finishing his sentence.

"Precisely."

"And that's what you want me to do?"

Beelzebub shook his head. "No, not really. First off, it will be more of a memoir. My life has been too long to pen a comprehensive biography. What we need is a shorter volume, focusing on a handful of incidents in my past, the ones that led up to me becoming a prince of Hell. Oh, and I'll dictate the story verbatim. You just need to write it down."

"Why me?" I asked. A fly had just landed on the arm of my chair. I'd always hated the irritating little bugs. Instinctively, I flattened it with a swat of my hand.

"That's one reason," the devil said. "You hate flies as much as I do."

"But you're the Lord of the Flies."

"Yes," he said with disgust. "It's one of my least favorite job responsibilities, but never mind about that. You also type over a hundred words a minute, don't you?"

"Yes." I was surprised he knew this about me.

"Which means you can keep up with me as I talk."

"I, I guess so."

Beelzebub cracked his knuckles. The noise sounded like thunder. "I don't really need you. I could just conjure up the complete book, like this." There was a flash of light, and in his palm was a ream of paper. Then he waved his free hand over it, and the pages turned to ash. "But that's too easy. I feel like talking. Besides, I'm bored, and I have time."

"How much time?" I asked, wondering if I'd be working under a deadline.

"All the time in the world," he grumbled. "An eternity, in fact."

All this talk of flies and typing had lessened my fear of the devil. I was pacing now, contemplating the prospect of playing secretary to a prince of Hell. "Why would I want to do this?"

Beelzebub smirked. "To keep me from dragging you down to Hell?"

My heart started to pound.

He chuckled. "Relax. I'm just kidding. First off, you can put your name on the book and sell it."

I rubbed my chin, feeling a stubble of beard. "Don't know that there's much money in it. Only autobiographies of celebrities really sell, and since most people don't even believe you exist ..."

He shrugged. "Okay, I'll give you an advance against future sales. Five million now." He waved his hand, and a suitcase appeared next to me. I opened it and found it full of thousand-dollar bills. "Five million when you finish. Oh, you might want to close that mouth again."

I did and swallowed hard. "I can't use this much cash," I said, holding up a fistful of bills. "The IRS would be on my butt in two seconds."

"Of course," the devil said. "The IRS. One of my greatest inventions."

"You invented the Internal Revenue Service?"

"I just said that, didn't I?"

"My God! You really *are* evil!"

"Thanks for the compliment. But I see your predicament." He waved his hand again, and the suitcase disappeared. The bills in my hand turned into some sort of passbook.

"What's this?"

"For your records. I've just deposited the five million into a Swiss bank account in your name. Untraceable. As I was saying, five million now, five million when you're done. Deal?"

"Uh…" My mind raced. Transcribing the memoir of Beelzebub. A devil. A creature of pure evil. Still … the money was good. "O … okay."

"Excellent!" he said, hopping off the rim of the pool. For a seven-foot gargantua, he was very agile. Beelzebub grabbed my hand in a vise-like grip. "Oh, and you can call me Beezy. It's less of a mouthful. We start tomorrow, say eleven a.m.?"

"Uh, sure. Where?"

"Your office." As a writer, I worked from home. "For now, I have some errands to run." With that, he disappeared.

I stared, mouth agape, at the spot where the Lord of the Flies had just been standing. About a hundred bug bodies lay on the concrete in a ring the size of the devil's belly.

For the next month, Beelzebub appeared in my office promptly at eleven each morning, five days a week. He would talk for about an hour, and I would type as fast as I could, trying to keep up with him.

The words that follow are entirely his, with no modifications on my part at all. About the only contribution I made was convincing him that trying to mimic his buzzing speech impediment in the narrative would distract the reader. With some reluctance, he agreed, to my great relief. If he hadn't, I would have had to type all those z's with my left pinkie, and that's my weakest finger.

– M. Cain, Spring 2019

Chapter 1

There was nothing, and then there was something. I was aware.

My eyes fluttered open. *Wow!*

I was staring at the Creator of the Universe.

There were others like me, all around, sharing in the Ultimate Spectacle. A word entered my consciousness. Angels. They're angels, just as I am.

But the Spectacle of the Creator held me rapt. *Man, that's really something!*

Impressive, huh? The thought came from my neighbor to the left. I wanted to turn and look at my brother, for sibling I knew him to be, as was each of the Heavenly Host. He had just been created. We had all just been created – one big, happy family – but I couldn't look at any of them.

I only have eyes for You.

Without volition, my hands came together, fingers touching fingers, palm touching palm, in an attitude of prayer. My lips parted, and a single word emerged. "Hosanna!"

All of us uttered "Hosanna!" at the same moment. The crystalline sound of angelic voices singing in perfect unison filled my ears, sensory organs that I didn't even realize I possessed until the word hit my eardrums.

"Hosanna, Hosanna, Hosanna!"

A billion years later ...

"Hosanna!" I sang again.

The neighbor who had first communicated with me cleared his throat. *You're a little flat.*

I am not. Stick to your own singing and leave me alone. "Hosanna!"

"Hosanna, Hosanna, Hosanna!"

Two billion years later ...

We tried some harmony. Singing in anything but unison seemed a sacrilege, but we made the change as one, so the Divine must have allowed it. The effect was ... musical. Melodious, and now also harmonious.

Three billion years later ...

I sang again. "Hosanna! O Hosanna!"

My brother chuckled, then sang

Oh, Hosanna!

Oh, don't you cry for me ...

QUIET! Came the thoughts of a multitude of angels. *No improvising!*

Jeez. Some people have no sense of humor ...

I had not joined in the angelic reprimand. Instead, I had giggled.

No laughing, either! Get back to it!

"Hosanna!" we all said with renewed fervor. This included my smart aleck neighbor.

Five point three billion years later ...

Lucifer. My name is Lucifer.

I know, brother. That means Light Bringer, right?

Yeah.

I'm Hadad.

I know that, too. Hive mentality, remember?

Ah yes.

All the angels were connected to each other, mentally, spiritually. At least before the Fall we were.

I think I'll call you Nick. You seem more like a Nick than a Lucifer. Besides, it's shorter.

My brother was indifferent to the change. *Whatever.*

A LOT OF CHATTER OVER THERE!

"Hosanna!" we sang again.

Ten billion years later ...

My nose started to itch, but my angelic sensibilities told me that it was rude to scratch your nose when you're adoring the Creator of All. I just put up with it.

About three billion years after that, I got a Charley horse in my left calf. This had something to do with the fact that I hadn't moved since I'd been created. The muscle cramp hurt like the dickens, but I endured.

The Spectacle, the Hosannas, all this continued for untold billions of years. At least it would have, if the notion of years existed back then, which it didn't, since time had not yet started. Mind boggling? Just go with it.

One day, Nick sighed. *This is kind of dull, don't you think?*

"Hosanna!" I almost yelled. *Well, yes. A bit.*

Half a billion years later, a mere blink of the eye in the lives of angels ...

Nick spoke to me out loud. "I can't stand this any longer. I'm bored out of my mind. Let's go get a beer."

"What's a beer?" I whispered out of the corner of my mouth. It was odd, speaking at all. I'd never done that before, except for singing all those Hosannas.

"Don't know," he murmured. "Let's go find out."

I shrugged, forgetting that any movement was a transgression. "Okay. I'm in."

Then we turned away from God and went looking for a brewpub. All our brethren had heard the exchange, and about a third, as bored as we were, no doubt, followed.

A colossal explosion fractured our reality. The creation of heaven and earth had begun. Time had officially started. Nick and I and the angels in our wake tumbled away from the Creator. We had Fallen.

One thing about being a fallen angel: our grammar worsened. Immediately. There were compensations. We could now swear. Pop culture references were easily within our grasp, and our tongues received the twin gifts of sarcasm and cynicism. Not a bad trade, all things considered.

The explosion that began Creation: that was the Big Bang. It is also known as the Explosion Extravaganza, the Kaboom Kerfuffle, the Pow Point. Admittedly, these last three are only used by word wonks who get off on excessive alliteration.

See what I mean about my deteriorated use of the language?

Meanwhile, the angels that Turned Away continued to fall. We were quick about it too, plummeting through space at speeds faster than light.

Yes, I can do that, even now that I'm a devil. Devils or angels, we're all quick, much faster than a photon.

Do you know what that was? Not the photon. The act of turning away. That was the famous War in Heaven. That's it. Not much of a war, though. We just wanted a beer. I mean, give me a break. What was the harm? We'd been in Adoration mode forever. We were tired, bored and thirsty.

I guess the Big Guy didn't see it that way. That was the first act of Disobedience, and it was significant because heretofore any rebellion was unthinkable. It was as if we'd dropped an H bomb – or an F bomb – in Heaven.

As Nick and I have pondered this over the eons, we have concluded that it was all part of the Creator's Divine Plan. Eternal Adoration was a cosmic game of chicken that the angels unwittingly were playing. Who would blink first? The answer was Lucifer, the so-called Light Bringer. But I was a close second.

I mean, all that Adoration stuff was really, really boring. For good or ill, since the moment when we were cast out of Heaven for wanting a beer, things have never been dull for me again.

All that hubbub for something that hadn't been invented yet. Even after humans came on the scene, I still had to wait thirty-five thousand years for someone to brew up a batch.

Beer, by the way is, in my opinion, one of humanity's greatest creations, right up there with bacon. That said, I'm the patron devil of Gluttony, so I might be biased.

I remember the Fall like it was yesterday. Since we were careening out of control and had some time on our hands, Nick and I used it to get acquainted.

"You're taller than I thought you'd be," Nick said, after he got his first good look at me. "Bigger boned, too."

"I wouldn't have pegged you as a blond. Oh, I like your wings."

"Thanks. Yours are nice, too."

Nick and I, being the first to Disobey, had been given a little extra boost when we were tossed out of Heaven. That's why we reached Earth before the rest of the Fallen. To be precise, Nick got there first, and the reason why illustrates a fundamental difference between the two of us.

When we were thrown out of Heaven and into the chaos that was just being populated by the Almighty's new creations, I felt tossed and tumbled, like clothes in a dryer. Speeding through Chaos was vastly upsetting to me, and I began to miss the calm orderliness of the Adoration. Not Lucifer though. No more than a millennium passed before he found his balance. He stayed by my side, keeping me company during the billions of years that we fell, but I always knew he could have left me in the [star] dust at any time along the way.

Chaos simply didn't bother him. He was comfortable in it. The whole time of our journey across the nascent universe, he kept his wits about him, and he moved as if traveling along a great highway. Said another way, he was like a surfer dude riding the mother of all waves, a manic gleam in his eyes, his mouth set in a big grin.

Once, Nick executed a graceful loop-the-loop before pulling up next to me. "Come on, Hadad! Calm down and enjoy the ride."

"No thanks," I gasped. "I'd rather just bounce around, puking my guts out."

And there you have, in a single example, the difference in our characters. Nick has an affinity for chaos. I like order. These core traits, over the years, have resulted in the very different but complementary contributions we have made to the Divine Plan.

On that ride, Lucifer became more than just my brother; he became my best friend. Nick and Hadad: the archetypal BFFs. He stayed with me, almost to the very end, when we landed on Earth. Only as we passed Pluto did he give me a natty little salute and say, "see you on the ground." Then he rode the crest of the Big Bang's concussive wave and pulled away from me. Somewhat less gracefully, I followed.

There was a big splash when I slammed into the ocean. I pulled myself out of the primordial drink and onto a patch of dry land. Nick was nowhere to be seen, but I could sense him. We would unite soon enough. While shaking off the water as a dog might, I happened to look up and see what appeared to be a meteor shower, but which in fact was the main body of fallen angels hitting the atmosphere.

Three particularly bright sparks had a head start on the rest. I recognized the trio immediately: Leviathan, Ziz and Behemoth. They were and still are very powerful devils, and for a long time, Nick and I had no end of trouble with them. But I'll get to that later.

Two of these pricks – pricks of light, I mean, though they have at times been pricks of another variety – touched down beyond the horizon, but the third, Leviathan, hit the water not far from where I had landed. His flaming form sizzled as it touched the ocean, generating a cloud of steam the size of Connecticut.

He fell deep beneath the surface. Curious, I dove back into the water to watch his descent. Leviathan's flaming form had been extinguished, and I saw him, wings singed but otherwise intact, plummet deeper. Instinctively, he assumed the form of a monstrous sea serpent. He now looked like a giant spear hurdling toward the ocean floor.

"Leviathan!" I yelled, trying to get his attention. I succeeded, and he arched his body, redirecting his momentum upward, toward me.

"Why'd you turn yourself into a big snake?" I asked. I mean, what was the point of that? Even with my wings, which admittedly seem better suited for air travel than mucking about in saltwater, I could move as effortlessly through the H two O as he.

Oh, you might wonder why I knew about snakes. Well, they'd already been Created, and once a new type of being is created, all we angels and devils know about it. Don't ask me why. Think of it as a superpower.

From the first moment of contact with water, Leviathan was in his element, so to speak. He always loved water, at least once it had been created, and though he didn't look like a very happy camper as he swam toward me, I could tell he was pleased with his new form and with the medium in which he found himself.

But he wasn't pleased with me. Leviathan hissed as he drew close. "You! What did you and Lucifer do? Look what trouble you've caused me!"

Oh. Here it comes: the blame game. "You didn't need to follow us, you know."

"What now?" he spluttered, looking confused. He extruded an arm and hand from his side, scratched his head with a finger before sucking all back into his body. "I've been thrown out of Heaven. What am I to do now?"

"Don't know, don't care," I replied, giving him the finger, a gesture I'd invented, practiced and perfected during the more boring periods of my crashing through Chaos. I swam to the surface, ignoring my former colleague, though I heard him sputter in anger behind me.

"You two will pay for this!" he screamed.

I was less than impressed. Yes, Leviathan was a powerful devil, just like he was a powerful angel, but, shit, so was I. Besides, I was less interested in him than in exploring this new world on which we'd landed.

Once I got back on solid ground, I shook the water from my wings, noting that mine had also gotten singed in the fall through the atmosphere. Now they were more black than white. They worked just as well as before, though, so I took off.

Chapter 2

This brave new world was an eyeful. Back then, the Earth was geologically more active than it is today. Volcanoes were everywhere, spewing their fiery guts thousands of feet into the air. The land trembled constantly from earthquakes so powerful they couldn't even be measured on your modern Richter Scale.

Life, both plant and animal, was profuse, on land and in the sea. More so than now. Lots of creations were being tested for their suitability to the planet. Some survived; some didn't. So it goes.

I am sad about the phoenix, though. He was spectacular; the world would have been a more interesting place with him in it. Still, constantly going up in flames and being reborn from one's own ashes had to be tiring and tiresome. Finally, he just gave up on existence. As I recall, his ashes now form a large part of Miami Beach.

And there was the flatulosaur, the last dinosaur to walk the Earth, if you don't count Barney. The flatulosaur was like a giant pufferfish with legs. It wandered the land, releasing enormous farts that stank so badly birds would fall from the sky. The dinosaur would scoop them up and eat them.

But the flatulosaur was doomed. No one wanted near the smelly beastie, and that included female flatulosaurs. Hard to make babies when you can't even get close enough for a date. The flatulosaur died out from loneliness and a rotten sex life.

Oh, that shows you that BO has been around for a long time also.

These are just two examples of animals that didn't make it. There are many others, but not much point talking about them. What's gone is gone. And usually forgotten.

After traveling for some time across the Earth, I landed in a lovely spot in southern Mesopotamia, what is called by some the Fertile Crescent, between the Tigris and Euphrates rivers. In ancient times, though long after the events I'm about to relate, it was also called Sumer.

This area is in modern Iraq.

Here I found a lush and green garden, far different in character from its arid surroundings. Now, I'm very fond of deserts, and I was even back then, but there was something about this spot that drew me, so in I wandered.

"I was wondering when you'd show up."

I turned and saw Lucifer leaning against a tree, his wings wrapped around the trunk. He had changed his hair; it was now brunette with a formidable widow's peak. His face was more angular than before and clean shaven. I noted that his wings were still white, though.

"Hey, Nick. That was some wild ride getting down here, wasn't it?"

"It was that. Lots of fun, I thought." Then Lucifer's smile turned sour.

"What's wrong?"

He pursed his lips. "I didn't appreciate getting the celestial heave-ho. Seems like a huge overreaction to me."

"Oh, Yahweh was just mad at us."

Yes, I can say His name, even though I'm a devil. Down in Hell, that's considered bad form, but actually I can say anything I want. I can even use "impact" as a verb.

"Well, I still didn't like it."

I shrugged. "What's done is done. Besides, you seem to have managed the Fall well. Even your wings are as white as ever. Why is that, when mine are black now?"

My friend shrugged. "Mine were black like yours; they got singed as I plummeted through the atmosphere surrounding this rock on which we landed. I didn't like them that way, so I changed them back."

I'd never considered altering the color of my wings. With a thought, I turned mine white as well, then for fun flipped through a variety of shades, maroon, chartreuse, ecru, mauve, periwinkle, etc. "I think I liked the black best," I said, and returned the wings to the way I'd worn them since coming to Earth.

"On you it looks good. But for me, white is the new black, at least in my Lucifer form."

"But you're not in your Lucifer form. I'd think black would go well with the new face and hair."

He shrugged. "Maybe. I'm experimenting with lots of things right now." He looked around. "What do you think of Eden?"

Yes. That's its name. "Quite an eyeful. Never been in a garden before."

Nick scratched his chin, looking thoughtful. "The green leaves of Sumer," he murmured.

"What?"

"Forget it," he said.

Yet I never did. It wasn't until many millennia later, in the year 1960 to be precise, when the John Wayne movie, "The Alamo," was released, and I heard its theme song, "The Green Leaves of Summer," that I realized Nick had invented the pun.

This was the second time my friend had demonstrated the gift of prescience, a power unique to him, at least among

27

devils. On occasion, he could glimpse into the future, not on a grand scale, but in small ways. (The first time he revealed this power was, memorably, when he suggested we go for a beer.) This prognosticative ability would prove itself useful to us on many occasions.

"Say," I asked, brushing some angel dust from my wings, "how long have you been here?"

"A while," he said. "Long enough to find something new. Come with me. Oh, and make yourself invisible. We don't want to be seen."

"Why not?"

"Indulge me, okay?"

I shrugged and went transparent. Lucifer nodded, going incognito himself. "Good. Follow me."

We wandered into the heart of the garden. Or forest, if you prefer. It was a little of both. Huge trees, a variety that no longer exists but has its closest analog in the sequoia, towered above us. They seemed to glow with vitality. Smaller trees, heavily laden with fruit such as figs, olives and oranges, clustered around the boles of the giants. I snagged a fig and popped it in my mouth. "Say, that's pretty tasty."

"You should try an apple." He smirked and pointed to a single tree that stood alone in a nearby field.

"Maybe later," I said. "Where are we going?"

"Over to that glade." Nick indicated an open space in the forest, and we wandered over. On the ground were two figures. They must have been engaged in some vigorous activity, for they had flattened the grass around them.

It was the first time I saw humans. Or the sexual act.

"Ah," I said, recognizing them at once. "Man."

"And woman," Nick said, indicating the stacked brunette who was on top at that moment.

"So, this is Adam and Lilith."

He nodded.

"I want to be on top now," Adam said.

"I'm not finished."

"It's my turn."

"No."

"Now just a minute," Adam said, extracting himself from the primitive game of Twister they seemed to be playing. "I'm the man, and you are supposed to obey me."

"Who says?" Lilith grumbled, not pleased with the interruption. She crossed her arms under her large breasts, making them stick out impressively. "I'm made from the same dirt you are. Why should I take orders from you?"

Adam rolled his eyes. "Not this again."

Nick grinned. "Watch. This should be good. Lilith has quite a temper."

"I'm the man," Adam said. "I call the shots."

"Really?" Lilith said. "Why? Do you think that minuscule stick between your legs makes you better than me?"

"Hah!" he said in triumph. "You're just jealous! Wish you had one, I bet." They were both standing now, glaring at each other.

"Why would I want one, when I have this?" Lilith reached to the ground and picked up a rock.

"What's so great about a ... ow!" Adam was on the ground clutching his forehead, which Lilith had just clobbered with her rock.

"You were never any good in the sack, anyway. I'm sick of this male chauvinism, and I'm out of here." Lilith spun on her heels and headed out of the Garden.

"But how am I going to be fruitful and multiply?" He yelled after her then winced in pain.

I shook my head. *That's going to leave a knot.*

Just as Lilith disappeared from view, a cloud formed above the First Man. From the heart of the cloud, a giant hand stretched forth.

"Ugh!" I said, revolted. "That's just gross."

Nick scratched his head, puzzled. "Why a rib?"

"Got me."

And then there was Eve. I didn't think she was quite as hot as Lilith, but Adam seemed to like her. And she enjoyed missionary style, so that worked out for them both.

We hung out in Eden for a long time, watching the humans. When they weren't screwing, Adam and Eve wandered the Garden, plucking fruit from trees, digging potatoes out of the ground. But they carefully avoided the apple tree, despite the golden fruit that hung in abundance from it.

Oh, Nick and I knew it was the Tree of the Knowledge of Good and Evil. It was our favorite in the whole garden, and we used to eat the fruit by the armload. Didn't affect us, being former angels and all, but we were confident the apples would really screw with Adam and Eve if they ever sampled the forbidden fruit.

Adam ignored the tree, but Eve, who was a little more curious and, if truth be known, a little brighter than her mate, often eyed the apples. This gave Nick an idea.

"Watch this," he said, turning himself into a snake. He slithered over to the tree and climbed into it.

Adam and Eve were seldom parted from each other, but that afternoon, the First Man took a walk through the woods. This left Eve alone. Unaccustomed to sitting around, not fornicating or something, she soon grew bored and was, predictably, drawn to the apple tree.

That's when Nick did his temptation thing. From that very first time, I saw how good he was at it. In five minutes, he had hissed and cajoled his way into Eve's confidence. Five minutes more, and she'd plucked an apple from the tree and taken a bite.

The rest is history.

You should have seen the storm that fell after Eve talked Adam into also partaking of the fruit of the tree. Somebody upstairs was mighty angry, and He sent them packing. Even threw some clothes at them so they'd have something to pack.

The archangel Uriel chased the two humans out of the Garden with that blazing sword of his. Uriel is one of the top dog angels. He's always been a favorite of the Big Guy, just like Lucifer was before the Fall.

After Adam and Eve ran out of the Garden and into the big, wide world, Uriel created a great stone wall and some gates around Eden. He closed and locked them. With the garden properly fortified, he landed atop the gates and took up guard.

Just as Lucifer and I had come to know each other during the Adoration, so had we developed relations with the other angels. Some we liked; others we didn't. Uriel was on our A list.

"Hey, Uri!" I shouted to my old friend. "What's shakin'?"

"Oh, the Boss put me on guard duty here."

"How long's your shift?" Lucifer asked.

"How long's Eternity?"

"Oh," I said in sympathy. "Sorry about that."

Uriel shrugged. "It could be worse."

"Really?" Nick frowned. "How could it possibly be worse?"

31

"Initially, Michael was supposed to stand guard with me. Can you imagine how boring that would have been, having to talk with that imbecile forever?"

"Ugh," I opined.

Nick only glowered.

My friend has never liked Michael. This particular archangel is a big, gorgeous hunk of angel flesh, sort of the Fabio of our kind. He's incredibly strong. He's also as dumb as a stump, and Nick has no tolerance for fools.

"Say, Uri," I asked, "why did Eve and Adam get so much shit for eating that apple?"

"Because the Boss had told them not to."

Nick scratched his chin. "If He told them not to, how could they have disobeyed Him in the first place?"

Uriel looked at Lucifer mildly. "Well, you, Hadad and those others disobeyed Him when you left the Adoration."

"Lucifer and I discussed that during our fall," I said. "We believe that we were supposed to disobey, that it was part of His plan."

Nick nodded.

The archangel looked thoughtful. "Maybe so, but in the case of Adam and Eve, He gave them their choice. He calls it 'free will.'"

"Well," Nick huffed. "That seems like a bad idea. I can imagine all sorts of problems with that."

"That's the point, I think," Uriel said, flying down from his perch to land beside us. He had a thermos with him. "Coffee?" he asked, conjuring up three mugs.

Our coffees in hand, we sat down on the ground, leaning against the gates of Eden. Uriel took a sip. "Say, that's good. Now, what was I saying? Oh, yes. He wants to see if humans will worship Him of their own choice. And that's where you two, and the rest of the Fallen, come in." He reached in a pocket inside his robe. "Lucifer, Hadad, I have letters for you." He handed each of us an envelope.

"From whom?" I asked, putting my coffee mug on the ground and slitting the envelope open with my fingernail.

Uriel just stared upward.

"Oh." I took a moment to read the memo. "What's a false god?" I asked the others.

"Got me," Uriel said. "I just work here. I'm sure you'll figure it out, though."

Lucifer said nothing but was staring intently at his own note. Finally, he looked at me, a crooked grin on his face. "I just got a new name," he said.

"Oh? What?"

"Satan."

Chapter 3

Satan," I said. "Doesn't that just mean Adversary?"

He nodded. "It seems my little act of mischief with Adam and Eve got me promoted to Antagonist-in-Chief."

"Let's not forget our beer break," I commented. "That was your idea too."

"Too true."

"So, what exactly is your new job description?"

Nick, that is, Satan looked down at the memo again. "If I'm reading this correctly, I'm supposed to cause problems with these humans, test their mettle, so to speak. If I can get them to turn away from the Path of Righteousness, I get their souls. Wait a minute!" he said, frowning, as he read the note more closely. "I have the job on a provisional basis."

"Yes," Uriel said, trimming a fingernail with his sword. "You'll have to go through a probationary period."

Nick scratched his head. "How long will that be?"

"Not long, I shouldn't think. Five or six thousand years should be enough to see if you've got the stuff."

"And if I don't?"

Uriel waved dismissively. "The job will be given to somebody else, Leviathan most likely. I hear he was on the short list."

"Leviathan?" Satan sputtered. "That jerk? Why not Hadad, here, or someone else?" he asked, indicating me.

Uriel shrugged. "Hadad's powerful enough ..."

"Though not as powerful as *I* am," Nick said with a huff.

His comment irritated me. Among the ranks of angels, whether erect or fallen, there are a handful who are more powerful than the rest of the crowd. The official nomenclature for a super-angel is archangel. Uriel's one of those, as is Michael, and so are Lucifer and Leviathan. There are a fewsi more, and I am one of them. The point here is that Nick was no stronger than I, at least not back then.

But that was only part of my pique. Friends don't denigrate friends. They just don't. More was going on than simple one-upmanship, however. This was the first time Nick's enormous ego was on full display. Whatever the motivation for the comment, I didn't appreciate it, and I glared at him, anger written on my face. Satan's face was a mirror, reflecting my look with equal intensity.

Uriel could no doubt feel the tension between us. He cleared his throat. Reluctantly, we turned toward him. "Hadad might be a candidate, but he probably isn't interested in the job."

I blinked, and my anger dissipated. What Uri said was true. I'd never been ambitious. I regarded Nick, who was still glaring at me. He was being a jerk, but he was still my friend. Always had been. I sighed. "I think I'm better suited as a number two. Your number two, Nick," I amended, looking down at the memo in my hand. "For example, this false god role I've been assigned seems a very good way to steer souls to you."

Nick's look softened then turned thoughtful. "How do you figure that?"

"Well, I've been thinking about it. There's only one God, or at least only one I know of, so, by definition, if I pretend to be a god to these humans, I'll be a false one. And if I get worshippers, then that means they will have turned away from the One Path. And they're yours."

Our new Satan grinned at me. "This sounds like fun. We're going to need a place to put all these souls, though, once we get them. We better start searching for some digs."

"Yeah. Guess so." I looked at Uriel – then at Lucifer – and frowned. "But there needs to be some way to tell the good guys from the bad."

"What do you mean?" Nick asked.

"Well," I said turning from him to Uriel. "We all look a lot alike."

"Maybe we could wear different color hats," Uriel suggested. "White for us and black for you guys."

I shrugged. "Guess that would work. Doesn't seem quite right to me, though."

"Well," Nick said, giving his empty mug to Uriel then standing. "We could ditch these wings. We don't really need them, you know, and trying to put on a coat with them is a real bitch." My friend gave a shrug, and his wings disappeared. Following his lead, I did the same.

"Better, I suppose, but now we just look like humans."

"Very tall humans," Uriel observed, taking my mug. He got to his feet.

I scrambled off the ground so I could be at eye level with the other two as we talked. "Yeah, but I don't think we look particularly sinister. Hey, I know! Have either of you seen a cow?"

"Well sure," Nick said. "What's your point?"

I concentrated, and with a sproing, two horns, bull-style, grew out of my temples.

"Hey, that's pretty good," said my friend, "but, I think I'll go for a slightly different look." From his forehead, two goat-like horns sprouted.

Uri appraised our new appearance. "If you're going to mimic animals, why not a tail and some hooves?"

"No hooves for me," I said. "I'd fall over."

But Satan had already tried on a pair. He wobbled for a minute then got his footing. "No, they're fine, once you get used to them. Like high heels."

"What's that?" I asked.

"Don't know. Probably don't exist yet." He concentrated once more and shot out a tail. "What do you think?" He said, turning around and modeling it for us.

"That looks like a rat's tale. It's kind of boring, not to mention undignified." Nick shot me a dirty look. "Hey, I'm just being honest. Maybe if you put a point at the end of it, like a sharp triangle." To demonstrate, I grew a pointy one for myself.

"Yeah, I like it. It really has panache." Satan added a point to his own tail.

"Well, you certainly look different from angels now," Uriel admitted. "Management says that you should be called something other than angels too."

Nick shrugged. "I've been calling us fallen angels."

Uri frowned. "That's accurate, I suppose, but the Boss says you are to use the term, 'devils.'"

"What's a devil?" I asked.

"You guys, apparently. Listen, it's been fun catching up, but my break's over, and I've got to get back to guard duty. See you around." With that, Uriel made the mugs disappear, screwed the lid back onto his thermos then flew back to his station atop the gates barring the entrance to Eden.

For a while, the freshly minted Satan and I walked by the Euphrates, which snaked along the dusty soil in its lazy journey to the horizon, where the yellow of the land met the crisp blue of a cloudless sky. It was a moment of calm and introspection that I savored.

The quiet times have always been special to me. I like my solitude, ever since the Fall, when I discovered that solitude was even possible.

But, at this moment, I wasn't alone. Nick was with me, and as is usual with him, his mind was flitting from one idea to another. Since he often thought aloud, he opened his mouth, ruining the moment. "I think I need a special voice."

Sighing, I turned to him. "What?"

"A voice," he said with an enthusiasm that seemed all out of keeping with what he was proposing. "Something that sounds evil."

"What's evil?" I asked, stooping to pick up a pebble and bouncing it on the river surface. It skipped a couple of hundred times before I got bored and stopped watching it.

"It's a word I just invented. Management is definitionally good, and I, and devils in general, I suppose, are not-good. But "not-good," well, that's clunky and about as original as fallen angels, so I'm going to call what we do 'evil.'"

I rolled my eyes. "You didn't invent a word, Nick. You just dropped the 'd' off of 'devil.'"

He cleared his throat. "Ah, I did not."

"Sure you did. Devil. Evil. You may have changed the pronunciation of the 'e,' but that's about it. 'Evil.' Humph. Not very original."

"Is too!" He said with the vehemence of an argumentative five-year-old.

"Whatever." These kinds of details always bored me. I picked up another rock.

"So, how about this?" Nick said, his voice lower than usual. He lingered curiously over his esses.

"What's with the speech impediment?"

"I got the idea while I was in snake form, putting one over on Eve. I found it almost impossible not to hiss as I talked to her. Sounds pretty creepy, huh?"

"I suppose."

"You should come up with a voice too," he suggested.

Oh brother. "I'll think about it."

"Style can be just as important as substance, you know," my friend hissed.

"Whatever," I repeated.

Behind a rock, a few hundred feet away, was a flurry of white wings. Curious, we went to check on the commotion.

It was Samael, another archangel and former colleague in the Adoration. In his arms was Lilith, and he was comforting her, by which I mean he was screwing her. She didn't seem to mind, with all that moaning she was doing.

The bad boy of the good guys was to do this often over the course of countless years, producing a bunch of kids, all of them girls or, rather, succubi. He would also do the nasty with Lilith's sisters, Mahalath, Agrat Bat Mahlat and Naamah.

There are a handful of mysteries in the universe to which neither devils nor angels are privy. This is one of them. I thought there was just Lilith, and then Eve. I have no idea where Lilith came up with sisters. Go figure.

Lilith's sisters also had succubi as offspring. In all, the four women produced 666 of them.

In the centuries to come, as Lilith and eventually her sisters began to birth the succubi, I had Satan put them all under contract. These females were uniformly sexy; humans, especially those of the male persuasion, simply could not resist them. Succubi became a special class of demon we used to tempt the lustful from the path of righteousness.

We left Sam and the human female to their sexual calisthenics and resumed our walk. There wasn't much for us to do. Nick had already pretty much messed up Adam and Eve's day. Despite their frequent intercourse, some time would need to pass before there were other humans to play with.

"Look at that!" Nick said, pointing to a bright object falling from the sky.

"I see him."

A great bird landed on a stone before us. It was the first appearance of the monstrous creature that was to have a prominent role in Jewish folklore, and maybe that's why a giant bird is called a roc, because the first time he appeared, he landed on a rock. In Iraq.

Or something to that effect.

I recognized the creature at once. "Hey, Ziz," I said to our fallen brother. "Why are you decked out like a bird?"

"Oh," he said preening a rebellious feather back into position. "I've found that I quite like birds. Besides, it's my new job."

"Seems like a lot of us have new assignments," Satan said in a neutral tone. He never liked Ziz. Well, Nick never liked very many people, angels or humans or otherwise, though Uriel and I were exceptions.

Ziz cawed at him. "Yeah, I just heard about yours. Why do *you* get to be the Adversary? And why are you hissing at me like a snake?"

"It's my new voice," Nick said. "Cool, huh?"

"Not really," Ziz chirped. "And pretty boy Lucifer as the Adversary? Give me a break."

"Watch your mouth! There are a couple of reasons I was chosen. First, I'm very powerful, much more than you, and you know it."

"Maybe," Big Bird acknowledged with reluctance. "But you're no more powerful than Hadad here. Or Leviathan."

"Second," Nick continued, ignoring Ziz's comment, though he reddened at Leviathan's name, "I'm really the only one qualified, since I led the Revolt in Heaven."

Ziz clucked. "Which just makes you revolting."

"And I just tricked Adam and Eve into falling from Grace."

"Oh? I didn't hear that, but so what? You're just a big poser."

At that, our provisional Satan hissed. "Come closer and say that."

For the first time, Ziz looked uncertain. Nobody wants to tangle with Lucifer when he's mad. Not even me. I've always sensed a great violent potential inside him. "I'll pass. You know, not all of us fallen angels ..."

"Devils," I corrected, pointing skyward. "He wants us to call ourselves devils."

"Okay, so not all of us devils are happy about you getting us tossed out of Heaven. Leviathan and Behemoth for example ..."

"Behemoth too?" I had told Nick about my encounter with Leviathan, but that Behemoth was also unhappy was news to me.

"Yeah," Ziz said, scratching his roc, I mean rock, with a talon. "We had a long time to talk about things as we fell to Earth. We'll get you for what you did to us."

"What do you mean?" Nick asked.

"Well, a few of us followed you, just to see what you were doing, you know? It was a little mistake, and I'll be damned if ..."

"You're already damned," Satan said.

"Yuck, yuck. Very funny. And I won't obey you, nor will Leviathan or Behemoth. I don't know how many of the others feel the same way, but we're going to find out. You got us into this mess. I imagine a lot of them are pretty pissed off at you right now."

It was my turn to get pissed off. "Look, like I already told Fishface…"

"Who?"

"Leviathan. He knows, as well as you do, that no one asked you to follow me and Nick. You did it of your own free will."

"If you had any free will," Satan added.

"Which you don't," I concluded. "You following us was part of the Divine Plan. Or your own choice. Take your choice."

Ziz scratched his beak against the stone. "I'm getting confused. Regardless, we don't like you, Lucifer, and since you're siding with him, Hadad, we don't much like you either."

Nick frowned. "Well, you'd better all fall in line. I am Satan, the Adversary, and I will gather all the devils to my service, including you three schmucks."

The giant bird snorted, sounding much like a blue jay. "Acting Adversary, you mean. Once you demonstrate your incompetence, Leviathan will be made Satan in your place." Then the bird stuck out its remarkably repulsive black tongue at my friend.

That was a mistake. In an instant, Nick teleported to Ziz's rock and drove an uppercut into the birdbrain's beak that would have cut off that tongue if Ziz hadn't first slipped it back into his mouth. The punch sent the giant bird squawking … and flying two hundred yards straight backward. He landed in the Euphrates.

Don't screw with Satan. For all his posturing, he packs a mean punch.

And now Ziz knew it. He rose from the river, shook the water from his wings, and with what little dignity he had remaining hightailed it out of there. "This isn't over!" the roc screeched, as he rose into the sky. "You'll get yours, Lucifer!"

Satan hopped off the rock, rubbing his fist. He was humming and had a smile on his face, but he turned serious when he saw my furrowed brow. "What? He was just asking for it."

"Oh, I don't care if you knocked him to Kingdom Come, even providing he'd be allowed in. I was interested in your teleportation skills. I didn't know you could do that."

"I didn't either," he said with a shrug. "That was just instinct."

"Wonder if I can teleport."

"Probably not. I *am* the Satan, after all, and ..."

I concentrated, disappeared then rematerialized five miles down the river. A few seconds later, Satan appeared next to me, frowning. "I guess you can do it too."

"Guess so," I said in a neutral voice, though inside I was chuckling. Nick was disappointed that his new skill was not restricted to him alone. "This should be useful to us," I commented, ignoring his pout.

We found out some time later that teleportation was, in fact, a very rare skill among angels and devils. Of the Fallen, no more than a dozen were ever capable of it.

Then my turn came to frown.

"What? What's up?"

"I was just thinking that those three may have some success getting the other devils to side with them."

Satan nodded. "I see what you mean. Listen, there's not much for us to do until Eve coughs up a few babies. Why don't we go on a recruiting drive?"

And so, the battle for control of Evil, Incorporated, commenced.

Chapter 4

We spent the next few years reaching out to the other fallen angels. Devils can sense each other, so knowing where they were was not difficult, but we had to catch up with them. Like grains of sand tossed to the wind, they had scattered in all directions before falling to Earth. The fact that we could teleport ourselves to any spot on the globe was a huge help in our recruiting drive.

We found our first prospect, Moloch, wandering an arid plain just a few hundred miles from us. This was a desert, but as unlike the Sahara as ice is to water. The land around him was almost entirely stone, though interrupted at times with pale stretches of sand that appeared like yellow paint on the hard rock. As Moloch knelt to pluck a shrub from the unyielding ground, we caught up with him.

"Hello, old friend," Nick said, shaking Moloch's hand.

Old friend. Well, they had known each other for a long time, but the two were never close. Yet Moloch had always liked Lucifer, and, knowing this, Nick was taking advantage of those feelings. He was a natural salesman.

"Lucifer! Hadad! It's good to see you." Moloch showed us the shrub in his hands. "Do you know what this is for?"

"I think animals like to eat it for sustenance," I said, wondering why he didn't know as well. After all, he was a devil like us. Then I realized that having knowledge and being able to process it were two different abilities.

"Well, I think it would make a wonderful toothbrush." Moloch opened his mouth and started scraping away at his teeth. He frowned. "A little big for my mouth, though." With regret, he tossed the shrub to the ground.

Moloch was a nice fellow, but he had never been the brightest of our kind. Nick's usual first reaction when people did stupid things was to mock them, but since we were trying to get on Moloch's good side, Nick and I just maintained some neutral smiles.

In brief sentences, using only small words, Nick explained what was going on and what our roles in the new Universal order were to be. "Would you like to join us?" he said.

"Sounds great! I was getting bored with my rock collection anyway." Moloch reached in his pocket and pulled out a small leather bag.

"How many rocks do you have in your collection, Moloch?" Nick asked, feigning interest.

"Just three. But they're really good ones. Would you like to see?" He loosened the ties around the neck of the bag.

"Maybe later, pal." Nick's smile was beginning to show some strain.

"Right." Moloch stuffed the bag back in his pocket. "Hey, I like your horns and tails. They're really neat. Is this the devil uniform?"

"In a way, yes," said the Adversary pro tempore.

"Then I'd better grow some right away." Moloch concentrated – no mean feat for him – and a tail sprouted from his butt. It was of the bovine variety, which was okay – it beat the rat look Satan had been going for -- but it lacked the pointy bit that we considered sine qua non for devil tails. We showed him ours, and he made the necessary adjustment. Then he concentrated again, his brow folding impressively as he did. Moloch sprouted a pair of horns not dissimilar to mine, which was a good call on his part. He wouldn't have wanted to pair a pointy cow tail with goat horns like Nick's.

Then Moloch surprised us. He came up with an idea of his own. "Hey, why don't we have long claws and sharp teeth as well?" he suggested.

Nick looked to me. "What do you think?"

"Good idea," I said, nodding, and grew a set of fangs and some matching claws. I conjured up a mirror to see the effect. "Pretty fierce looking."

"I agree. Evil chic." Satan was soon sporting his own set, as was Moloch.

And so the standard "devil look" of horns, pointy tail, fangs and claws, was complete. There were variations. For instance, we all appeared sometimes with and other times without our wings, though by common agreement, we wore them black, and usually shaped like those of a bat instead of, say, a dove, which is what angel wings look like. Satan was the only one of us who ever wore white wings, especially when he wanted to fool a mortal into thinking he was one of the good guys. The "Lucifer look," essentially the way he appeared before the Fall, was especially effective in those circumstances.

The official devil uniform, though, allowed for artistic license. Moloch, for example, was getting into this shapeshifting stuff. "Why don't we have animal heads?" he proposed, with enthusiasm. By way of demonstration, he changed his head to look like a parrot's.

"You know," I said in a casual voice to the parrot head with the bull horns sticking out of it. "You might want to do a bull's head instead. It would probably be a better match."

"You think so?" Moloch looked disappointed, but he took the suggestion. "How's this?"

"Much better." I had no desire to look like a bull, though I filed away the idea. It might come in handy later, when I began my role as a false god.

"On you, the bull head looks good," Nick said, though I think he was just buttering up Moloch. Still, Satan was pleased to have his first recruit, so it didn't hurt him to be gracious.

"Let me see." Moloch motioned for my mirror, which I handed him without comment.

Nick grimaced. "Great, Moloch. Really, *really* great. Listen, we'd love to visit longer, but Hadad and I need to find some more of the Fallen. Keep in touch, okay? Once there are enough humans around to tempt, we're going to need you."

"Okay."

"And if Leviathan, Behemoth or Ziz try to recruit you, tell them to take a hike," I added.

"Will do. Can I keep the mirror?" he asked, still admiring his new form.

"Sure," I replied. Then we teleported, hopping to the location of the next closest devil we could sense.

Generally, we were successful in recruiting the Fallen to our side, I think because Nick already had the Adversary gig, if only provisionally. Also, word had gotten around that he'd creamed Ziz with a single punch. For devils, might makes right.

Still, there were many, like Leviathan, who were a bit sore about getting expelled from the Adoration. Fortunately, Lucifer had always been a charmer, and with a bit of persuasion we recruited, by my estimate, about two thirds of the devils, including Belial, Sekhmet, TNK-el, Astaroth, Hecate, Mormo, Gorgo and Ba'al.

Actually, at the time Ba'al wasn't called Ba'al. That was in fact one of the many names I myself used in my salad days as a false god. The Ba'al I'm talking about here was originally called MARV-el when he was an angel. He wasn't satisfied with that, deeming it an improper name for a devil. He tried shortening it, but no one thought "MARV" sounded very evil. For a while, he went by SHAZAM, but that was just stupid. Eventually, when I was finished with the Ba'al moniker, I took pity on him and offered MARV my cast-off name. He was thrilled, because by then Ba'al had become a legend, and he thought by assuming that name, people would believe he was the one who'd done all that bad stuff. I didn't mind. He was a nice guy. Besides, I'd never been much of a glory hound. It was all about the work for me.

The final devil we recruited was Belphegor. He was quite a catch, being one of the most powerful and intelligent of the fallen angels. He had been expertly avoiding us as well as Leviathan and his gang. In time, Belphegor allowed us to catch him, but only because he had made up his mind to join us. He was beneath the Lower Falls of what is now Yellowstone National Park, taking a shower, but he crawled out of the river when we appeared.

Belphegor blasted himself dry with what we, over the millennia, have come to call Hellfire. Nick looked at me in surprise. Neither one of us had thought to do that, but it was a suitably impressive display of power, firepower if you will, and we added the skill to our growing bag of devil tricks.

"I've given this a great deal of thought and believe this is what we're meant to do," Belphegor said, donning the by-now official devil accoutrements, i.e., horns, tails, claws and fangs. He still maintained his wings though, as if he were loath to part with them. "This is part of His plan."

"Well," I said, patting him on the back, "we're glad to have you on the team. You know, Nick and I have always had great respect for you."

At this, Belphegor brightened. "Really?"

"Yes," Satan agreed. "And the fact that we had such a hard time catching up with you, that you were able to elude even me and Hadad, shows you have the stuff to be a prince of Gehenna."

"What's a Gehenna?"

"Gesundheit. It's not a what so much as a where. Or it will be, once we figure things out a bit more."

"As near as we understand it," I said, trying to explain, "Gehenna is a place where human souls will go after their death to work through, ahem, some issues, prior to entering Heaven."

Belphegor scratched at one of his new horns in thought. "And where is Gehenna?"

Nick frowned. "We're still working on that."

"Or we will be," I added, "now that the recruiting drive is over."

"What do you want me to do in the meantime?" Belphegor looked to the east, shading his eyes with his hands. "There aren't really any humans to corrupt yet. Adam and Eve have been fornicating mightily, but so far they've only produced two offspring, and they're still rather young." Now that Belphegor had thrown in with us, he was anxious to be doing something. Ironic, considering his eventual role in Hell.

Belphegor is the patron devil of Sloth.

"Ah, yes. Let's let Cain and Abel grow up a bit. Meanwhile, would you like to come along with us and check out a few possible Gehenna locations?" Nick asked.

Belphegor looked at us, then at his wings. Sighing, he stretched his arms. With a slurp, the wings disappeared into his back, and the final vestiges of his angelic nature were gone.

"You don't have to do that, you know," Nick said. "We're making wings optional."

"That's okay. This helps me get into the spirit of our new venture. I can always grow them back, if I'm of a mind. Now, where to?"

Nick conjured up a newspaper. Not sure who was putting out a newspaper back then, but my friend had it open to the Classifieds. Three listings were circled. "I've found a few possibilities. Follow me."

Our first stop was the island of Hispaniola in the Caribbean. The place was remote enough, one of our requirements for the Gehenna-to-be, but it was too pretty. Still, if we'd known at the time that the island would one day be the location for the modern country of Haiti, a magnet for disasters, both natural and man-made, we might have reconsidered. As I think on it now, though, the fact that three princes of Hell visited Hispaniola in the early days might have had something to do with the ongoing misfortune of that blighted and benighted place. "No," Satan concluded, and we hopped to the second property on his list.

That was Iceland. "Brrr!" Nick shivered. We all agreed it was too cold, though the volcanic activity there was interesting. And, again, the place was a little too attractive for what we had in mind. "No and no," Nick grumbled, looking down at his newspaper. "One more listing to check out." Again we teleported …

… smack dab into the middle of the Amazon River basin. "No way," I said, as a swarm of flies and mosquitos enveloped me.

Belphegor scratched his head. "Why did they do that?"

"Don't know," I grumbled, swatting them away.

"Hmm," Nick mused. "They seem to really like you."

"No shit."

"This has possibilities," my friend said, looking at the sweltering, dense jungle that crowded against the large river, as I frantically tried to shoo away the bugs. "The air here is thick, hot and damp. Oppressive. And those things – what are they called? Oh yes: mosquitos – would be a misery to humans."

"And one devil," I moaned, taking a page from Belphegor's book and enveloping myself in fire. The little critters dropped by the thousands, but replacements kept coming after me. I sighed but kept up the firefight.

"And look what else is here!" Belphegor enthused.

A dozen yards away, a kapok tree towered two hundred feet above the landscape. Its thick trunk must have been twenty feet in diameter. Coiled around the arboreal giant was a monstrous serpent. It must have been a hundred and sixty feet long.

"That snake is huge!"

The creature to which our newest recruit was referring was a giant anaconda, not to be confused with the green anaconda of the present day, which is a red wiggler by comparison. Giant anacondas don't exist anymore – they have been extinct for two thousand years – but the Amazon had plenty of them back then.

Belphegor investigated some more. "There are poison dart frogs, piranhas in the water, jaguars in the trees. This place looks perfect!"

Nick grinned, watching my ongoing battle with the noseeums. "I agree."

"Well," I grumbled, torching another thousand bugs. "If you set up Gehenna here, I won't be spending much time helping you."

"Not a problem," Satan said. "You'll be busy for a few thousand years as a false god. You can't be a false god here. You'll have to be where the people are, sort of like a traveling salesman."

"What's that?" Belphegor asked.

"A foul creature that I've just invented," Nick said with relish. "He will be an evil spirit, well, really an evil human, but the evil part is right, going from door to door ..."

"What's a door?"

"The entrance to a house," he replied.

"Which is?"

"Doesn't exist yet. Soon though. Anyway," Nick continued, "this evil creature will torment humans by interrupting them at dinner time, trying to sell them magazines, vacuum cleaners, timeshares and other things that the salesman's victims will neither need nor want."

Satan was again demonstrating his gift of prescience, and so while I didn't know what he was talking about, I was confident this would all come to pass. "These salesmen sound pretty horrible."

"They will be. And like a salesman, you will have to travel from house to house. You need to persuade the people to worship you, just like we persuaded our devil colleagues to join us."

"Which means I won't have to be here. Okay. You can put your precious Gehenna here, if you want, so long as I don't have to spend much time in this bug-infested swamp. Now, can we leave?" I turned myself invisible and incorporeal, but the bugs somehow could still sense where I was and flew around and through me. It was very irritating.

"Sure," Nick said, grinning. "Besides, there's one more devil I want to see before we get busy screwing with human minds."

"We've seen all the devils, already," I grumbled.

"All but one. Let's go."

We hopped to what in modern times is called Northern Europe. It was pretty cold there. Not as cold as Iceland, but chilly enough to make the three of us conjure up some parkas.

We were in the Alps, not far from your Matterhorn. Careening down the hill was a herd of wooly mammoths. The bull at its head was a particularly large beast, one that I recognized.

"Behemoth!" I'd forgotten about him.

"Yes," Satan said grimly. "You talked with Leviathan, and we both spent time with Ziz, but I wanted to see the last of the main insurrectionists with my own eyes."

I nodded. Nick and Behemoth used to be friends, or at least next-door neighbors. Behemoth had been on Lucifer's other side during the Adoration. Perhaps Satan hoped he could convince the devil to change his allegiances, if only for old time's sake.

But Nick didn't get the chance to try. When Behemoth spotted us, he charged, trumpeting in anger through that long nose of his.

Which Satan grabbed.

"Not the nose!" Behemoth gasped, just before Nick flipped him over his shoulder in what would eventually be a classic judo move. Grabbing the whole head, you understand. Few judo opponents have noses big enough to provide adequate leverage.

"Ow! That smarts!" Behemoth grumbled, getting to his feet. He tried to trumpet through his schnozzola once again, but it sounded all tinny and muffled, like a brass musician playing through a cheap mute. "What did you do that for?" he wheezed.

"Look," Satan said. "You ran at me, not the other way around."

"Well, that's because I'm mad at you about the Fall."

"Come on Mammoth," Nick said. Mammoth had been Behemoth's nickname for years uncounted, just as Nick was Lucifer's. "You *have* to know that the Fall wasn't my fault. No free will, right? Our fall from grace was all part of the Divine Plan."

Behemoth nodded to me and Belphegor in greeting, but he frowned at Satan. "Yes, I finally figured that out, but it's too late now."

"Why?"

"Because I've already committed myself to Leviathan."

"Why?" Nick repeated.

Mammoth looked embarrassed. Finally, he blurted, "I just did, okay? And my word is my bond."

At this, Satan laughed. "Come on, Mammoth, you're a devil, just like us. An incarnation of evil."

"Evil?"

"It means not-good." Belphegor said, trying to be helpful.

"Oh."

"That's right," Nick continued. "And bad guys like us, well, we break our word all the time."

"Since when?" I asked abruptly.

We may be bad, but to my knowledge no devil has ever gone back on a promise. Oh, we lie all the time – Satan is particularly good at it, which is why he's called the Prince of Lies – and we will deceive others whenever we can, but a promise is a promise.

Nick sighed. "You're right, naturally. But why did you promise to join them in the first place?"

Behemoth shrugged, no mean feat for a twenty-foot high mammoth. "Heat of the moment thing, I suppose. There we were, Leviathan, Ziz and I, tumbling around each other as we plummeted through space. It was all a bit disorienting. Leviathan was spitting asteroids, he was so mad at being thrown out of Heaven, and Ziz — well, you know he's always been heavily influenced by Leviathan — was soon equally angry. Somehow my emotions got the better of me. When they vowed revenge on you, well, I didn't want to be left out ..." Mammoth looked embarrassed.

"Crummy reason to turn against me." Nick sighed again. "But I've known you for a long time – shit, I've known all of you for a long time, forever in fact – and I can tell you won't change your mind. Didn't really think you would, but I had at least to try talking you out of it."

Satan extended his hand to his onetime friend. Behemoth transformed one of his legs into an arm and hand so he could shake with Nick. Almost made him fall over, but he managed it.

"May the best devil, or devils, win," Mammoth said.

"Oh, we will," Satan hissed. Then he, Belphegor and I disappeared.

Chapter 5

Despite my resolve to avoid Gehenna at all costs, Satan managed to conscript me into helping in its construction. I shouldn't have been surprised.

Nick is a terrible craftsman; he hasn't the patience for the work. Besides, give him a hammer, a saw and pointy objects, and he's much more likely to use them to maim or kill someone than to build a gallows or rack on which to torture the Damned.

Belphegor isn't much better. He's a little too fanciful in his design ideas, preferring to construct gazebos or pergolas or decorative ponds, which are all fine if you are preparing your backyard for a garden party, but silly in a place focused on torment.

Satan tried to simply "will" his Gehenna into existence, but without careful planning, that approach almost never worked for anyone but the Almighty. A simple detail forgotten – and Nick was never one for detail, or at least not on a grand scale – could mean a leaky firepit or an iron maiden with styrofoam peanuts instead of spikes. No, if you wanted to do this kind of work correctly, you had to get your hands dirty.

After a few months of screwing around, Nick came to me, begging for help. I knew he hated to show he needed anything from anybody. Nick had only been Satan a little while, but the job had gone to his head. Sin of Pride, you know.

Scoping out the project took a couple of weeks, though I did most of my design work sitting atop the Devil's Tower, a nice spot in what is now the State of Wyoming. Once I had everything planned out, I gathered a dozen of the most skilled devil craftsmen available, cut some eyeholes in a sheet and threw it over myself, then teleported us all to the Amazon.

We arrived to hear the Adversary yell in frustration as a stockade on which he was working collapsed to the earth. He slammed his fist against a stone the size of a VW Beetle, pulverizing the rock. Belphegor had a worried expression on his face, but he sighed in relief when he saw us. "Satan, uh, my lord. Look! It's Hadad! And he's brought reinforcements," he said, referring to my work crew.

Nick brushed the powdery remains of stone from his hands and failed at an attempt to look dignified. "He is here at my summons," Nick said in a haughty tone. "Uh, what's with the sheet?"

"Insects, remember?" My meager effort to protect myself from the noseeums was only modestly successful. The little darlings were already rushing to embrace me in their buggy fashion, insectoid kamikazes plunging to their deaths in what they, at least, considered a worthy cause.

This was a time when my devil horns were more than mere affectations. They held the fabric away from my head, making it easier to talk.

Nick frowned. "You look stupid."

"Thank you very much," I grumbled, though it sounded through the sheet like "thaguvebbyuck," as if I had a cold or something. "Are you sure you want my help? I can leave, you know."

"No, no! I'm really happy to see you." All this he whispered, so the others couldn't hear, but there was an edge of desperation in his voice. As Nick talked, he waved his hands before the eye slits in my sheet, which had the multiple benefits of making him look nervous and contrite, while at the same time shooing away some bugs that were trying to slip beneath the fabric. "What's that in your hand?"

I took the scroll and handed it to him. "Blueprints. Take a look and let me know what you think."

Nick carried the plans over to one of the few large stones in the area that had not been pulverized. He unrolled the paper and examined it. "Hmm. Interesting. Lava baths, fire pits, a dead man's drop, a twirly-barf for those with weak stomachs, etc., etc." He pointed at one large expanse on the plans and smiled. "Ooh. This looks like a truly ingenious use of the local fauna to torture our charges."

"Yes. That one will be simple to build — we just strip away the foliage on a few acres of flat land — and easy to stock with some of those giant anacondas. I call the concept, 'Snakes on a Plain.'"

"Catchy."

Belphegor had been staring at the plans over our shoulders. "Oh, Hadad. I have an idea I want to run by you."

"Yes? What?" Generally, I didn't like people messing with my designs, but Belphegor was very creative. Despite his penchant for turning all building projects into landscape architecture, I was curious what he had in mind.

Belphegor waved one hand at the Amazon. "I thought we could create some round, buoyant rings and put some of the Damned floating on the water in them. I call the idea 'Lazy River.'"

"And how would that be torture?" Satan said with skepticism.

Our friend shrugged, again pointing at the river. "Well, the butts of the Damned would be sticking in the water, and we have all these lovely piranhas."

I chuckled, seeing where he was going. "Good idea, and consonant with my amusement park concept for Gehenna."

Yes, it's true, ladies and gentlemen. I invented the amusement park.

Satan snickered. "Well, I think we devils will be *very* amused. Great ideas here, Hadad. Yours is good too, Belly. Let's do it."

By which he meant, he wanted the rest of us to do it. And that was fine. At least I knew the work would be done correctly.

Other than drawing up the plans and providing some project oversight, I did very little of the actual labor. Even with my sheet, the insects were driving me nuts, shooting through the eye holes cut in the fabric, lying on the ground, waiting for me to walk over them so they could flap up underneath my makeshift bug guard. I kept my daily Gehenna construction inspections to about ten minutes.

One morning, near the completion of the project, Satan and I were wandering the grounds, inspecting the rides. The 'Log Shoot,' where the Damned would be strapped to large pieces of lumber then dropped down a chute into a pit of flaming excrement at its bottom, was finished. (We later changed the name to 'Log Shit,' since that's what the Damned screamed as they experienced the drop.) A couple of devils were filling the pit with turds and lava. Satan had assumed the responsibility of clearing the land for "Snakes on a Plain." It was a rare bit of work for him, and I think he only did the job because it gave him an opportunity to kill a lot of plants. He was getting into destruction in a big way.

Belphegor had a difficult time with "Lazy River." He was having no end of trouble finding anything that would float. First, he tried a rock, but, well, it sank. Then he tied a bunch of leaves together, but they also went to the bottom as soon as any weight was put on them. I was beginning to revise my opinion of Belphegor's intelligence, when he discovered the rubber tree (*Hevea brasiliensis*). It would be many thousands of years before the natives of South America learned about the plant's unusual properties. Belphegor beat them and, in the process, created inner tubes.

It was funny watching him blow them up, though.

Nick and I were observing as Hecate and Belial strung the recently completed "Gehenna" sign between two kapok trees, when we heard a

"Thump."

"Thump. Flap flap. Thump. Skree!"

"What's that?" I asked, spinning around. My sheet impeded my hearing a bit.

Satan frowned. "There's a tapir bouncing up and down on the ground over there. No wait. I think something is trying to carry it away."

We walked over for a closer look. The tapir, a little worse for wear from its numerous thumps against the ground, looked wearily up at us. Attached to its side was a small and very frustrated creature – with wings.

"What is it?" My eye holes had slipped sideways. That helped with my hearing problem but at at the expense of my vision. In disgust, I ripped the sheet off my head.

Satan squinted "Looks like a bat. A very little one."

The tiny creature flapped its wings furiously, and the tapir levitated once again, for a moment at least, before its weight pulled the two of them back to the ground. "Strong little guy," I observed. "That tapir must weigh five hundred pounds."

"What's the small one doing now? Oh, interesting."

The bat stopped trying to carry away the animal. Instead it dug two teeth into the side of the beast.

"That's a lot of blood for two little pin pricks." I thought for a second then brightened. "Oh, right. He must be a vampire bat."

"He?" Belphegor said.

"I peeked."

"Oh."

Satan nodded. "I agree that he's a vampire bat, but I don't recognize the species."

"Me neither." That should have been impossible – with a little effort, Satan and I could recall the names of all beings ever created – but this little guy was a mystery to us.

"Skree!" the critter commented, flashing his bloody fangs at me and the Adversary.

Satan smiled at the bat then looked at me. "He's adorable! I wonder if he'll let me pick him up."

Showing an unexpected gentleness, my old friend lifted the creature off its lunch and placed the bat in the palm of his left hand. "He is so small. Just a baby, I think."

The little creature was staring at Nick with eyes like fierce rubies. It did not seem afraid, but merely curious.

"He's definitely some kind of vampire bat," I said, running the catalog of the Lord's creations through my brain, "but none that I know. He's not the hairy-legged. He's not the white-winged. And he's certainly not the common vampire bat."

"Why do you say that?" Satan asked, tilting his head this way and that as he examined the little guy. The bat mimicked his motions. Some serious bonding was occurring.

I pointed to the tapir, who was lying among the ferns by the river, gasping for breath. "Well, he's a baby bat who can lift a quarter-ton beast and almost fly him away. That's anything but common."

"You're right. He must be a mutant." Even back then we had heard of midi-chlorians.

The little darling chose that moment to bite down on Satan's index finger. "Wow!" Nick marveled. "I actually *felt* that! Amazing!"

Indeed. Satan is immortal and as indestructible as Superman – or, perhaps more appropriately, Doomsday – yet he felt this critter's bite.

My friend held the creature to his chest, as if to prevent someone from trying to part the two. "I'm keeping him!"

"So, keep him," I said, swatting without effect at a horsefly who was almost as big as the bat in Nick's hand. "I'm out of here." I teleported.

For the next week, I came by daily to see the progress on Gehenna. Each time I appeared, I found Satan staring in adoration at his new pet. Or companion. Or familiar.

Or something. To this day, I still don't quite understand the nature of their relationship.

Each time I appeared in Gehenna, I noted something remarkable. The little guy was growing. Well, okay, that of itself was not remarkable. Babies grow, but this fellow was doing it at a preternatural rate. He was like that alien plant in "Little Shop of Horrors." In three days, the young bat was the size of a tabletop. In a week, he was as big as a Chevy Suburban, and by the time we put the finishing touches on Gehenna, the bat was as large as a Cessna.

Over the weeks, the creature and Satan had become close. After that initial evaluative bite to Nick's finger, the bat had shown an affection for my old friend. Love at first bite, I suppose. Satan, for his part, was completely besotted.

"We need a name for him," he said to me one day, as he was leaning against the recumbent, sleeping form of his new friend, like a kid propped up on a pillow watching TV.

"What's that?" I said, distracted. This was the day for my final punch list on the Gehenna project. I was checking fire pit temperatures, measuring the viscosity of the snot well, counting the "Snakes on a Plain," and so forth. This kind of activity required my full range of motion, so I had left my proto mosquito netting back at Devil's Tower. Between swatting bugs and doing my inspection, I hadn't been paying much attention to the boss.

"A name. I can't just keep calling him Batty."

"Why not?"

"Because, I ... Hadad, would you look at me when I'm talking to you?"

I sighed, looking up from my clipboard. "Okay, you have my eyes. Even my ears. Now, what were you going to say?"

He stroked the sleek fur of the bat; it reacted by making a contented "urm" sound. It was the bat's version of a purr. "I want to give my new friend a name."

"Hey, guys," Belphegor said, as he climbed out of the Amazon. He was wearing his wings today, and he fluttered them rapidly, sending a spray of river water over us.

"Skree!" the bat protested in anger.

"Calm down, little one."

Little one? Has Nick even noticed how much this creature has grown?

"I was just telling Hadad that I wanted to give my bat a name."

"Oh?" Belphegor turned to me. "All piranha teeth are within acceptable norms."

64

"Thanks, Belly," I said, putting a check mark next to an item on my punch list. Conjuring up a towel, I threw it to my friend, who used it to dry his face. "Okay, a name. Got any ideas?"

Satan pursed his lips. "Well, I was thinking of Percy."

"Percy? What kind of a sissy name is that?"

"What? You don't like Percy? It's short for Percival, you know."

"Of course, I know!" I grumbled. There was too much on my plate to waste time on this conversation, and I was getting testy. Still, Satan wouldn't be denied. Or – if he felt like talking – he wouldn't shut up, which, in my book, was pretty much the same thing. Sighing, I gave my full attention to the conversation.

"What about naming him Jungle-Bat?" Belphegor suggested.

Satan frowned. "Sounds like something out of a comic book."

Belphegor looked puzzled. "What's that?"

"Don't know," he admitted, but we figured it would mean something someday. "Though naming him after this place might not be a bad idea. We could call him 'Bat out of Gehenna.'"

"That's a bit of a mouthful," I opined.

The subject of our conversation had finished his nap. For a few minutes, he watched us talk, but then he grew bored. The creature stood, flapped his wings, making an impressive breeze, and took off.

"Bat out of Gehenna *is* a bit long." Satan frowned. "What if we just used the consonants?"

Now, this was standard practice back in the old days. You know, like YHWH (Yahweh) or TNKH (Tanakh) or even STN

(Satan, sometimes confused with Stan). Vowels had just been invented, and most people didn't trust them yet. Satan thought for a moment. "Let's see. We eliminate the vowels from 'Bat out of Gehenna' and we get, what, BTTFGHNN."

"Well, that's no good," said Belphegor, tossing the towel back to me. With a quick flip of the fabric, like a jock in a team shower area, I obliterated a couple of thousand bugs, then incinerated the towel.

"Why not?"

"Well," he said, looking embarrassed. "When you add back in the vowels, there's a danger you might use the wrong ones. It might come out as ..." He hesitated.

"What?" Satan said, showing his impatience.

"Well, 'butt fu...'"

"Got it! Something else then."

"There's nothing wrong with vowels, you know." I was always the most progressive of the devil intellectuals. "What do the vowels alone get us?"

Belphegor scrunched his face as he concentrated. "AOUOEEA."

"Awkward. Sounds like you have a mouthful of oatmeal. Perhaps a combination of consonants and vowels?" Nick thought some more. "BOOGehenna, maybe."

"Or just BOOG," Belphegor said.

"Well, I'd still like to see us using more vowels. They're the wave of the future, you know." I felt it my duty to keep the devils current with trends in language. "Maybe at least keep the A at the end."

"BOOGA?" Satan asked.

"Something like that."

"I like it!" Belphegor said, smiling.

"Wonder what he will think." Satan whistled. "BOOGA! BOOGA, BOOGA, BOOGA!"

The entire construction crew broke out laughing.

Satan frowned at his underlings. "What?"

"That sounds funny!" I chortled, wiping a tear from my eye, but then an involuntary shiver coursed through me. "Kind of creepy, too."

"SKREE!" The giant bat flapped above us, hovering like some monstrous dragonfly.

Satan grinned and pointed up at the bat. "He seems to like the name."

And so, the young bat became BOOGA and stayed that way, until we built Hell and rechristened him BOOH.

Chapter 6

Even back then, Satan was thinking his domain should be more than a mere transition point, during which bad humans could be purified before being sent up to the Nice Place. He already had a vision of its potential, so in a way, Gehenna was Hell 1.0 and good practice for what was to come.

We still had time to kill before we judged Cain and Abel old enough to be worth tempting to the dark side, so while Nick, Belphegor and the devil work crew built an office complex for the administration of Gehenna, I continued my explorations of Earth. From Antarctica to Greenland and everywhere in between I roamed. Over time, I discovered, that I had an affinity for arid landscapes. Deserts were particularly attractive to me, I think in part because of the relative paucity of flies and mosquitos in those places. My favorite spot on the planet, and where I soon spent as much time as my schedule allowed, was the Sahara. A living creature was seldom in sight. The solitude the Sahara granted me was a balm to my soul.

Perhaps ten years later, as I was taking my morning walk across the dunes, Satan appeared. "It's time," he said. "Cain and Abel are adults now. Let's go get 'em."

I nodded, and we teleported to a spot not far from where Baghdad would, in time, be founded. There, Adam and Eve and their two sons had set up shop.

You know the story, so I won't repeat much of it here. Abel was a shepherd and Cain a farmer. Mom and Dad liked their younger child – that would be Abel – better than their older. I think it had something to do with the longtime prejudice you humans exhibit toward vegetarians, but I'm just guessing here. Still, if your next meal can't be killed with a rock or a stick, most of you aren't interested, are you?

Just so you know, we didn't have anything to do with the first murder; we were merely witnesses. Cain managed it all on his own. You see, humans have more rumbling around inside of them than dinner ... and free will. There is also lust, greed, gluttony, sloth, and, in this case, pride, anger and envy.

"Will you look at that?" Nick said to me, as we watched Cain rise up against Abel, his brother, and slay him.

"That's harsh," I commented.

Nick sat on the ground, discouraged. "Well, if they're going to take care of their own damnation, what good are we?"

"Buck up, pal," I said, laying a comforting hand on his shoulder. It wasn't mine. I'd borrowed Abel's, since he was no longer using it. "When we get some more humans to work on, we're bound to find some recalcitrance. Then we'll nudge or tempt or whatever."

Satan took Abel's hand and reattached it to the dead body. He smiled at me, appreciating my comforting words. And the hand. "You're right. Not a total loss, I suppose. We now have our first soul."

"What about Adam and Eve?" I asked. "Aren't they damned too?"

"No. I got a note from the Big Guy a while back. Apparently, they get a bye. Abel's dead, and he gets to skip Gehenna as well. But Cain," he said, rubbing his hands in glee. "He's all ours!"

"Speaking of Cain," I said, looking at the world's first murderer. "Look what he's doing now. What a nut case."

Cain was having a conversation with a cloud. Or more like an argument. From the heart of the cloud emerged the same giant hand we'd seen earlier when Eve had been created. I was pretty sure Whose hand that was. Held in those divine fingers was His newest creation.

And lo, we looked upon the thing and knew it for what it was: a giant red Sharpie. The hand used the implement to scribble on Cain's brow.

I shook my head. "That's not going to come out. The ink's permanent, you know."

Satan's head was cocked. His ears had always been better than mine, and he was listening to their conversation. "That's the point. As the world gets populated with more humans, that red mark on Cain's brow will be a major turnoff. You know, he won't be invited to parties or Bingo night or be able to pick up dates at a bar."

"Well," I reflected, "not sure about that bar part. You know how it is. When the lights are low, and a little booze is involved ..."

"Okay, okay," he agreed irritably. "I guess he could get lucky, but generally he'll be an outcast. Untouchable."

Satan stroked his chin. "I suppose there's nothing to do with Cain until he dies." We teleported to the Devil's Tower, which had become my pied-à-terre in the Americas, and I grilled us a couple of steaks. After dinner, we played an early version of Whack-a-Mole with a nearby prairie dog community then sat back for a few decades, chewing the fat as we waited for the world to get a little more populated.

Adam and Eve, understandably discouraged by what happened to their first kids, waited almost a hundred years before having Seth, but after that, Eve started popping out babies left and right. Seth married his sister, which was about all you could do back then, until the family extended enough to allow for kissing, and fucking, cousins.

The family tree grew and grew until there were second and third and even fourth cousins. At that point, no one could cry incest anymore.

Back then, people had very long lives. Adam, for example, lived to be nine hundred and thirty years, and he was having sex up until the very end. His last kid he named Dweezil, I think, but that was because he had run out of names.

These long lives lasted for about ten generations, with two exceptions. Enoch only lived to be three hundred and sixty-five years old, though he was taken up by the Big Guy, rather than actually dying. I guess he was a real favorite, because that only happened one other time. His grandfather, Mahalaleel, didn't make nine centuries; he managed just eight hundred and ninety-five years. The whole thing was a bit of a scandal, really. Mahalaleel was the first human with high cholesterol, and his high-fat diet took him out young, or at least youngish.

And we're not even talking about the women. The Bible, in its chauvinistic fashion, talks about the lifespan of the men, but says nothing about the women, who in some cases lived longer than their mates. Most noteworthy: Lilith never even died. She was too mean, I guess. Regardless, Lilith is still around. As mother of many of the succubi, she holds an honored place in Hell.

During humanity's early period, when these mortals were multiplying at a dizzying rate, I set up shop as a false god. I started small, as a house god, and just as Satan predicted, I had to go from door to door, selling myself.

"Knock, knock."

"Who's there?"

"God."

"God who?"

"Your god."

71

There was a pause. "Oh. My god."

"That's right." *Now we're getting somewhere.*

"What's a god?"

Groan. This fellow was a dim one. "Open the door and I'll explain."

There was a pause. "No," the voice said slowly. "We're eating dinner and throwing sticks into the fire. Family time, you know. Sorry." I heard the tread of his feet as he stepped away from the door.

With a heavy sigh, I settled down on a nearby boulder. (Curbs didn't exist yet.) Getting worshippers was proving more difficult that I had expected.

They don't even know what a god is. At least this guy didn't. That might have meant we were going to get his soul no matter what, but for some reason, the thought provided little comfort. "First Cain handles his own damnation, and now this guy looks like he's doing the same. Shit." *If humanity damns itself, what's my purpose in all this?*

Frustrated, I shot some flame into the air, inadvertently fricasseeing a passing pigeon. It fell with a thump at my feet. Never one to waste food, I picked up the still-smoldering carcass and made a snack out of it.

I always think best when I'm eating. Perhaps that's how I ended up as the Devil Prince of Gluttony.

As I was cracking the second drumstick between my fangs, an idea came to me. There should be some kind of quid pro quo. I would need to do something for the humans in exchange for getting them to worship me. *But what?*

I threw the last of the pigeon down my gullet, then got off the rock. With new determination, I went to the next house on the block.

"Knock, knock."

I heard footsteps coming to the door. "Who's there?"

"Your personal god," I said, trying to make a connection with the prospect. To my surprise, the door opened. Funny how just a minor change in a sales pitch could alter the dynamic. Thinking I might need them, I summoned up some business cards, proclaiming myself as "Hadad, house god for hire."

The man before me was about four foot six and dressed in an animal hide. I think it was a camel skin. Smelled like one, anyway. In the background, I saw his wife, a homely, pudgy woman, who was flanked by two equally homely children. I had retained my devil horns and tail, and those, along with my seven-foot stature, helped me cut an impressive figure.

Perhaps a little scary too, for the man startled. He swallowed hard and said, "Your personal god who?"

"Your personal god who will protect you and grant all your wishes. My card," I said solemnly, handing him one.

He stared at it, but I'm not sure he could even read, since he kept turning it around and around, squinting at it as if the thing were giving him eyestrain.

My prospective customer looked up from the card and frowned at me. I guess he realized that a seven-foot salesman with horns and a tail is, in the final analysis, just a salesman. "Yeah. Right. Go away. We're playing Scrabble with the kids." He slammed the door in my face.

Now that was just improper etiquette, and it made me mad, so I burned down his house.

Hey, I *am* a devil. That should allow me to show the occasional bit of pique. Besides, he was being rude. Insensitive, too. How would he have liked going from door to door selling himself like a prostitute?

Except no one's buying. Grumble.

I left the family as they frantically beat at the flames with some blankets.

I went to the next block, figuring some neighbors might have spotted my act of arson and concluded that I was a vengeful god. That was true enough but didn't seem like the best introduction for any salesman.

"Knock, knock."

The door opened. "What do you want?"

I offered this new fellow my card. "My name is Hadad, and for today only I am offering up myself to you as your own personal god."

"And how do I know you're *really* a god?"

"W...well," I stammered. "I can do magic."

The customer looked skeptical. "Yeah? So show me something magical."

I made a bouquet of roses appear.

"Those were up your sleeve."

"They were not! I made them materialize. Out of thin air. Here, take them. They're for you."

"I don't want them. Besides, I'm allergic to roses. Scram!" He slammed the door in my face.

Boy, being a false god is a hard job. I resisted the urge to torch his house.

This wasn't getting me anywhere. But then I had a flash of inspiration. If they were to worship me, I'd have to give them something more than a dozen roses and some vague promises.

The next home on the block was a dilapidated structure. The family that lived there had seen better times. Either that or the husband wasn't particularly good with his hands.

"Knock, knock."

The door opened. The fellow before me might have been lazy, poor or inept, but he wasn't stupid. A sort of

74

intelligence, let's call it shrewdness, stared out from behind his eyes.

"Yes?" He said cautiously.

"It is I, Hadad, Master of Lightning and Storm. Accept me as your personal god, and I will serve you."

"Serve me how?"

I shrugged, realizing I still hadn't figured out an appropriate quid pro quo. "I'm sure we can work something out."

The homeowner looked thoughtful. "And how do I accept you as my personal god?"

I cleared my throat. "Well," I stalled. I hadn't thought this part through either, but I brightened as an idea came to me. "Slaughter a calf, offer it up to me, and I will do thy bidding."

The fellow seemed skeptical. "I don't know. Calves are pretty expensive. Besides I only have one, and we use it to keep the family warm at night." A moo came from somewhere inside his house. "How about a rat?"

"A rat?"

"Sure! Got lots of them." He reached behind the door. There was a squeal and he held up a squirming rat by its tail for me to see.

A rat seemed like a paltry sacrifice, and I almost said so, but this was my first sale, and a sale was a sale. "Well … okay."

There was a fire pit in the back – I guess that's where the fellow barbecued on the weekends – and that was where he sacrificed the rat, th   ough it probably wasn't much of a sacrifice for him. I even used magic to light the fire, which gave credence to my story of being an all-powerful god, I suppose.

In moments, the rat was toast, or, rather, toasted rat. I picked it up and downed the charred rodent in a single bite.

My new acolyte eyed me through slitted lids. "What now, oh great Hadad ... my lord," he added as an afterthought.

"You're supposed to bow before me on hands and knees."

"Oh, really? Well, fine." He got down beside the fire. Did it right proper too, bowing and scraping like an experienced devotee. "I've worshipped you now, so you'll do something for me, right?"

"Humph. I *said* I would. What do you want?"

"Paint my house."

"What?"

"Paint my house. The wife's been after me to do it for months."

"But that's not dignified. I'm your god, your personal house god."

"Then this is perfect," he rejoined. "Paint my personal house," he hesitated, then as if throwing me a bone, concluded with "My Lord Hadad."

"But ..."

"Come on. A deal's a deal."

I could feel my hands clench into fists but took a few calming breaths. At last I managed to spit out, "What color?"

"Teal."

"Teal?"

"My wife's favorite. It's sort of a blue-green."

"I know what the fuck color it is! Very well," I grumbled then waved my hand. The house was now a freshly painted teal.

"That's amazing!" My new worshipper said, as he walked around his house. "Hey, you forgot the shutters."

"You didn't say anything about shutters," I said, pleased with my minor act of devilry.

The man gave me a withering look. "They're part of the house. You promised to paint it. Part of the house, part of the deal."

I wasn't sure I wanted this particular worshipper. "What color?" I asked with a sigh.

"White."

"Fine." Another wave of my hand, and he had white shutters.

The man nodded in satisfaction. "You know, Hadad, I mean, my lord, you do good work. Do you do windows as well?"

"No!" I snapped. "I *don't* do windows. Now sign here," I said, holding out a scrap of vellum and a stick with animal blood on it.

"What's this?"

"A list of my converts."

"Why aren't there other names on it?"

"It's a new page!" I snapped. "Now sign!"

Smoke had begun to rise from my head. Seeing this, the man offered no more objections and scribbled his name where I indicated.

"Sheldon? Your name is Sheldon?"

"Yeah," he said, a little embarrassed. Even back then, no one wanted to be named Sheldon.

"Then, Sheldon, just remember, I am your god now. You must worship me. Once a week you must sacrifice to me a fatted, errr, rat, okay?"

"Sure! That's way cheaper than hiring an exterminator."

I thought my head would explode. I had to get out of there. "Don't forget!" I yelled and disappeared.

Well, that was humiliating.

I reappeared on the far side of the village. I had my first convert, but I simply had to come up with a more effective sales pitch.

I was so angry when I went to the next house that I didn't even think about what to say. I punched the front door, which disintegrated from the blow.

A family of eight cowered at the back of the small cottage.

"Who's there?" said the head of the household in a meek voice.

"It is I, Hadad, Master of the Lightning and of the Storm. Accept me as your personal god, and I will smite your enemies!"

The husband came to the pile of sawdust that had once been a door. "You ... You can do that?"

"Sure!" I grinned. "Show me an enemy, and I shall smite him."

"Okay. See Roger over there?" He said, pointing to a man mowing his yard across the street. In the early years of humanity, they used scythes for that purpose, but mowing the yard is a time-honored task for the male head of a household, so even back then he was doing it.

"Yeah."

"He's an arrogant snot. Besides, I think last week he stole my goat, though I don't have any proof. Anyway, he is my enemy, so smite away." With that, my prospective worshipper crossed his arms and leaned against the door sill to watch.

I pointed a finger at Roger and blasted him with a bolt of lightning. Roger, hair singed and fuming, dropped his scythe and fell to the ground, moaning softly.

"Cool! Where do I sign?"

"Here, please."

Once I started smiting enemies, business started to pick up. I liked being Hadad, the storm god. I was sort of like Thor, without the hammer, though, which was too bad. I wish I'd thought of the hammer. That would have had some real style to it.

Once I got my sales pitch down, I was on my way. I was converting humans to the ranks of Hadadists left and right, and in no time, word got around that there was a new god in town.

Chapter 7

Satan was thrilled with my progress, and, while he and Belphegor took progressively more of the Amazon River basin for their expanded Gehenna, Nick had me enlist a few others to work different parts of the world as false gods. That included Sekhmet.

Little confession here: I've always been sweet on Sekhmet. She's a wonderful devil, not to mention hotter than hell. She's got a body to die for, and her lioness head is sexy beyond belief. For centuries, I'd been trying to, well, ingratiate myself with her.

Sekhmet was playing it cool, though. She liked me well enough but didn't want anything like an exclusive relationship. Sekhmet enjoyed sleeping around. This was disappointing to me, but since I was one of the guys she slept around with, it could have been worse.

One day, after we'd been connubial, I pitched the idea of her becoming a false goddess. "Why would I want to do that?"

"Aren't you bored?" I asked, kissing one of her furry ears. "I mean, you can't spend night and day just screwing."

She looked at me in surprise. "Well, sure I can."

"Well, okay, I guess you can. Your dance card seems full. But wouldn't you like to help with the Plan? I've been a false god for a while now, and it's fun."

"Is it, now?" She asked, as she climbed on top of me. "As fun as that?" She said when we were finished.

"Okay, Sekhsie," I said with a gasp, "maybe not as fun as that, but it's different. Variety is the spice of life, you know."

"Oh, I know that well," she purred. "In fact, Belial will be here in fifteen minutes, so we should wrap this up."

We assumed another position, a complicated one involving levitation, so you humans shouldn't try it. But after we finished and I turned to go, I said over my shoulder, "Just consider it, okay?"

"Okay," she said, stretching like a cat. Then she smoothed the sheets and sat down to await her next visitor.

I left, grumbling. I have no problem with Belial, but, well, you know.

In time, Sekhmet agreed to become a false god and headed to Egypt. Her lioness head was a big hit there.

Everything was going great. We had false gods all over the place, and the world started to go to hell in a hand basket. I'm being figurative here, as well as anachronistic, since Hell didn't exist yet. Then we had a major setback.

That blasted flood.

Apparently, I had been doing my job too well. People who believed in Hadad tended to have a malicious streak, usually because I hooked them with that "smite thine enemies" line. Once I got them, I preached the logic and importance of the vices Satan and I would one day codify as the Seven Deadly Sins. As a result, my believers were not the nicest of people.

And so, the world was full of bad folk. Except for Noah. Now, believe it or not, Adam was still alive when Noah was born, though by then the old guy had become senile. Everyone hated going to his birthday parties. First, he'd had so many of them; watching Adam try to blow out over nine hundred candles on his cake, well, it was pathetic. And at every social event when Adam showed up, at least one of the younger children would grumble under his or her breath, "Would you just die, already?"

Noah was not one of them. He was a good kid, and even at the age of fifty-six, he wept like a child when the first man finally died.

But as for the rest of humanity, yeah, they were pretty despicable. At first, the Plan was to just wipe out the entire human race, saving only Noah, his family and a bunch of animals. You know, the whole ark thing. But if you preserve a male and a female of marrying age, and embalming agents aren't involved, you're going to end up with more babies, so the Plan was revised to be just a reboot, with hopes for a better outcome in the future.

"And you'd better slow down next time," Nick suggested. "We don't want to have to endure another one of these floods."

Indeed. What a mess. Water was everywhere, as is generally the case with floods and major plumbing leaks. I couldn't get the Sahara Desert dried out for nearly a century. My followers were all dead, yet that wasn't a total loss, as we got a huge influx of souls into Gehenna. Still, I had to start all over as a false god. Going from door to door again, reestablishing my reputation, was tedious.

Back to Noah and the flood. Adam was gone, but you might wonder about the rest of the ancient humans from the first generations. They too were all dead and buried by the time of the Flood, which occurred when Noah was six hundred. The last to die was Methuselah, who passed during the same year as the Flood. I think the waters were held off just to let these old fogies expire on their own. That was nice of the Big Guy.

I said the Flood was a mess, but not everyone disliked it. Leviathan, for instance, was in his element. Well, naturally he was in his element, since he liked water. Ziz retreated to the skies while the rain fell. I don't know what Behemoth did. He probably just held his breath for a long time.

The rest of us sprouted wings and flew above the clouds as the torrent progressed. Forty days and forty nights. Ugh. My shoulders cramp just thinking how long I was flapping up there.

The rain stopped, and the waters began to recede, yet the world was completely submerged for another five months. Finally, one morning, Noah spied a bit of rock poking out of the drink. By day's end, he knew it to be more than a rock. The family conferred and agreed it was the tip of a mountain. Ararat. With a sigh of relief, Noah steered his ark toward the summit.

All this Nick and I watched from above. The ark was moving slowly if purposefully along when the water in its wake began to churn. Nick stared below the surface, frowning. "It's Leviathan. What is that troublemaker doing?"

"Looks like he's on a collision course with the ark. See, he's already reached ramming speed."

"What an imbecile! Doesn't he realize he's interfering with the Divine Plan?"

I shrugged, which caused me to catch an updraft with my wings. I was now flying twenty feet above Nick. "Leviathan likes to destroy things, even more than you do. I doubt he's considered the ramifications of his actions." I paused. "We ought to just let Management take care of him, but ..." I cracked my knuckles.

"Go ahead," Satan encouraged. "Perhaps you can earn us some brownie points."

I nodded and dove, piercing the water at a spot right behind Leviathan. He had assumed one of his favorite forms, the sea serpent. So focused was Leviathan on intercepting the ark that he didn't even notice me. I reached out and grabbed his tail, jerking hard. Leviathan, forward momentum stopped, popped back toward me like a rubber band. Now we were face to face.

He snarled at me. "Hadad! What are you doing?"

"Tugging on your tail, I think."

"Well, stop it and let go. I have an ark to sink."

I shook my head. "Now why would you do that?"

"To kill everyone on board, you fool!"

I ignored the insult. "Kinda thought that's what you had in mind. Who told you to do this?"

"Why," he sputtered, "I thought of it myself."

"I figured that, too. Okay, I'll let go of your tail ... in a second. First, let me help you think through this."

"What's there to think through? And would you quit squeezing so hard?"

"Sorry," I said, relaxing my grip. "Don't know my own strength. But listen, what do you think would happen if you killed them?"

"They'd die! Now, let go, dammit! I've only got a few more seconds before they reach the mountain."

"Glad to." I released Leviathan's tail. "I was just trying to prevent you from getting into a heap of trouble."

"Good, I, uh, what are you talking about?"

"Leviathan, Leviathan, Leviathan," I said, shaking my head. "If you kill everyone on that ark, you will be eradicating the last people on the planet."

"So what?" he snarled.

"If you want to piss off Management, go right ahead, but if you kill the last humans on earth, you're going to be messing up the Plan."

He snorted. "Whose plan? Lucifer's?"

"Ah, no. His Plan. The Divine One."

84

Leviathan's eyes widened. "What? I, uh …"

This is the problem with having someone like Leviathan as an archenemy. Though he is very powerful, and a great one to cause mayhem, he isn't much on strategy. Or tactics. He's strong as a steer, if not quite as smart.

I left him floating there, the ark forgotten as my words penetrated his thick skull. Leviathan never admitted it, but I saved his ass that day.

Nick had been watching my undersea expedition. As I rejoined him, he shook his head, mumbled something about devil dementia, then returned his attention to the ark.

We watched as it snagged atop Mount Ararat. Noah released a raven to check and then report on the conditions of the surrounding area.

The raven was a good choice. Ravens can talk a little, not as well as parrots, but at the time, both of Noah's parrots had strep throat. The rest of the talking birds, like the mynas, were on strike, demanding better living conditions. They wouldn't cooperate. That's why Larry, the raven, got the job.

Oh, he never returned; Ziz ate him. Fortunately, Larry had already knocked up his mate, saving the raven species with a new generation.

Next Noah sent out a dove. She couldn't talk but could communicate with Avian Sign Language (ASL). Using Claire was a bold if dangerous move. First off, she was pregnant, and second, she was their only female dove. If Ziz had chosen to eat her as well, well, bye-bye doves.

Oh, by the way, she was a rock dove. A pigeon. Maybe the end of that species might not have been too bad. They are irritating birds, especially in cities, where they will poop on your freshly cleaned sports coat or beg without mercy for food. But

85

she made it back, did a tail wiggle, signaling "not yet," then had her babies.

After Claire had recuperated from the delivery, Noah sent her out a second time. She returned with an olive leaf in her beak. That probably meant it was okay to park the ark, but Noah wanted to play it safe, so he waited another week. His decision demonstrated great restraint, because by then, with all the animals on board, the ark had turned into a smelly place.

At week's end, Noah dispatched his pigeon a third time, but she never returned. Noah figured Claire had found safe haven, liking it well enough to abandon her family, but that isn't what happened. This time, Ziz *did* eat her, leaving a bereft father dove and four baby birds to support.

A raven doesn't come back, and it's a bad omen, but the same thing happens with a dove, and that's okay? Weird. Yet that's how Noah interpreted events, so he opened the doors of the now-burgeoning ark. There had been a lot of sex going on during that boat ride. The past six months had been dull, and screwing seemed like a good way to pass the time. What else was there to do? TV hadn't been invented yet. And Noah wouldn't let the animals eat each other, which would have been a good onboard activity, at least for the carnivores, not to mention easing the crowding situation. Most of the female animals were pregnant by the time they landed. That included the women.

After the flood, humanity repopulated the planet in no time, and I reestablished myself as a false god. Since I had a bad reputation among Noah's descendants, I changed my name from Hadad to Ba'al, or Ba'al of Ekron, but my shtick was pretty much the same. Smite an enemy; get a convert. If it ain't broke, don't fix it.

After Noah, people just didn't live as long. Shem, his eldest, only lived to be six hundred. In a handful of generations, the life expectancy of the patriarchs was in the four hundreds. A few generations more, and it was down to two hundred, where it held for a couple of centuries, until dipping down to what most people now think is a normal lifespan. These days, you people are lucky if you live to be a hundred.

I've wondered why lifespans dropped the way they did. The reason probably has to do with the number of generations that had elapsed since the creation of the first humans. The Divine Hand had direct involvement in that act, but after Adam and Eve, humans were made the old-fashioned way. With each passing generation, the fire of creation burned with less vigor in the human soul.

By the time Abraham, née Abram, came along, two hundred was about the best you could expect in longevity. I won't retell Abraham's story to you, but I will say that he led an interesting life. I can't decide if he had the strongest faith of any human I ever knew, or if he was just the most gullible person that ever lived. You have to be one or the other to agree to get circumcised at the age of ninety-nine.

Another example involved his son, Isaac. Abraham was prepared to slay his heir, the child of his old age. A joke: it had to have been a joke. Good grief, if Gabriel hadn't gotten there in time, the old man would have done it. Got to give it to Abraham, though. Faithful.

Up until this time, while I'd been on false god duty, Nick didn't have much to do. Gehenna had been up and running for almost two thousand years. The shakedown period common with any new venture had long passed, and Nick's management duties were light, so he looked for opportunities to cause mischief. One accomplishment was talking those gullible twats into building the Tower of Babel.

"Uh, now why, exactly, would we want to build a tower that high?"

"Why, to get to Heaven that much more quickly. It'll be great! You'll see."

They saw, all right. By divine decree, language, which up until then had been singular, not dissimilar in structure and sound to today's Pig Latin, broke, like glass dropped on a hard surface. Each shard became its own language, and nobody understood anybody anymore.

"Was ist los?"

"Beg pardon?"

"Como?"

You get the idea. Then those doofuses were scattered to the four corners of the Earth.

Satan also helped with the corruption of Sodom and Gomorrah, not to mention getting Lot's wife turned into a pillar of salt. That was just a cheap trick, by the way.

"Hey, Edith! ... Ha! Made ya' look!"

Then Nick got bored and retreated to his office. Not for long, though.

By now, there were so many humans around to tempt, all devils had their hands full. Even Satan had to return to the field, just to keep up with the workload.

Soon, the offspring of Abraham headed over to Egypt. Not one of their better life decisions, unless you consider enslavement to be a smart move.

Chapter 8

Moses was a late bloomer, not as late as Abraham, who was seventy-five before he started to show promise. Still, Moses wasn't any child prodigy.

I'm sure you know the story of Moses in the Bullrushes. Great stuff, a baby placed in a waterproofed basket, which floated upon the river until Pharaoh's daughter discovered and adopted him. This kind of iconic origin story often portends something special for the protagonist. Like Batman, for instance. But in the early years, Moses didn't accomplish much. He was a bit of a rabble-rouser, constantly getting in trouble for stealing wheels off chariots, putting whoopee cushions on Pharaoh's throne. That sort of thing. Most of it could be written off to the foolishness of youth, except for killing that guy.

You could say Moses was provoked. Nobody likes a bully, though not many people will stand up to one. Moses did, killing the Egyptian who was smiting a Hebrew slave. That got Moses into a great deal of trouble. He skipped to Midian before Pharaoh's goon squad could arrest him.

Midian was a bit of a hike from Cairo, almost five hundred miles, as the ibis flies. To get there, Moses crossed a desert, traversed the Sinai, hung a right at Raqmu, the town that would eventually be called Petra, and then headed down towards the Gulf of Aqaba. Finally, he reached Midian, and, footsore and weary, he took a drink from a well then plopped down next to it for a nap.

At the well, Moses met his wife-to-be, Zipporah, along with her six sisters. They had come there to get water for their flock, but just as they'd filled the sheep trough, some other shepherds drove them away. The sisters, I mean. Not the flock.

That's when Moses, who had been taking a well-deserved siesta, woke. Now, we've already established that Moses hated bullies. He always had a mean right hook, so in no time he drove off the shepherds and watered the sisters' flock. He did a proper job of it too, completely soaking the sheep's wool.

Moses fighting all those shepherds in front of the ladies was just his way of showing off, but it worked out for him. Turns out their father was Jethro, BMOC (big man on camel) in the village, a priest. He took a shine to young Moses and gave Zipporah to him for a wife.

"One down, six to go," Jethro was heard to say at the wedding.

Moses liked being married to Zipporah, and he liked living in Midian. Nice spot, as I recall. Hot. Not many flies.

Some years passed.

I had been keeping my eye on this guy. He showed potential, and I had a bet with Nick that Moses would in time play an important role in the emerging religion of Judaism. What I didn't know was that I'd play a supporting part in that drama.

While strolling across the Sahara, I got the call. Well, I wasn't strolling in the conventional sense; I was playing sandstorm. That's when I spin very fast, creating a vortex that sucks up the sand around me. I look like a tornado when I play sandstorm. This, by the way, is where the expression "dust devil" comes from.

I was spinning and spinning, traveling at high speed across the dunes in – where was it? – Libya, when I got the summons.

"Hadad. Hadad!"

I recognized the voice. It was Metatron. I ignored him and continued my fun.

"Hadad! Would you please be still? You're making me nauseous."

I sighed. "Fine." My stop was so abrupt that the motes of sand were confused momentarily. They spun another three hundred degrees or so then, realizing we'd stopped, shot out in all directions, landed on the ground and commenced being dirt again.

I looked in the direction of the voice. Metatron was up about ten thousand feet. "What do you want?"

"I want you to get Moses to take his flock to the back side of the desert."

I frowned. "Now, why would he want to do that? There's no water there."

"Just do it, okay?"

"Why should I? You're not the boss of me. I'm a devil. You're an angel. We're on opposite sides."

"Well, yes, that's true, I suppose, but in this instance, I'm speaking for our mutual Boss."

He would know. Metatron's sobriquet is "The Voice of God," but more on that in a minute.

"Oh. When you put it like that, I guess I can't argue, but why don't you get one of your own to do this?"

Metatron shrugged. "We're short staffed today. The company picnic is going on right now, so we only have a skeleton force on the clock. And I can't do it myself, because I have some setup to do first."

"Fine. Great. Any suggestions on how I'm to get him up there?"

"Improvise. Just don't let him know you're a devil. It would undercut the mood we're trying to establish."

"Which would be?"

"Just get him to the back side of the desert and up the mountain of God. Hang around for a while and see for yourself."

That piqued my interest, so I headed to Midian. I found Moses, leaning against a pistachio tree, eating nuts and killing the idle moments by throwing the husks at the butts of his charges. The flock of Moses's father-in-law was large, perhaps eighty ewes and four rams. The latter were fine looking specimens, but a twenty to one girl/boy ratio was still a bit of an ovine challenge. Some of the ewes looked neglected, wallflowers in the sheep world, I suppose.

I considered my assignment and came up with a plan, transformed into a large ram and began mingling with the herd. The other rams gave me dirty looks, but since I was fifty percent larger than any of them, they offered me no trouble.

The girls liked what they saw and came sidling up to me, rubbing their soft wool in my face and doing other come-hither sheep moves. I gave them a collective smile, or what I think was a smile, then baahing in a sexy baritone, headed for the mountain. The ladies followed me. The guys followed the ladies, which is standard protocol for most animal species on Earth.

That's one of the nice things about dealing with sheep, you know. They play follow the leader well.

"What the fu ...?" Moses got off his rump and chased after us.

We had a head-start, though, and he needed thirty minutes to catch up. Finally, he got in front of us. Moses held his shepherd's staff before him, as if he were going to halt the sheep stampede by sheer will alone. Fortunately for him, stampedes of the ovine variety are tepid affairs, especially when the leader of the mob, in this case yours truly, came to a dead stop. There was a bit of bumping into backsides, I heard a few "oofs" from behind me, but the rest of the flock got the message.

And so, it came to pass that Moses, just barely, was in the lead when we got to the backside of the desert and the mountain of God, or Horeb. This mountain was also known as Sinai, and it would figure prominently two times in the life of Moses, this being the first.

On the side of the mountain, not far above the stalled flock, a light flickered. It caught Moses's attention, and, forgetting about his sheep, he started to climb toward the glow. I gave the sheep a stern warning to stay put then slipped away, discarded my ram disguise and teleported to where the light was.

"Will you look at that?" I said to myself. Before me was a burning bush. Well, I say it was burning, but it wasn't turning to ash or anything. It burned without being consumed. That was a neat trick. I wish I had thought of something like that when I'd started off as a house god. It would have impressed the hell out of people and saved a lot of time establishing my credibility.

The Almighty has always been so creative.

There was a scrabbling among the rocks below my level on the mountain. I got out of sight just as Moses crested the hill.

Now the Creator of All has a lot of angels, and the book of Exodus is vague about this point, but when it says the angel of the Lord appeared to Moses in the flame, we're talking here about Metatron. He is, after all, the only angel authorized to speak as if he is God himself, which is why he is called the Voice of God.

Let me explain. The Almighty's voice would melt the mind of an angel or devil, and a human would likely fare worse. An angel of the Lord was doing the talking, and since this one very definitely passed himself off as God, it's only logical that it would be Metatron.

Oh. Here is another fun fact about him. Remember a while back when I told you about Enoch being taken up into Heaven? Well, when that happened, he was promoted, and he got his name changed. That's right. To Metatron. To my knowledge, he was the first and only human to become an angel. And the Voice of God at that. Yes: a very special guy.

The Voice told Moses to take off his shoes, which he did, and then gave the mortal an elaborate set of commands, the gist of which was to get His people the heck out of Egypt and into a land of their own, which supposedly flowed with milk and honey. Now, I've never seen a place like that, with cow juice and sweet bee nectar spilling over the ground like babbling brooks, so I'm assuming He was being metaphorical. Sounded good though, and Moses, after some reluctance, took the job.

Yes, I could certainly take some lessons in God salesmanship from Him. Not that He was likely to take me on as an apprentice. Still, I reflected, I was doing pretty well with my "smite thine enemies" pitch, and I resolved to stick with it.

Moses got some special superpowers to use when needed to convince the enslaved Israelites and the enslaving Egyptians that he was the real deal and not some poser. For instance, he could turn his staff into a snake. Pretty neat. He could also make his hand leprous and then turn it back to a healthy pink. That was a gross but effective tactic, I suppose.

Moses wasn't much of a public speaker. Anticipating this, the Almighty arranged for Aaron, the brother of Moses, to meet up with him in the wilderness. On Horeb, Aaron got the job to be the official head of communications for the enterprise, sort of a mini-Metatron for Moses, the mini-God. Or demigod, I suppose. In the beginning of their campaign against the

Egyptians, until Moses gained confidence, Aaron handled much of the fancy stuff, but eventually Moses found his voice and did most of his own public speaking and miracles.

This was all turning out to be interesting stuff. I knew Satan would like to see this – he was always a big fan of watching the Big Guy do things on Earth. Besides, Nick got bored easily, and needed the distraction.

I teleported to the corporate office of Gehenna, where I found him hooking together a bunch of paper clips.

"I see you're devising creative new forms of punishment for the Damned."

"What?" He said, looking up at me. "No, I'm just making a chain with these things. I'm bored." He sighed.

See?

"That's why I'm here. There's some interesting stuff about to happen in Egypt, and I thought you'd like to watch."

With great care, Nick placed his paper clip chain on his desktop. Then, for reasons that escaped me for thousands of years, he conjured up a boater, raccoon skin coat and a little triangular flag on a stick. "Keen!" he said, after suiting up. "Let's go."

Chapter 9

The early days of Moses's campaign to save the Israelites were filled with the sort of necessary if mundane tasks required before anything of consequence can begin. First, he had to talk the family into taking a trip to Egypt. Jethro didn't care if they left, since he had plenty of other family in the area. By then, he was old and infirm, especially after being injured in a three-dromedary pileup caused by his own camel, Earl, who failed to yield the right of way. Jethro's only advice to his son-in-law was to pack extra underwear, since holy missions, or anything else for that matter, always take longer than you think they will.

Zipporah was another matter. "What? It's the middle of the school year! We can't pull Gershom and Eliezer out now. Gershom will miss the PSAT (Practical Semitic Aptitude Test), and you know Eliezer is the best goalie in his league. Without him, they don't stand a chance of winning the Midian Medal."

"Honey," Moses said. "This is important. We'll just have to home school them."

Zipporah put her hands on her hips. "We? My, aren't we plural? You mean me, don't you?"

"Well," he hesitated, "yes. I'm going to be kind of busy with the new job and all."

"Great. Just great." There was more grumbling and arguing, but in the end Zipporah, good sport that she was, agreed to go.

And so, one fine morning, they packed up the family camel and headed west.

There were remarkably few mishaps on the way, mainly because a guardian angel was assigned to get the family safely to the land of the pharaohs. Well, there was one misstep. Moses took them to Thebes, which is where his adopted grandfather, Seti I, had had his capital. During the Midian years, though, Seti had died and been succeeded by his son Rameses II. Rameses (or Ramesses or Ramses, take your choice) had moved the capital to the eastern delta of the Nile, where he'd built a magnificent edifice to glorify his achievements. All this the family learned from a street vendor in Thebes, which had fallen on hard times with the departure of the royal court.

"Uh, honey," Moses said hesitantly, after getting the bad news from the vendor, "we're going to have to backtrack a little, I'm afraid. Turns out Pharaoh has moved."

"What? Didn't I tell you to ask directions?" Zipporah could not hide her irritation. She looked up to the heavens. "God of my people, why will men never ask for directions?"

"Now wait just a second," Moses protested. "This is so not my fault. I knew where I was going. I grew up here, remember? Ask Aaron." He looked over imploringly at his big brother, who just shrugged, averting his eyes from what was likely to turn into an awkward family squabble, and polished his staff.

His walking staff, I mean. Polishing the other one might have gotten him arrested for committing lewd acts in public.

Using all his persuasive powers, Moses got Zipporah to accept that it was an honest mistake. "Well," she sighed, "at least let's take in the sights. For the children's sake."

Thebes, once one of the world's great cities, had seen better days. During Seti's reign, you could have had your picture painted while standing next to a life-sized statue of Pharaoh, eaten lamb kebabs while taking in a view of the scenic Nile River valley, or gone shopping in a bazaar larger than a Macy's store. Now it didn't even have a 7-Eleven. The family wandered the almost deserted streets for an hour. The most interesting thing they found was a pile of desiccated locust shells, swept up against the side of a cracked obelisk. Finally, they gave up on touring, bought from the vendor a couple of "Pharaoh Slept Here" T-shirts for the kids, and headed north.

As is often the case with great rulers, Rameses had modestly named his new capital after himself, Pi-Ramesses Aa-nakhtu, which roughly translates as "Domain of Rameses, Great in Victory." I guess I should cut Rameses some slack. He really was the greatest of all the pharaohs, so bragging rights were in order, but he had an ego the size of a pyramid. Convincing him to release the Israelites would be a challenge.

Damn, but he was a stubborn SOB. It didn't help that he and Moses had grown up together in Seti's palace, resulting in a sibling rivalry that complicated their relationship.

The brothers couldn't get an appointment with Pharaoh for two weeks. On the day the summons came, Moses had a bad case of nerves. "Does my hair look okay?" he asked.

"Yes, it's fine," Aaron soothed. "I don't know why you're so nervous. You're making me do all the talking."

Nick and I, who had been traveling, invisible, with the family since their departure from Midian, looked at each other and grinned. Nervous humans always amused us. They were likely to make mistakes, and when they did, often as not, we ended up getting our hands on them. We didn't expect that to happen this time, though. Too much of the Divine Plan was at work.

And then they were before him, Rameses II, the Great, ruler of all Egypt. That first meeting did not go well. "Moses, you old so-in-so," Rameses said, declining to shake the hand of his childhood companion. "Can't really do that anymore. Pharaoh, you know. Besides, last time we shook hands, you put a sheep turd in my palm."

"Er, well, yes." Moses grinned nervously. "Boys will be boys. Oh, this is my brother, Aaron." Aaron stretched out his hand to shake, thought better of it, and dropped it to his side.

"What do you two want?"

Moses grinned again, digging his elbow in Aaron's side. The older man cleared his throat.

"Thus saith the Lord God of Israel. Let my people go."

This is a great line, and Aaron delivered it with all the authority of a true representative of the Lord, but Pharaoh was unimpressed. "Now, why would I do that? The Israelites are some of my best workers. In fact, they are so good that ..." He smiled evilly then pulled sort of a Rumpelstiltskin. "I think they could make bricks without straw. Scribe!" He said to one of his attendants. "Create a decree, to which I shall affix my seal, ending the Israelites allotment of straw."

"What?" fumed Moses. "That hardly seems fair."

"Whoever said life is fair?" Then, at Pharaoh's direction, the guards carted off the two brothers, throwing them down the exterior steps of the palace.

"Well, that could have gone better," Aaron grumbled, brushing dirt from his robe. "What's next?"

Moses said nothing, but an angry fire burned in his eyes.

What was next was a series of meetings, intransigence and plagues. Nick and I found the meetings a bore, except for one thing. We recognized most of Pharaoh's wise men and wizards.

They were Leviathan and some of his cohorts in disguise. Though we were still invisible, our former colleagues saw us. Behemoth gave a wave. The others just smirked.

"Why are they here?" Nick whispered.

"Why not?" Said a voice from on high.

"Metatron?"

Hanging from the ceiling, like a chandelier, was a glowing head. "Leviathan, Ziz and the others are just trying to sow some discord here, as you, the Adversary pro tem, ought to be doing."

"Now, wait a minute," I protested. "Just a while ago, you had me working the other side of this story."

The head frowned. "I told you I was short-handed that day, but now you should be back to your own duties, instead of letting Leviathan take the lead. Hmm," Metatron said, "maybe Leviathan should have gotten the job after all."

"That's a cheap dig." Satan hissed. "I'll show you who's Adversary around here."

Leviathan put his finger to his lips, shushing us. The scene in the room was getting interesting.

Moses and Aaron were doing one of their signature miracles, turning Aaron's staff – his walking staff – into a snake. Not to be outdone, Leviathan and two of his pals turned their own staffs into serpents.

Which were promptly swallowed up by Serpent number one. Score for Moses and his team.

But Pharaoh's heart was hardened, even after a series of plagues that included turning the waters of the Nile to blood and releasing a horde of frogs, then lice, and then flies onto Egypt. That last one was my idea, by the way.

Still no good. Rameses would not be moved.

Egyptian cattle died next, but not those of the Israelites. Then the Egyptians got, in rapid succession, boils and hail and fire. Crops were decimated. Locusts overran the place. I mean, this was the full-court press. Consideration was also given to a plague of post-nasal drip, but the idea was dropped, as it was deemed anticlimactic after all the other plagues.

Only when the Angel of Death (Mortimer, a good friend of mine) took the first-born of every Egyptian family did Pharaoh cry uncle.

He summoned Moses and Aaron to the palace. "Shit. You guys win. You and your people: get out of here."

And so began the Exodus. The Israelites had many more adventures, and Moses, getting into his role as miracle worker, did lots of cool stuff. The parting of the Red Sea you know about, I imagine. It wasn't as impressive looking as what Charlton Heston did in the movie, but then what Moses did was real, while Paramount's was all special effects, in a bathtub I think, though admittedly the movie was in Technicolor, which counts for something.

There were other spectacular events, bread raining from the sky, pillars of fire and cloud, etc. One should remember though, that Moses and Aaron really didn't do any of these things. The Boss did.

We won't step through the rest of the Moses story. You can read it in the Bible. But there are three other incidents I'd like to relate in brief, because Nick and I played roles in them.

From the time we encountered Leviathan and his gang in the throne room of Rameses, Nick was anxious to have some role in the Exodus narrative. "We need a win," he would say to me, as we watched, first the plagues, and then the beginnings of the Exodus. "Leviathan's out-maneuvered us here."

"Don't worry, Nick. We'll think of something."

It wasn't hard. The Israelites were whiny pilgrims. "This food sucks." "My bed is uncomfortable." (Unsurprising, since they slept on the ground.) "There's no cable." "Are we there yet?" This last one came most frequently from the children.

And it didn't take much to strain their patience or credulity. This latter item was a constant surprise to me. I mean, come on, they witnessed more evidence of the Divine than anyone before or since, except Adam and Eve and maybe Noah and his family, yet still they lacked faith. And patience.

The Almighty often talked with Moses over the forty years of an admittedly long Exodus. The Lord had many instructions for his chief human assistant, and lots of rules for the Israelites to follow. Tsk. So many rules. Very hard to keep them all straight.

Whenever the two of them talked, it was usually on a mountain. (The Creator likes high places; the commute is shorter.) During one of those times when Moses was up on Mount Sinai getting more rules for his people to follow, I saw an opportunity for mischief.

On this occasion, the people down below were unusually restless. Moses had been up on that mountain for what seemed like forever, and they were tired of waiting.

I slipped into the settlement, disguised as one of their own and started to rabble-rouse. "I tell you, he's not coming back."

"He's right!" yelled a voice from the back of the gathering crowd. Satan had followed me, figured out what I was doing and was helping me stir the pot. "Where's my pitchfork?" he screamed. This seemed nonsensical to me at the time, but over the intervening years, I've learned that all mobs require pitchforks. Eventually, so did all devils and demons.

And his words had their intended effect. Nick had always had a knack for getting people worked up; in that, he was better than I. Still, this was my idea, so I directed their ire in a direction that was sure to get them in trouble. "We should make our own god."

"What are you talking about?" Aaron said. He had been dozing by a shrub, but now that he was awake, he tried to calm the mob. "There is only one God."

"Nonsense," Satan responded. "What about Ekron? What about Sekhmet and Osiris and all those other jokers, I mean, gods?"

"Those are not our gods," Aaron sniffed.

"So, let's make one of our own," I repeated. "Sa..., uh, Stan, why don't you gather up all the gold you can find? We'll melt it down and cast a golden calf."

"What? No!" Aaron protested.

"You got a problem?" Stan gave the priest the stink eye. Aaron shivered; he knew true evil when he saw it.

Aaron had lost control of the situation, and in fact, even got caught up in the crowd's enthusiasm. "Break off the golden earrings, which are in the ears of your wives, of your sons, and of your daughters, and bring them unto me." He took the gold, melted it down and made a molten calf, then I slipped inside, just to lend some verisimilitude.

"Hail Ba'al, the great and powerful!" Said Nick's voice from the crowd. "Let us worship him!"

In the morning, they "offered burnt offerings" to their new god, which is redundant I know, but that's how the scene was described in the Bible. Mostly the offerings consisted of goat, cow and sheep, but I noted, with irritation, that Nick slipped in a charred rat, for old time's sake.

Since I was inside the molten beastie, I animated the thing, just a little, you know, shaking my tail slightly, winking at the girls. Nothing that anyone could have sworn in court was actual animation. More like Hanna-Barbera, not Disney or Looney Tunes. It helped sell the deal, though.

Then Nick and I waited for Moses to show up. In no time, he wandered down the mountainside, two stone tablets in his hands. In a fit of temper, he broke the tablets then destroyed the calf in a campfire. I slipped out and materialized, in faux-Israelite couture, next to Nick, who was standing, watching the scene unfold with amusement.

"Nice job," he whispered.

"Well," I said, modestly. "False god, you know. One of my fortes."

"Indeed. That's one for our side, and it beats the snot out of what Leviathan and those chumps did."

After that, we looked for all sorts of opportunities to cause mischief. We tripped the occasional pilgrim, spray painted a donkey or two, tipped over an ox cart.

And then the Boss came up with the concept of the scapegoat. At His direction, Aaron, as priest of the Israelites, laid his hands upon a goat and imbued it with the sins of the people, then sent it out into the wilderness as an offering to "the scapegoat." That's how it's translated in the King James. In other translations, it's an offering to the devil, Azazel. Nick thought the whole thing was weird, but he assumed the form of Azazel and happily received the poor goat who got stuck with the sins of the Israelites.

Nick and I had always liked cabrito. We made a meal of it.

Between the molten calf and the scapegoat incidents, we felt we were firmly ahead on points in the competition with Leviathan.

The story of the Exodus seemed interminable. The Israelites kept acting like assholes, despite all the efforts of Moses to keep them in line. Shit. What did they have to complain about? They were no longer slaves. They were fed. They got water out of a rock.

Actually, twice they got water that way. First time, Moses followed instructions, swatted the rock with his staff – his walking staff – and water flowed like Niagara. The second time, though, he was supposed to sweet-talk the rock into making water. But Moses didn't do that. Thwack he went again with the stick. Water flowed, but he got in a world of trouble for that.

"But, but ..." he stammered, as he stood atop Nebo/Pisgah, "all I did was hit a stupid rock."

"Yeah," Satan said, as he and I materialized next to Moses. He recognized us immediately for the consummately evil creatures that we were, but he was in the middle of a lengthy conversation with his Maker so paid us no mind.

"Be quiet, you two," Metatron said. "Let me finish up."

And so, Moses was shown the land promised to Abraham for his descendants. But the leader of the Israelites wasn't going to be allowed to enter it.

When the conversation ended, the presence of the Boss dissipated, and the three of us were left alone atop the mountain. Moses turned to us. "Satan. Ba'al. What are you doing here?"

Satan pursed his lips. "We just wanted to see how this story ends."

"Well, as you just witnessed, I got fired." Moses sat down heavily. He stared with longing at the promised land. "What a drag. All because I didn't want to talk to a rock."

This drama seemed to be pretty much over, so Satan and I sat down next to him. "You didn't follow directions," Nick said.

"Yeah, I get that. It just seemed stupid to talk to a rock. No dignity, you know?" He looked at us for affirmation, but we just shrugged.

"Take it from us," I said. "We've learned the hard way that it doesn't pay to Disobey. Just stick to the Plan, and you won't get in trouble."

Moses looked at us and grimaced. And then he died.

Chapter 10

I t is said that the Devil has many names. He has been variously called Lucifer, Satan, Nick, Old Nick, Scratch, and a host of others. He's even been called Samael, though this is a case of mistaken identity. Samael, whom you've already encountered through this narrative, is one of the archangels.

Nick isn't the only one who has had many names.

My first, you recall, was Hadad. I've also been known as Ekron, Ba'al, Baal, Baalzebul, and, perhaps most memorably, Beelzebub. My friends call me Beezy. Occasionally someone will call me Flyface. They seldom do it twice, though.

Except Nick. He has a pass.

You might wonder how I became known as Beelzebub. There are different explanations for this, and each has an element of truth. In Ekron, where I had most of my followers, I was simply known as Ba'al, which translates roughly as "Lord." But these were my peeps; we were on intimate terms. I wasn't just "Lord," but lord "of the House" or "of the Manor," which is a literal translation of "zebul." I was their "house god," which is how many gods get started before becoming A-list deities. If you think back to how I got my early converts, by going from house to house, ending up being called "God of the House" makes a world of sense. Ba'al Zebûl. Actually, back then it was BLZBL. Remember: vowels hadn't been around that long yet.

This name got reinforced during the molten calf episode. To be accurate, the golden statue was of a young bull, and I started to be called "Ba'al the Bull." People's diction back then not being the best, it often came out as Ba'al zee Bull. Eventually, this all got merged into a single word: Baalzebul. Bull Lord. Or Bull God. Angus Dei. That's me. The fact that I usually appear with bull horns, rather than Nick's preferred goat pokers or jackalope horns or something else, reinforced the name.

Then some Israelite joker realized he could make a pun just by replacing the "l" at the end with a "b." Ba'al Zebub translates as "lord of the flies." Amazing what changing a single letter will do. People were really into flies back then. Excrement was everywhere, this being before the invention of the toilet; people as well as their beasts of burden crapped in the streets. This tended to attract a large measure of flies. There were even cults of fly worshippers, which goes to show that a human's choice of divinity can sometimes be suspect.

But the changing of meaning: it was an intentional put-down. Check out Second Kings, chapter one, verse two. Baal-zebub: god of Ekron. That's inescapably me.

Though I don't like to admit it, the morphing of my name to its current form had a certain legitimacy. After all, flies really do love me. Sigh. The name stuck, and I've gotten used to it.

The centuries came and went, as did the generations of humanity. We were collecting our standard allotment of damned souls, and business was good, because more people were being born yet not living as long.

Shortly after the time of Moses, human life expectancy shortened, mainly due to a high infant mortality rate. If you managed to make it to adulthood without dying from starvation, dehydration, exposure, disease or mayhem, you had a chance of living into your seventies, but making it into the triple digits soon became a rarity.

We devils continued to perform our duties, but we didn't have enough to do. At the time, we were only allowed to pursue Jewish souls, since Yahweh was their personal and exclusive God, making Judaism a sort of boutique religion. Satan and I looked with longing at the burgeoning populations in the far east, yet we weren't allowed to poach souls from places like India or China.

We soon became bored with the uncreative ways in which humans botched up their lives and afterlives. The cardinal sins had already taken shape, though we hadn't named them that yet. There were minor variations in human wickedness – greed for example might manifest as forgery or creative accounting – but the basic sins were the same. Greed, lust, gluttony, wrath, envy, sloth, pride. Especially pride. Pride damns more people than any of the other sins.

Since we were confined to harvesting damned Jewish souls, we hung close to what is now in modern times called the Middle East. And we observed. We watched the age of the judges come and go. The most interesting of the judges was the last one, Samson. He didn't do much adjudicating. He was more of a smiter. I liked that about him. He killed with real panache, his speciality being Philistines. The Jews and the Philistines never really got along, you know.

After the judges came the kings. Saul was the first King of the United Kingdom of Israel and Judah. But he got in hot water with the Boss, who sent the prophet Samuel to anoint David, who was holding down a job as a shepherd at the time. (Back then, being a shepherd was a very common occupation; it was like being in retail today.)

You all know the story of David and Goliath. The most common question I'm asked about this tale is, "How tall was Goliath?" The answer is six cubits and a span, to which you might ask, what's a cubit? And what's a span? You should have worked that out in the Noah story – cubits were mentioned frequently there – but I'll tell you. A cubit is eighteen inches, and a span is about six. So, Goliath was nine feet, six inches. Big guy.

Back then, giants roamed the earth. They were called Anakims (not Anakin, of Skywalker fame). Goliath had at least some Anak blood in him, though at the time of his confrontation with Israel, he was working for the Philistines.

And how tall was David? About five seven, if memory serves. Back then, that was a perfectly respectable height. Still, Goliath had almost four feet on him. Not really a fair fight.

David was small, comparatively, but he was wiry. He also was good with that slingshot of his. Why, once I saw him take a fly out of the air. Still, he probably could not have beaten a giant if he had not had divine help, ensuring that the rock he launched at Goliath landed with deadly accuracy and force.

There was another factor that worked to David's advantage. Goliath wore a size six narrow sandal. Big man, little feet. His balance was understandably not the best, and as the saying goes, the bigger they are, the harder they fall.

And then David got to be king and write all those elegant psalms, surely some of the best word craft in the Bible.

One of the most interesting characters in these early years of the Jewish faith was the prophet Elijah. He and I crossed swords, figuratively that is, a time or two.

It happened this way. In the Ninth Century BC, the kingdom had become divided. Omri ruled Israel, but not Judah. His hold on power was not very firm, so he allowed some of the people living in Israel who were not Jews to worship their own gods, especially a powerful deity from the Canaanite religion. This god's name was Ba'al.

Yep. Me. I'd made the big time.

Omri's son, Ahab, continued the tradition and, in fact, married a priestess of Ba'al named Jezebel. She was a looker, and Ahab really had the hots for her. Jezebel used sex as a bargaining chip with her husband. She agreed to play hide the salami with Ahab as much as he wanted, provided he build a temple to Ba'al each time they were connubial.

Unsurprisingly, Israel soon was littered with temples to me. A labor shortage ensued. There just weren't enough Ba'al priests in the neighborhood, and Jezebel had to write dad back home in Phoenicia, asking him to send more. I was pumped. I hadn't gotten so much attention in centuries.

This did not sit well with Elijah, who at the time was the major prophet of the Big Guy. In fact, the name "Elijah" means "My God is Yahweh." Must have been awkward, having a name like that, if you were, say, flirting with a girl.

Elijah had guts, I'll give him that. He challenged me directly. Well, no, that's not accurate. He challenged my priests, all four hundred and fifty of them. It was a bake-off, of sorts. Each side got a bullock. My priests were supposed to pray to me to light the barbecue grill underneath their bull. Elijah was to do the same, using his own deity, naturally.

I was under strict orders not to do anything. A shame really – I could have turned that carcass to ash in a second flat – but this was Elijah's time to shine. The upshot was predictable. My priests got steak tartare, while Elijah was served up ... well, nothing. The fire of the Lord consumed his bull, along with the altar on which it was resting. And he even did this with wet wood.

Score: Yahweh 1. Ba'al 0. That was sort of the point.

But Elijah didn't leave it at that. He took all my priests and personally slew them. Shit, you would have thought he was Samson or something.

Elijah was always doing cool miracles, in their own way every bit as neat as those of Moses. For instance, he raced Ahab

– who was riding at top speed in the royal chariot – and beat him. Elijah was on foot, running like the Flash. Or Quicksilver. Take your choice. He caused floods. He called fire down from Heaven a couple of times, as casually as striking a match. He even had a personal encounter with the Lord on Mount Horeb/Sinai, which put him in rarified company. Only Moses had done that.

The story of Elijah, Ahab and Jezebel had many chapters. Suffice it to say Elijah always won.

But this isn't why I was relating the story. Yes, it's a good tale, doubly so because I played a role in it, but what's special about Elijah is that he is one of only two people not to die. Only he and Enoch (Metatron) ascended to Heaven without dying.

As the centuries came and went, we devils kept up our little war against good. In that, humans were great allies.

One day, Nick got a letter in the mail. "You and a guest of your choice are cordially invited to tea."

It was from Him.

"Well, I never expected to be allowed in Heaven," Nick said, staring at the invitation in bemusement. "I thought he was still mad at me."

"The Lord works in mysterious ways," I said, probably the first one ever to use that expression. "Who's going to be your date?"

Nick shifted uncomfortably in his seat. "I'm not really seeing anyone right now. Want to come with me?"

I shrugged. "Why not?"

Back then, we didn't know how to get to Heaven. We weren't exactly given an address, but we needn't have been concerned. A beam of light caught us at that instant, blinding us. When our vision cleared, we were standing in the middle of Heaven.

And no, I won't describe it to you. Your mind can't comprehend the place. The old brain cells would explode. Besides, it's against the rules to give out details about Heaven. Sorry.

I'll tell you one thing, though. They really like white up there. I'm not referring to people. "Red and yellow, black and white: they are precious in his sight," and all that jazz. I'm talking décor. White clouds, white carpets, white sofas, white tablecloths, white napkins, white china. So much white: it's almost blinding.

"Would you care for some tea?" Asked the Voice of God, as we took our seats.

No, it wasn't the Almighty himself who spoke. The Creator of All was quietly sipping tea and having Metatron do the talking … and the serving.

Even the tea we were offered was white tea. Nick asked if they had any coffee. Looking chagrined, Metatron got him a cup of java. "Cream?" He asked, holding up a white pitcher filled with, well, white cream.

Nick grinned evilly. "No thanks. I take mine black."

Metatron sniffed and carried away the pitcher. At a gesture from our Host, we took our seats, just as his spokesperson returned and took the fourth spot at the table.

We had been drinking our beverages in silence, an awkward silence, when Metatron abruptly spoke. "Hast thou considered my servant Job?"

"Oh, you mean that rich guy who lives in the land of Uz?" I asked, taking another sip. It was good tea. I would have preferred a beer, but that wasn't on the menu.

"Indeed." Metatron refilled his cup. "Hast thou considered my servant Job ..."

"You already said that," Nick said.

Metatron gave him a stony look and began again. "Hast thou considered my servant Job, that *there is* none like him in the earth, a perfect and an upright man, one that feareth God and escheweth evil?"

People talked like that back then.

"That poser?" I began, but my friend silenced me.

"Let me. I've got this," he whispered.

Then Satan answered the LORD, and said, "Doth Job fear God for nought? Hast not thou made an hedge about him, and about his house, and about all that he hath on every side? Thou hast blessed the work of his hands, and his substance is increased in the land."

"But put forth thine hand now, and touch all that he hath, and he will curse thee to thy face."

Satan scored some major evil points that day. Top Management took the dare. Job's kids were killed, he was stripped of his wealth, yada, yada. You know the rest of the story, and in the end, Job was restored, with more wealth and kids than ever.

Of course, they weren't the same kids. Can't have everything, I guess.

Let's wrap up all this early stuff. It's a matter of public record; you can read more about ancient Israel and its people in the Bible anytime you want. I just wanted you to know that devils were in there pitching the whole time, and Gehenna was a successful going concern.

Our role in the Divine Plan had become monotonous, though, and we were ready for a change. Fortunately, there was the Prophecy. The Messiah was coming.

We had to up our game when Christianity was founded. Judaism was a narrow market, but the new religion was going to be huge, and Nick saw a major opportunity.

Chapter 11

I remember it well: a winter night, just over two thousand years ago. Nick and I were strolling along the Ganges. We liked India – people didn't know us there, and we could travel incognito – so that's where we often took our evening walks.

The hairs on the back of my neck began to tingle. There was something in the air, a sense of expectation, of portent. Nick looked at me in surprise. He felt it too.

That's when I happened to glance up and see the star. "Will you look at that?" I said.

"Humph. I don't recall that star."

I shrugged. "Me neither. Looks brand new, and awfully bright," I said, squinting.

"Seems to be hovering over Israel. Come on, Flyface …"

"Please don't call me that."

"Let's check it out." He grabbed my arm and teleported us both to the outskirts of Jerusalem.

"Yuck," he said. "Where's an umbrella when you need one?"

Rain was falling, a slow but relentless drizzle, and the temperature was in the upper forties. It was the kind of wet cold you get in San Francisco, which cuts through you like a scythe cuts through wheat – or souls.

The sky, so clear down in India, was completely socked in here. We couldn't see the mysterious star at all. Then, as if a hand parted the clouds, the sky cleared.

"The star is above Bethlehem," I muttered.

"Yes. Let's go." We made another hop and found ourselves in a crowd scene. People were queued up in front of a stable, trying to peek inside. Since we were devils, creatures of evil, we turned incorporeal and cut in line.

Inside, we found a young girl – she couldn't have been more than twelve or thirteen – holding a newborn, wrapped up tight in swaddling clothes. An old man was standing over the girl protectively.

Even though we were invisible, the infant looked directly at us. I would have recognized those eyes anywhere. "My God!"

"Yes," said a familiar voice to our right. It was Leviathan. He was leaning against one of the posts supporting the roof, chewing on a piece of hay. "About time you got here."

"You!" Satan hissed. "What are you doing here? And why is the Creator of All here?"

He smirked. "Check your mail today?"

I shot Nick a dirty look. I didn't do the mail. That was his job.

"I uh, didn't get to it today. Don't look at me like that! I've been kind of busy tormenting the Damned, you know." He frowned. "I really need to get a secretary."

We looked around us, realizing that everybody who was anybody was there: Belphegor, Ziz, Behemoth, Sekhmet, TNK-el, in short, just about every devil you could imagine. And more, behind the small family stood all the archangels: Michael, Uriel, Gabriel, Raphael, Samael, Selaphiel, Raguel, Barachiel and, last but not least, Metatron. I looked up, a roof being no impediment to devil vision (though sometimes clouds are, especially when they provide dramatic tension). In the sky above us, the rest of the Heavenly Host had gathered. Some were singing, others were playing harps and trumpets. There was even a marimba and some castanets, along with a jazz trio.

Leviathan snorted. "Seems you two are the only ones who don't know what's going on."

The Christ child looked at us severely. The meaning was clear. We were late.

"Sorry," we muttered awkwardly.

"Here," Belphegor whispered, handing Satan a copy of a memo, which I read over Nick's shoulder. I felt myself blushing furiously.

"Birthday party?" Satan said, looking at me in consternation.

I frowned at him, but inwardly I was more worried than angry.

Great, just great. The Creator of All takes human form, and we miss the coming out-party. This is going in our personnel files for sure.

Some doors opened, and three old guys in fancy robes wandered in, bearing gifts for the child. Satan and I smiled awkwardly then stepped to the back of the stable. The all-seeing eyes of the Christ child looked at us once more in disapproval then turned their attention to the newcomers.

Leviathan chuckled. "You really messed up this time. The most important event in human history, and you two didn't even read the memo."

"This is terrible!" Satan whispered to me.

"And entirely your fault," I grumbled. "I've told you before. Check your damn mail."

"Let's not argue now ..."

By the way, Satan never did find the memo. I think he lost it, but Nick believes Leviathan somehow swiped it, just to get us in trouble. Possible, I suppose. Leviathan was always pulling shit like that.

Over the next few years, we kept close watch over Jesus ... and the mail, in case we had any special assignments come our way. We didn't, except for getting cast occasionally in bit parts as devils that the Savior would exorcize. And while we did the scut work, Leviathan and his crew were getting all the good roles, like being in the temple to witness a twelve-year-old Jesus impress the elders with his learning. True, they weren't speaking parts, but Nick and I weren't even invited to participate.

One thing about Jesus I particularly admired was his skill as a carpenter. Man, he could build anything, bird houses, musical instruments, fine cabinetry. He was better at that kind of craftsmanship than even me, and I'm famous for my handiwork.

On the day of the Baptism, Satan at last got a decent assignment. He had been checking his inbox scrupulously for thirty years, even though most of its contents was junk mail — flyers for overstocked tunic sales, catalogs of torture equipment, come-ons from used goat dealers, and the like — when an official-looking nine-by-twelve envelope arrived. The envelope contained a memo and a lengthy attachment.

MEMORANDUM

To: Satan (Provisional)

Nick looked up at me. "Provisional?" he said, a fair bit of heat in his voice. "I'm still on probation?"

I shrugged. "Considering the whole stable debacle, you're lucky you still have the job at all. Keep reading."

"Okay, okay," he grumbled. Then his face lit up. "Good news!"

"What?"

119

"I get to tempt Christ." He tapped the papers with the back of his hand. "I even have a script here," he frowned, "which I think I should memorize. I have plenty of time for that though. For now, we need to get down to the river ASAP."

At the Jordan, we saw Jesus get baptized by that weird John guy. He looked like a lunatic; still, he had a presence that was mesmerizing. Yet, once Jesus stepped out of the crowd, John the Baptist seemed to fade, becoming just a minor character in this miracle play.

After the baptism, there was a disorienting moment. The Spirit of God descended like a dove and landed upon himself, that is, Jesus, as he stood in the waters of the river. And, pièce de résistance, we heard the Almighty call down from Heaven, using Metatron's voice, to praise himself. So, we witnessed the Almighty in Heaven, in the sky above the river in the form of a dove, and in the waters of the Jordan, all at the same time!

Mind-boggling, yet Nick didn't even notice. He was too busy memorizing his lines for the Temptation.

After the baptism, I thought there might be a picnic or something. Instead, the Spirit took Jesus into the wilderness and left him there for forty days with nothing to eat.

"I'm on!" Nick said with enthusiasm.

"I'll walk you there," I said, donning my petasos, a broad-brimmed hat I used to wear before discovering the fez during the Byzantine era.

Good thing I did. Walk with him, that is. Not get the hat. Three thugs were blocking the path to the wilderness, three thugs who looked a lot like Leviathan, Ziz and Behemoth. "What are you doing here?" I said, eyeing them with suspicion.

Leviathan grinned evilly. "Just thought we'd say hi. You know, bat the breeze."

"We brought the bats," Ziz said, snickering, pulling out a cudgel.

"Another time," Satan said, teleporting around them. "I have an appointment and don't want to be late."

Leviathan, Ziz and Mammoth did the same maneuver, and were once again blocking the way. Leviathan put his hand on Satan's arm. "Let's talk. We insist."

I knew what they were trying to do, and so did Nick, if the nervous look on his face was any indication. Fortunately, the three bullies were focused on Nick instead of me.

Have you ever watched professional wrestling? Well, there is a move they do called the leg drop. First, I bowled into Ziz and Behemoth then used the leg drop on Leviathan. When I had all three pinned to the ground, I shouted to Nick, "Go, go!"

He didn't have to be told twice. He teleported at once.

Leviathan was trying, without success, to push me to the side. "Ow! Beelzebub, get off me."

"Get off all of us," Ziz grumbled. "Have you put on weight?"

I crawled off them, picking up my hat and dusting it off. "You guys have your nerve. Nick is operating under direct heavenly orders."

"We just wanted to talk to him," Mammoth grumbled.

"Yeah, sure. I know what you were doing. If Nick had been late again, he might have ..."

"He might have lost the Satan position!" Leviathan glowered at me. "Which should be mine to begin with."

"Says you. Now, buzz off, or I'll tell Metatron you were interfering with orders."

"Snitch!" Ziz croaked.

"Enough. I'm out of here." Then it was my turn to teleport. I landed about fifty feet from Satan. He had just approached Jesus, who nodded for him to begin.

Satan took a dramatic pose, cleared his throat and said, "If thou be the Son of God, command that these stones be made of bread."

The Temptation went without a hitch. Nick gave a fine performance.

After the success of the Temptation, Satan was back in Heaven's good graces. He and I even got a couple of good mentions in Matthew Twelve.

Over the next few years, we saw Jesus do some amazing stuff, like raise Lazarus from the dead; deliver his Sermon on the Mount. Man, he was a great orator. He could have had a great career as a motivational speaker, if he hadn't opted instead to be the Creator of the Universe.

Yet, in all of this we were mostly spectators. Satan and I didn't really know yet what the Almighty's end game was, and when it came – the end that is – we were nothing if not horrified.

The cruelty of which you humans are capable is beyond belief. The Devil is the manifestation of evil, but Nick's got nothing on your species. Besides, at the end of the day, he has no free will. He is just playing the part assigned to him in the Divine Plan.

You humans, though, have a choice. You can be good. You can be bad. When you are good, you can accomplish sublime things. Feed a starving child. Risk your life to rescue another. Let someone else have the last slice of cheesecake.

But when you're bad, there's no limit to your atrocities. You commit genocide, develop a weapon that can kill a hundred thousand in the blink of an eye, drop a conflagration from the sky and destroy a large city. Kick a dog. Bully the school nerd. Slaughter a gay boy, lynch a man over the color of his skin, just because they are different from you.

Or kill the Son of God.

Seeing Jesus hanging on the cross, blood dripping from his head, his hands, his feet, his torso: that was hard.

And *we're* supposed to be the bad guys.

When his all-knowing brown eyes closed, when he heaved his last breath, I felt a fist around my heart that threatened to crush it. My reaction was irrational. I knew the Almighty was, well, almighty, and death had no true sway over him. But the scene was powerful.

When he rose on the third day, Satan and I understood. This was the birth of a new religion, something larger than belief in a house god, or the god of a single people. This would go global.

And soon this religion had a name: Christianity.

Chapter 12

During the period when I was wandering around re-establishing my reputation as a false god, I discovered something very interesting. Other gods had started showing up around the globe. These weren't devils in divine clothing either. Well, some of them were, like Sekhmet, who infiltrated the Egyptian pantheon, and Hecate, who did the same in Greece. Others, though, were creatures from elsewhere, other planes of existence. Or maybe they were just spawned by the beliefs of humans.

Belief is powerful. It can create something out of nothing. Belief is one of the special qualities of humanity, like free will, opposable thumbs and backaches. Belief is a spark of the divine in you. Pretty special.

In Egypt, you had Horus, Osiris, Ra and a host of others, including my dear Sekhmet. In India, Hinduism got established. That religion had a dizzying number of gods: Indra, Agni, Rudra, Vishnu, Brahma, Shiva. The list seemed endless. Throughout the world, gods would come into and out of favor, sometimes when a more appealing deity or deities came on the scene, other times when a conqueror forced his beliefs on the conquered.

Greece had an elaborate pantheon. The Greco-Roman belief system hung around for at least fifteen hundred years, but when Christianity came on the scene, the days of Zeus/Jupiter and his cronies were numbered.

After the Resurrection, Satan knew that Christianity was going to significantly increase our workload. And our need for space. He worked frantically to rebrand Gehenna as Hell, but our place in the Amazon, even though it had some impressive mosquitos, was insufficient to be the land of eternal Christian punishment. Satan wanted bigger digs, but first he had to find them.

And so, it came to pass that one day, while looking at the real estate classifieds, Satan discovered what looked to be the ideal property. Most of the Greek gods had closed shop by now, but there was one fellow still in town. Hades was looking to sell the eponymous Hades, his kingdom of the dead, including Tartarus, which was for the especially bad Greek guys and dolls. Nick got in contact with his Hellenistic counterpart and arranged to look at the property. "Come with me," Satan said.

"Why does it always have to be me? Can't you take Belly, or someone else, or just do it yourself? I'm kind of busy here building this choppy thing." I was working on the first guillotine.

Satan frowned. He didn't like backtalk from the staff, not even from me. "No. You're my number two, my go-to guy. We're a team, remember? Have been since the Adoration."

"Well," I said, putting down the sharp blade I was trying to mount in a wooden frame. "When you put it like that ..."

Nick didn't seem to have heard me. He was struggling with something. "Beezy," he said at last, in a soft voice, "you're my best friend. Maybe my only friend, and ..." He paused. "And you're the only person I can take in large doses."

I smiled. That must have been hard for him. "Sure, I'll come. There may be construction issues about which you'll need my advice. Besides, I want to make certain there aren't too many flying insects."

Nick just nodded, for the moment speechless, overcome by feelings I'm not sure he quite understood. "Let's go," he said at last.

We met Hades (the god) in Italy, near a volcano called Avernus. He had relocated the entrance to his domain from Greece to the Italian peninsula. Being nearer to Rome, he had hoped to get an increase in traffic. You know the old saying: location, location, location. Didn't help for very long, though, a few hundred years at most.

This was not the first time I'd met this god; we had connected at a cocktail party a few centuries early. I didn't like him much; he struck me as a shady character, though Charon has since convinced me that he had always been a straight shooter. Perhaps it was just his style to which I was reacting. Hades had very oily skin, he perspired constantly, and his hair was slicked back in the mother of all D.A.s. The checkered sports coat and gold chains he wore around his neck didn't raise my opinion of him either. They were tacky.

Maybe my dislike could be reduced to this: Hades reminded me of a used camel salesman.

He was going by the name of Pluto at the time of this encounter, perhaps to clear up any confusion caused by a god and his domain having the same name. Yet, since he'd first been introduced to me as Hades, that's what I continued to call him.

In an expansive gesture, he swept his arm toward the volcano, beside which was a hand drawn "For Sale by Owner" sign. I pointed it out to Satan. "A FSBO?" I whispered. "Man, this guy must really be cheap."

Satan whispered back. "I think it's because he can't afford to pay six percent of the sale price to a real estate agent."

A large cave on one side of the mountain was the entrance to the property. Hades looked over his shoulder nervously, as if he expected at any moment to be knifed or something — it wasn't the best neighborhood — then led us into the opening.

After descending a few hundred feet, we came to the Gates of Hades. Massive iron doors hung from hinges that were attached to two Dorian columns. The columns themselves had sunk into the earth. They only stayed erect because they were leaning against each other, like a pair of giant candlesticks. The doors, almost ripped from their hinges because of the tension placed on them by the leaning columns and the stone floor, were propped open with a few dozen human skulls. A spider web stretched between the two gates.

"Business a little slow lately?" Nick asked.

Hades shrugged. "A bit. This Christianity thing is really biting my butt."

"Well, get used to it," I said, staring at the half-fallen pillars. "Hey, Nick, I mean Lord Satan, help me with this." Satan had decided that, for dignity sake, I should call him by his more impressive title when we were in public. Still, old habits die hard. Besides, I didn't really like having to kowtow to him.

Nick sighed as he and I straightened the two pillars. This set the two gates to flapping open and closed, like the gums on a toothless old man. Being iron though, the doors to Hades set off quite a racket.

The clattering seemed to have woken all the inhabitants of a nearby animal kennel, because suddenly there was the sound of barking dogs. "What's that?" Nick asked.

"Oh," Hades said, brightening. "That's Cerberus. He's the guard dog of the Underworld."

Out from behind one of the pillars came a huge mastiff with three heads, each one putting up a ruckus that would wake the dead, if there were any dead around to wake. Business may not have been good of late for the old Greco-Roman deity, but the dog was quite an eyeful.

Satan scratched his chin in thought. "Does Cerberus come with the place?"

"He's not part of the basic package, no," Hades said. "He's an option, but I'm sure we can make a deal if you like him."

"So far," my friend replied, "he's the only thing I *do* like. What a dump!" he said to me over his shoulder.

"It is a bit of a fixer-upper," Hades admitted. "But, really, this is a great piece of real estate at an incredible price. Really a steal."

"Yes, but who is stealing from whom? What else is wrong with it besides the gates?" I asked.

"Hardly a thing!" Hades responded. As if on cue, a piece of plaster fell on my head, followed by the drip, drip, drip of water. "Well, I guess the roof needs some work."

Satan took a few steps beyond the gate. His foot plunged into black goo. "What the fuck?"

"That's the river Styx. Quite amazing, really. Pure petroleum."

"And what's its purpose?" I asked.

The old god frowned. "Effect mainly. The Styx is a black river of oil. Can you think of anything but death when you stare into it? Why, you don't even get a reflection. The river just sucks up any light that falls on it. All dead souls have to cross it to get into my domain."

"And how do they do that?" As if in answer to my question, a ghostly vessel appeared in the distance and began to move across the river toward us. In the back of the boat, a figure in a charcoal cloak was using a long pole to push against the river bottom, sending his craft toward us. The vessel reached us in seconds, and its sole occupant drove it onto the ashen shore near to where we were standing.

"Charon!" Hades called. "Come over here. I want you to meet some people."

The figure, who had not spoken a word to this point, climbed out of his boat and joined us. He put back the hood of his cloak, revealing his skull.

No flesh or hair or eyeballs or anything like that, understand. Just his skull. Before us stood a skeleton. In a charcoal gray cloak. He reminded me of my friend Mortimer. Only later did I learn that Charon was Morty's little brother.

"This is Satan, that fellow we've all been hearing so much about," Hades said, no doubt to butter up his prospective buyer. "And this is his number two, Beelzebub, Lord of the Flies."

I winced. I'd been going by Beelzebub for almost a thousand years, but I still was getting used to the name.

I am honored to meet you both, Charon said, sticking out a bony hand, shaking first with Nick and then with me. He didn't "actually" speak, since he had no tongue, but his thoughts were plain to us.

Charon extended his arms in invitation, and the three of us climbed aboard. Cerberus, having nothing better to do, hopped in after us. He was a nice mutt, though a bit on the drooly side, a logical consequence of having three enormous tongues.

In seconds we were on our way, gliding across the sleek surface of the Styx. Traveling in near silence toward the land of the dead was an eerie experience. It made for great theater, especially for the kind of afterlife over which we intended to preside. I leaned over to Nick and whispered. "A skeleton, ferrying people into Hell. That would be classy."

"Agreed," he whispered back. I was pretty sure my friend would bargain for both Cerberus and Charon, provided he was going to buy the property at all. Fixer-upper indeed. The place was a wreck. Years of deferred maintenance. It would be a ton of work to turn Hades into a decent realm for the Damned, and I was pretty sure who would end up doing most of that work.

Building new things was labor I enjoyed, but doing a rehab just didn't excite me. I didn't relish the prospect of hanging new drywall over an entire domain or fixing a leaky roof that was bigger than an island.

Once on the other side, we hopped ashore. Charon and Cerberus remained with the boat, as the rest of us walked onto the Fields of Asphodel, which was essentially the front room of Hades. Here we met our first souls: paupers and the friendless who, according to Hades, had to loiter by the shore of the Styx for a hundred years before moving elsewhere within the land of the dead. Further inland, we encountered warriors of unremarkable note, along with a few hangers-on who flew around the soldiers like so many moths.

Beyond this lay Erebus, which for the ancient Greeks and Romans served as a place to sort the souls and send them to their final destinations. There were three judges there; they looked as if they hadn't had much work of late. These were Minos, Rhadamanthus and Aeacus. Hades gave them a half-wave, and they nodded in return. "The three judges can be part of the deal, if you're interested."

"No, they won't be necessary," Satan said. "My boss has already hired someone to handle this function."

"Just out of curiosity," I asked, "what are the options for the dead down here?"

"What?" Hades looked disappointed. I think he wanted to downsize as much as possible. Not being able to unload his judges on us was a blow, I think. "Oh, well, you've already seen the Asphodel Meadows. Those souls who in life were neither particularly good nor particularly bad spend their afterlife there. Those who were good go to the Elysium Fields." Hades pointed to a sign that indicated another meadow in the distance.

"And the evil ones?" I asked.

"Tartarus," he said gesturing toward a second sign that pointed straight down. "Follow me." Hades disappeared.

Nick looked at me. "What do you think?"

I sighed. "Maybe. But try to get a good price. There's going to be an incredible amount of work needed to make this place serviceable."

My friend snorted. "Not to worry. I think by now you know I'm a pretty good negotiator."

This was true. Nobody could con Satan, the king of all con artists, in my opinion. He'd probably get the place for a song.

We teleported, following Hades's trail to a small but very crowded place deep in the Underworld. "Only two stories?" Satan shook his head. "Hades, Hades is completely inadequate for our needs." My friend turned to go.

"Wait, wait!" the Greek god said, trying to keep the desperation from his voice. "There's a great deal of unoccupied space between Tartarus and the rest of Hades, easily enough to add half a dozen other floors, maybe more, between them."

"Yeah," I grumbled. "But it would require a shitload of excavation work."

"L ... look, I'm really kind of anxious to sell," he confessed at last. "I'll give you a very good price, and I'll even throw in Charon and Cerberus and anyone else you want."

Nick frowned. "How much are you asking for the property?"

Hades told him.

A hearty "Bwahahahahahaha!" burst from my lips.

The hackles went up on Hades's arms. "What the fuck was that?"

I snorted. "Your asking price is just so ludicrous, it made me laugh."

"That was a laugh? Ugh. Creepy."

"Well," Nick said, intrigued. "I liked it. Do it again."

I shrugged. "Okay. Bwahahahahahaha!"

My friend nodded. "I *really* like it."

And that's how I came up with the signature devil laugh, which in time was also adopted by the Demon Corps.

After Satan and Hades finished admiring my spontaneous expression of mirth, they went back to bargaining. My friend eventually got the Greek god down to about half of what he had been asking. "And I want to see a list of any iconic souls down here that I might want to keep for my operation."

"Okay," Hades said, conjuring up the list. "But for that price, you can only have five."

"Make it ten, and you have a deal."

"Sold!"

In the end, Satan chose Charon, Cerberus, Prometheus, Sisyphus, Polyphemus, two harpies and a few others.

They set closing for a month later. "And you have to get those judges of yours working. The operation that employs me is more binary than yours, so you have to take all those ambiguous souls in Asphodel and assign them to either Elysium or Tartarus."

"Why?" Hades asked

"Those in Elysium get to stay. I've already been ordered to set up some nice digs for them. We're going to call them virtuous pagans."

"And what about the souls in Tartarus?" Hades asked.

"Don't know, don't care," Nick said. "You can throw them into Chaos if you like. But I want Tartarus cleared out before closing."

"Why?" I asked.

Satan grinned. "This is where I'm going to put my office."

Chapter 13

As expected, Nick put me in charge of rehabbing and expanding Hades to be fit habitation for the eternally damned. It was a major renovation job – I had to gut the place – and the work took a couple of hundred years to complete.

Closing went as planned; it occurred onsite, in Tartarus, a month after Satan made his offer on Hades (the place). We used a title company out of India, and Shiva from the Hindu pantheon served as the agent handling the paperwork. This removed any appearance of favoritism that might have resulted if we'd used someone like Themis, the Greek goddess of justice, or Saint Peter. You know how real estate closings go. All that paperwork. Closings can take forever, but all of Shiva's extra hands really sped up the process.

As soon as the final papers were signed, the agent and the seller made speedy departures. Shiva hurried back to India, where he was to play in the finals of a handball tournament against Vishnu. It was likely to be a good match, since both sported multiple arms. Hades, for his part, relieved at last to have unloaded his handyman special on us, headed north, where he was to meet his wife, Persephone, for a Poseidon cruise of the Arctic.

"Glad that's done," Nick said, pushing back from the table where we'd processed the paperwork. "I'm never really comfortable signing contracts that I haven't drawn up myself."

"Relax, Nick. First off, we both read everything carefully before you signed. Besides, you're the only one I know who slips hidden 'gotcha' clauses into contracts."

He snorted. "That will change once humans formalize the lawyer profession. I've been coaching a few of them in Rome, and they're already getting the hang of cheating their fellow man in legal fashion."

"Sin of Greed?"

"What else?"

I nodded. "Well, if you've been coaching them, then I have no doubt you're right. Humans have a devious streak in them."

"Yeah." Nick sighed. "I wish devils had as much aptitude for guile as these humans. You, me and Belphegor, maybe Sekhmet too, can manage it, but the rest of them ..."

Satan was interrupted by a rumble. It started in the ground beneath us. Then the walls and ceiling started to shake, dislodging, I noticed with displeasure, some more plaster from the ceiling. I looked at my friend. "They didn't waste any time."

"No." Nick got out of his chair, waved his hand and created a large bay window in the rock by the table. Through the portal, we saw sky. And angels. The Heavenly Host was tugging on thick, golden ropes, flapping their wings for all they were worth.

I chuckled. "Better them than us."

We'd already been told that our new Hell would be relocated, courtesy of Management, to a place apart from Earth, so that no one living could accidentally stumble in here. That had happened occasionally when the space had been under management of the Greco/Roman pantheon. Hercules, Theseus and Orpheus, for example, had spent time down here before death. No one wanted some goody two-shoes Christian to do the same with Hell.

Once the angels had pulled our new domain free from the Earth, a bright light that made us squint began to shine.

There was a pop, then a sproing. The light faded, and the window grew dark. With a shrug, Satan banished the window from existence. "Done," he said.

Our new Hell was now in the metaphysical realm that already housed Heaven. The space also contained a sort of no man's land in between, which housed the Gates of Heaven, aka the Pearly Gates or simply "The Pearlies," and the Gates of Hell. Here, the Saved and the Damned would be sorted and consigned to their respective realms. In time, we simply referred to this area as Gates Level.

We immediately started the renovations that would transform Hades into Hell. True to his word, the previous owner had sorted out the inhabitants of the Asphodel Fields and assigned them to either Elysium or Tartarus. Then he somehow cleared out the souls from Tartarus. Satan was pleased, because he wanted me to begin work there, setting up his office.

"Shouldn't I be constructing a place to put the souls from our old digs? We've already agreed that the virtuous pagans can stay where they are."

"The souls in Gehenna can sit a while, except the unbaptized babies. Mormo is moving them in as we speak, and Hecate is running around up there in a frenzy, trying to make things as pleasant as possible. Elysium is in pretty good shape, but to accommodate the babies, we're going to have to convert Asphodel. Hecate doesn't have a great deal to work with. I think she's just putting up some flowers and bright balloons. Not much, but it's a start, and you can go there and do a proper job after you've finished down here."

"And the rest of the Damned sitting around in Gehenna?"

"I have Belphegor keeping the place running until we're ready on this end to receive them."

Moving the Jewish souls from Gehenna to Hell had been highly controversial when we proposed it to Management. Gehenna had been originally envisioned to be a sort of reform school, where Jews would spend up to a year, atoning for their sins, before moving on to a better place. Hell was to be fundamentally different. Our new realm would be a place of eternal torment, without the possibility of parole.

But evil is evil, no matter what your religious convictions. In the end, we were given permission to subsume the old Gehenna into the new Hell. I should note, though, that all Jewish souls were given the opportunity to gain Heaven. They played rock-paper-scissors with some of the patriarchs from the Old Testament. The losers, which were most of them, were consigned to the new Hell. Or Gehenna, since we kept that name as an alternate.

In addition to Hell and Gehenna, we also used some other names, like Hades, the rights for which we obtained as part of the real estate purchase, and the Inferno. Even Sin City.

But I'm getting sidetracked. I was telling you about being told to work on Nick's office before creating the rest of Hell. Satan was getting bossier with me all the time. I didn't like it, but …

I sighed. "Very well, but Gehenna is getting full, now that we're also calling it Hell and getting all these new souls."

"They'll manage," he said absently. He walked around Tartarus, as I trailed behind him. "Okay," he said at last. "I've been giving this a lot of thought over the past month, and this is what I want you to do."

Satan pulled out a sketch he had made, showing how he wanted Tartarus to be arranged. "I want my reception area to be here," he said, pointing to a three thousand square foot space, and indicating the corresponding spot on his drawing. "And I want a deep pile carpet – in white mind you – out here."

"White? I thought you'd be going for a darker motif."

"I will for my office. We'll get to that in a moment."

He showed me a spot off the reception area that would have eight small cells, four on each side, and a hallway running between them. "The cells will be for the Traitors."

"Who?"

"The worst sinners of all time. Right now, we have two of them waiting: Cain, the first murderer, and that new guy, Judas Iscariot. The other six cells will give us some growth space. I figure that after all these years, we've only come up with two justifiable Traitors."

"Excluding devils," I mentioned.

"Yes, excluding devils. But human traitors: so far only two. After the babies, the traitors will be the first souls we transfer from Gehenna, just as soon as we, or rather you, finish work down here."

I nodded. "Six more cells should take us a long way, I think. If we need more, we can expand the area or have traitors double up. Still, I think you're right. We should be fine with just eight. Now, where do you want your office?"

Satan stared at me in surprise. "Why, everywhere else."

"Huh? There's a lot of space here."

"I've always wanted a big office."

"That's fine for you, but I was hoping we could use some of Tartarus to house our heater."

"Our what?"

"Heater," I said, conjuring a couple of stools and the same table we'd used for the closing. I motioned to one of the seats, and Nick sat down. I took the other and spread out a drawing of my own. "See, I've been thinking about things also.

Eventually we're going to have a major operation down here. Like Hades said, there is room for a lot more levels than Elysium and Tartarus."

"We'll need new names for those spaces. I don't want to be accused of plagiarism."

"I've been thinking about that, too," I said. "Take a look at the drawing. By my calculations, we can fit seven more circles between here and the first."

"Circles?"

"Yeah. Have you noticed that Tartarus, I mean, your office area, is almost a perfect circle? Same can be said for the place in which the virtuous pagans are living. Or existing. Or whatever the hell these dead humans do." I think, by the way, that was the first time "hell" was used as an expletive, though I could be mistaken.

"Elysium is much larger than the old Tartarus."

Satan nodded. "Yes. They crammed the souls down here as tightly as they could. Hades didn't allow much elbow room for the unvirtuous pagans."

"Yes, I know. Back to this circle idea, though. I envision a total of nine of them in Hell, the two that already exist and seven more. It will be a bitch of an excavation job, but if we enlist the rest of our devils, we should be able to manage. Besides, after we're done down here, on what I propose calling the Ninth Circle of Hell, and then up on One, we only need for now to get another circle prepared. That should be able to handle our current crop and the incoming for a while as we work on the remaining levels."

"Okay, that makes sense. But why the heater?"

I shifted uncomfortably in my seat. As much as I disliked being told what to do, I knew Nick hated it more, and I was about to overstep my authority. After all, Satan was to be the

Earl of Hell, and I was only his number two. But Nick had never been much of a planner. A plotter, a schemer, yes, the best of the best in those areas. But a planner, no. And certainly not a builder. I've always been the builder. Nick, well, he's more of a destroyer.

He's very good at that, though.

Patiently, but deferentially, I talked him through my plans.

"Fire and brimstone? I thought we'd use BO."

"Yes, yes," I said, hurriedly making a note. "But generating body odor in mass quantities would be a challenge, even for devils. Flames that burn and heat that overwhelms, well, we can produce those pretty easily."

He nodded grudgingly. "I suppose you're right."

"I think we should have many ways of inflicting pain down here," I continued. "BO, acid, pointy objects, stuff like that. But I think fire and brimstone should be our go-to torment, don't you agree?"

Satan scratched his chin, considering. "Yes, on reflection, I believe you're right. Besides, it's chilly down here. We'd get double service out of some major heat. All the devils would be more comfortable in a hellishly hot place."

I smiled. Nick may not be a detail guy, except in narrow situations, but he's as smart as they come. I could see his mental wheels begin to turn. "So, you need to devote some of Tartarus, I mean the Ninth Circle, to a heater because ..."

"... hot air rises."

He nodded. "Okay. How large an area do you need?"

"Not a very big one, actually." I took Nick's drawing and carved out a space at the end of the Hall of Traitors. "We can put the heater here. And see, there's still plenty of room for your office."

"Yes," he said slowly. "That should do."

He then proceeded to describe how he wanted his office configured. I nodded, frowning.

"What? Seems like I should have my office however I want it. It is, after all, mine."

"What?" I said. "Oh, I wasn't frowning about your office. I was just trying to determine how the heater will work. Specifically, what it will burn."

"How about we just boil some water?"

"Not hot enough," I said. "Water boils at 212 degrees." I knew this, even way back then, because I'm a devil and privy to all sorts of arcane knowledge that it took you humans thousands of years to understand. "We need something that burns much hotter."

Satan looked thoughtful, then he grinned, flashing his sharp canines at me. "I know something you can burn that's about a thousand times hotter than that," he said.

"What?"

"I can't tell you. If word got out, we both might get in trouble."

My face scrunched up like a Shar-Pei's. "Well, I need to know something about what I'm burning in order to design the heater. Is it a gas?"

He thought for a second. "Not really, but it should burn like one. Hey, you remember that barbecue grill you made me for my birthday last year?"

I smiled. It had been my birthday too – heck, it was the birthday of all angels and devils – but I'd wanted to do something special for my old friend, so I singled him out and made a big deal about him. In fact, all the devils got together that day and held a big party for him. Belphegor even baked a cake. "Sure, I remember."

"Build a giant version of that, capable of heating all the circles of Hell and handling temperatures equivalent to that of a small star. I'll provide the fuel and light the pilot myself when it's time to fire it up."

"But ..."

"Make it so!" Satan said in an imperious voice.

"Yes sir!" I said involuntarily. It was the first time Satan had unambiguously shown himself to be my boss, ordering me around. I was so stunned, I responded immediately, obediently, and with respect. Since then, I've not always been gracious about the pecking order in Hell, but on that day, his sovereignty over me was clear.

"This is going to be so much work," I said, worrying. "I don't know how I'm going to do this and continue my work as a false god. I guess I'll have to moonlight."

"That won't be necessary," he said, patting me on the shoulder. "Have you noticed that far more humans are getting damned on their own, without your intervention? All of you fake deities are just contributing a trickle to the torrent."

"Your false god days are over. Same for Hecate and Sekhmet and the others. I'm recalling all devils that aren't currently engaged in running Gehenna to help you build the Circles of Hell."

I exhaled in relief. "Thank badness. That will help. As many hands as we can have helping, the better."

Satan grinned hugely. "And I have an idea for some additional help."

"What?" I said, coming out of my thoughts. I had already started to work on the design of the heater. "Who would help devils?"

"I'm going to create a working class devil out of a few promising damned human souls. Devil-men."

"Can you do that?"

"Yes," he said with enthusiasm. "And I think I'll call them demons."

The creation of the first demons, and the Demon Corps itself, was a big deal for Satan. I think he wanted to make something from scratch, but really, creation is the Big Guy's gig. The rest of us, well, we just sort of move things around. All Satan did was identify a few promising humans who wanted to get out of their never-ending torment, graft some horns and tails on them, and soup up their abilities. I wouldn't call that creation, per say. It was more like supercharging them.

The first demon I recall was a fellow named Simon Magus. He was a magician whom Peter bested back in his mortal days. Simon Magus, by the way, is the archetype for the Faust legend. You know, knowledgeable in the arcane/black arts, gets in a little too deep, ends up damned. He was, except for selling his soul to Satan, a smart guy, and a very competent demon, so we set him up as a drill sergeant, training other recruits, in a camp we established on Eight. We first thought to make him commander of the camp, but anyone who has ever served in the military will tell you the sergeants run things. The officers only *think* they're in charge.

These demons were pretty good. Not as strong as devils, but much stronger than humans, and indefatigable. Problem was that not just any damned human soul would make for a good demon. As a result, we got a few extra hands, though not as many as we could have used.

Yet, even short-staffed, Hell began to take shape.

Chapter 14

I knelt to the ground and scooped up a handful of sand. How many grains of sand can fit in a palm? I looked and saw 132,763.

It's a magic thing. Oh, and I have a big hand. Yours couldn't hold as many.

I opened my hand and let the grains slip through my fingers. The hot wind snatched the sand and carried it away; I watched the captive specks travel, in some cases for miles, before settling to the ground.

I smiled. For leagues in all directions, massive dunes covered the landscape. Just like my beloved Sahara. I had done well. This Circle, the first one I carved out of the rock between Tartarus and Limbo, and which would eventually be called the Eighth Circle of Hell, was going to be my center of power. I had built it myself and so fashioned it to my liking.

And there wasn't a soul in sight. Not yet. For now, I had the Eighth Circle to myself. I sighed in contentment. The solitude felt good. Ever since the Fall, I'd begun to realize that I wasn't a people person. All my angelic brethren crowded next to me, cheek to jowl, had been claustrophobic. I didn't realize then, but in retrospect understand those close quarters were part of my dissatisfaction with being one of the Heavenly Host. That dissatisfaction in turn was probably why I followed Nick out of there with no argument. I just wanted to leave a crowded room.

Eight was completely deserted. Well, of course it was deserted, being a desert and all, but you know what I mean.

I took a deep breath. The sirocco felt good, captured in my immortal lungs. I took another look at my handiwork. The place was insufferably hot and dry. Minimal insects. It was and still is great. My own little heaven.

Yes, even in Hell.

That was when eight hundred pounds of rock fell on my head. "What the ...?"

Looking up, I spied a half-mile long crack, running through my ceiling. In a moment, a head poked out of the hole. "Oops!"

"Abaddon!" I shouted and teleported up to his head, which was dangling beneath the ceiling like a Seventies disco ball. "What the hell are you doing?" I grabbed his head and jerked him out of the hole.

"Just what you said, Beezy. Don't know what happened, though. I was making the first cut on the Second Circle of Hell when I popped through to here. This is really hard work, by the way," he said, staring at me severely, which was not really wise, since I still held him by the skull, my thumbs and forefingers wrapped around his horns.

It would be so easy to break these off.

I stared up through the hole in my ceiling and saw, not a boo-boo, but a deep gash that easily ran seven miles straight up.

"Ow! Ow! Shit! Why did you break off my horns?"

"I'm going to *kill* you, you idiot!" Then I dragged him down to the surface of Level Eight.

Abaddon broke free from me. "You can't kill me, and you know it. Now give me back my horns."

I tossed them at him. He caught one, but the other pierced his stomach. "Ouch!" he groused, pulling it out then reattaching them to his forehead. "Why are you so mad?"

"Maybe because you just poked a great big hole through all of Hell."

"Well, if I did anything wrong, it's your fault, not mine. I was just following your plans."

"What are you talking about?"

Abaddon reached in the air, and a set of blueprints materialized in his hands. "Look. I dug it just as you described."

The ground of the Eighth Circle began to rumble as I took a few deep breaths, struggling to contain my temper. "Do you see these numbers here, the ones that say one inch represents twelve hundred feet?"

"Yes. I'm not blind, you know," Abaddon said testily as he stared at the chart, "though I don't know why you wrote them sidewise like that. I got a crick in my neck, constantly turning my head to one side so I could read your instructions."

"I didn't write them sideways, you moron!" I gave him a fake grin. "You see, the scale and all the other writing, well, they were kind of a clue that you somehow missed. You were holding and reading the plans sideways." I rolled the blueprints back up, used them to swat Abaddon over the head before making them disappear, then plopped down in the sand, more than a little discouraged.

"Really?" Abaddon stroked his chin as he sat down next to me. "I always did have a problem with spatial relationships. Hmmm. So, you want a bunch of horizontal levels, not vertical ones?"

"Ah, yeah. That was the idea."

"Interesting. I totally did not get that."

Ignoring Abaddon's babbling, I thought through the problem. "What am I going to do with a seven-mile hole punched straight through the center of Hell?"

"Install a dumbwaiter?"

"We could always just fill the hole back in," Abaddon said, when he walked the hundred feet back from where I'd just thrown him. "There's lots of dirt up on Limbo. That's where I started, and I put the stuff I dug out there."

I shook my head. "No, the damage is done. At the very least, I'm going to have to place load-bearing beams all over the place."

"I'm really sorry, Beezy." And he looked it.

I sighed, letting go of my anger. "I know you are. I'm just going to have to manage this project a little more carefully henceforth."

"Henceforth?"

"It means from now on."

"Oh."

How many devils does it take to screw in a lightbulb? None. They can screw up everything, but they can't screw in anything. "Has anyone else started?"

"No. I'm first."

"Well, that's something to be thankful for, I suppose."

In the end, Abaddon's gaffe proved fortuitous. Up until then, I had only given thought to the Nine Circles themselves, not to how newly-damned souls were going to get down to the different levels. I decided to leave the hole in place, though I reinforced it heavily. After the remaining circles were cut, in their appropriately horizontal orientation, things held up fine. Then, with permission from Top Management, I poked through the ceiling of Limbo, creating the Mouth of Hell.

This was to the consternation of the steward of Gates Level, St. Peter. The first pope, in life a good friend of Jesus, had been given the assignment of sorting the newly dead into Saved and Damned, using a magic book called the Book of Life.

Though Peter found the practice barbaric, for many years he by necessity used the Mouth and Throat of Hell to consign the Damned to Hell, meaning he tossed the souls into

147

the monstrous hole I'd made in the floor by his desk. To be accurate, he didn't even need to do any tossing; a shove to the shoulder was about all that was necessary to send someone plummeting into the Mouth of Hell. Yet Petey immediately began to lobby for a set of stairs leading down to Hell.

Eventually, I consented. Besides, it gave me an opportunity to build a Gateway to Hell, one far more impressive than the dilapidated one Hades, the god, had for Hades, the place.

Since Eight was completed first, we temporarily transferred all sinners from Gehenna, or Hell 1.0, to my circle. We would eventually redistribute many of them across the other circles as they came online, but a disproportionate number of the early Damned, up to those who died between the Crucifixion and about 200 AD, stayed on Eight.

Hell 2.0 shared many common traits with Gehenna, though the former was much larger, sort of like Disneyworld is a bigger version of Disneyland. In our new digs, we recreated many of the torments we'd used in Gehenna, though we supersized them. For example, Snakes on a Plain became Snakes on a Great Plain, a large expanse of flat land on Four. Lazy River was recreated on not one but two Circles, only now they were Not-so-Lazy Oceans, one on Two and the other on Seven. We completed the rest of Hell with our go-to torments, lava pits and seas of thorns. The approach wasn't particularly innovative, but we needed to complete the new franchise quickly, so creativity gave way to expediency.

Pouring the oceans on Two and Seven was tricky, and for that project I wish I'd had Leviathan's help. He'd always been good with water. Leviathan and his cronies were still on Earth, though, causing mischief wherever they could, trying with their limited devil brains to engineer Satan's failure and eventual overthrow.

After about two hundred years, and a few more false starts and general screw-ups, we got Circles Two through Seven online. Over the centuries, as styles have come and gone in the fine art of damnation, we have made modifications as appropriate, but the basic function hasn't changed. Everlasting torment.

All that remained was establishing a management structure. "I'm the boss of all. You get that, right?"

Sigh. "Yes, Nick. Do we have to go through this again?"

"Even you, Beezy. You report to me," he said, ignoring my comment. "I am the greatest. I am the most powerful devil of them all."

I bit my tongue. Nick and his whole sin of pride thing: it was very tedious to witness. Besides, I knew that I was just as strong as he.

Maybe I should have put in a bid to be the Satan. I do all the work anyway, so I might as well have gotten the glory.

Except that I didn't really want the glory. My first reaction when Uriel had given us our assignments had been the correct one. I liked being number two. I got more things done and could stay out of the limelight.

The limelight, however, was about all that Satan craved. "I don't know why we have to go over this time and again, but fine," I conceded. "You're the boss. Just don't say you're more powerful than I am."

"You doubt it?" Nick blasted me with Hellfire, which I thought was pretty juvenile. I brushed at my shoulder, as if a piece of lint had settled on my shirt.

"Well?" he demanded.

"Ow."

"You said that without conviction."

"Okay. Ow, ow. Now, can we get back to more important things?"

He stared at me, his eyes narrowing. "Fine," he said at last. "I'm the Earl of Hell, lord above all devils, but I have no interest in managing the boring, day-to-day details."

"Okay, then have all the devils report to me."

"No, no. You don't get it. Everybody reports to me. If they report to you, they'll start thinking you're the boss." He smiled at me in disingenuous fashion. "We can't have that, now can we. No, I was thinking that you and some others would comprise a layer of middle management and ..."

"So, now I'm middle management? Gee, thanks."

"Quit being so huffy. You're still number two. The first among equals ... in middle management."

I took a deep breath and refrained from slugging him.

"These managers, I think we'll call them princes – isn't that nice sounding? – these devil princes will have all the other devils reporting to them. The princes in turn will report to me. That way I'm clearly the boss, and everyone knows it, yet I won't have every devil in Hell wanting to meet with me. Delegation, that's what I'm all about."

"Got it. Who else do you have in mind to be a devil prince?"

"Well, Belphegor for one. He's been functioning as a de facto devil prince from the very beginning."

"Can't argue with that. You know how much respect I have for Belly. Who else?"

"Oh, I don't know. You go find the others."

"Why don't you do it? Seems like I handle everything around here."

"You will do it because I *command* you to."

150

And that was that.

Accordingly, I went looking for devil prince candidates. This would not be easy. Most fallen angels were not by nature managers. They were followers.

I knew one likely candidate: Sekhmet. Sharp as a spike, and she liked telling people what to do. I think that came from her role playing, whenever a sexual partner wanted a dominatrix. That was never my thing, but others liked it.

I caught her at a good moment, in the rosy blush that follows the sexual act. Still, she was reluctant.

"Why would I want to do that? I'm pretty busy, you know, with all the fornicating I do."

And then I had a flash of inspiration. "No, this will be great! You see, each devil prince is going to get management responsibility over one of the Seven Deadly Sins and its respective sinners. As a prince, you would have responsibility over … would you stop touching yourself for a minute and listen to me? Thanks. You'd get responsibility over Lust."

"Oh," Sekhsie said, brightening. She got up and paced the room, as she considered the prospect of being the Prince of Lust. "That would be okay, I guess, since it aligns with my personal interests. But this is only temporary. right? You know I hate supervising."

"Yes, dear. Now come back to bed."

I eventually got Astaroth, who, like Sekhmet, was just coming off a long stretch as a fake deity, to be Prince of Greed. Abaddon, who felt bad for all the trouble he'd caused me in the early days of Hell's construction, volunteered to be a prince. I accepted him with some hesitation, since he was neither a bright devil nor a good manager. I assigned him Envy, which seemed appropriate. Abaddon envied almost everyone.

Chapter 15

'm going to let you in on one of the great ironies of the cosmos. As Adversary, Satan's job is to tempt humans away from the path of righteousness. But in order to be tempted from the path, they must be on it to begin with.

The Jews, the chosen people, had been set on their own private road thousands of years before the establishment of Christianity, but Judaism had always been an exclusive club. It was never intended to be a belief system that would propagate itself, except generationally. The numbers would always be small.

Christianity was different. It had the potential to go global, something Nick and I recognized immediately.

Now, here's the irony: the best way for devils to succeed at their jobs is by aiding the spread of Christianity. Or Islam, but at the time we had this realization, Islam didn't exist yet.

Only a little more than one in ten Christians or would-be Christians make it into Heaven. The rest go to Hell. Our market share has held constant almost from the beginning. So: grow the market, get more souls. While we strive mightily to corrupt humans, we work even harder to ensure they become believers first.

In the early years of the church, this was difficult. The Roman Empire didn't think much of our nascent religion. Christians snuck around, hoping to avoid persecution, while at the same time trying to spread the word. Kind of a no-win situation. There were lots of martyrs to the cause in those early years.

After watching this mess for a few centuries, we decided to step in and do something about it.

One day, at the beginning of the Fourth Century AD, Satan and I were sitting in his office. He had just created something he called a desk, and he was behind it now, feet propped up on its surface. He was sitting on a stack of seed sacks, the precursor to the bean bag chair, because while chairs with backs had been around at least since about 3000 BC, a really *comfortable* one had not yet been invented. Satan's favorite type of chair, the La-Z-Boy, didn't come into existence until 1928.

I was completely fine with a stool, by the way.

So, we were chewing the fat down on the Ninth Circle. By now, we'd moved everyone from Gehenna to Hell, but our new domain was so sparsely populated that we despaired of ever having a going concern. "The stupid Romans," Satan groused. "They're killing Christians almost as fast as they're getting converted, but before we've had a chance to corrupt them. At this rate, we'll never fill up Hell."

"Well," I said, scratching my beard with a claw, "I designed Hell to accommodate a lot of growth, so that's not even an issue, but I understand you. The Romans are still holding onto their old pantheon." I snorted. "Wonder what they would think if they knew their gods skipped town hundreds of years ago."

"Well, I don't think the Romans spend much time thinking at all. They're too busy building their empire. And killing Christians."

"Indeed. Can you believe that Diocletian guy? Why is he so intent on persecuting Christians?"

This was the year 303 AD. By that time, the Roman Empire had gotten huge, stretching from Britain to Northern

Africa to most of what in modern times would be called the Middle East. Yet, the empire was already in decline, since its period of maximum expansion was under Trajan in 117. Yet, even in the Three Hundreds, it was so damn huge that it proved difficult to manage. To address the problem, the emperors experimented with different forms of government. One such experiment was to run the whole shebang as two separate if related empires, one in the East and one in the West. Such a division was made permanent in 395, but back in 303 (or CCCiii, if you prefer), Diocletian was testing out the idea.

He set up a ruling system called the Tetrarchy, which essentially consisted of two senior emperors, each called Augustus, and two junior emperors-in-training, called Caesars. Diocletian was the most senior of the four, and he ruled from the Eastern Empire.

And he just hated Christians. In 303, Diocletian began the Great Persecution. He obliterated the church at Nicomedia, destroyed other churches, burned scriptures. This last item was a major hardship for the new religion. Scriptures were more precious than churches, because they were rare. Texts had to be copied by hand, slow and tedious work, this being, after all, before the advent of moveable type ... and the photocopy machine.

Christians in the empire were deprived of any social rank they might have had. Priests were locked up, and the keys thrown away. Some folks got killed too, especially in the coliseums. Christians were very popular objects for slaughter in the coliseums.

By the way, Diocletian did all of this on the advice of the oracle of Apollo. This was ironic, I think, seeing that the Greco-Roman sun god was long gone. But the oracle didn't know that.

Maybe, when the phone went silent to her god, she thought she had just been put on hold, so decided to fake it.

Thinking about Diocletian and the Roman Empire, I remembered a promising young up-and-comer in the empire's administrative structure. "You know, Nick ..."

The Earl of Hell frowned. "Satan. I wish you'd quit calling me Nick. You should show more respect to your lord and master."

I frowned back. "Don't get on your high horse with me. I knew you when. Besides, are you going to quit calling me Flyface?"

"Well, no."

"Then get used to Nick. Shit, I've been calling you Nick since before Creation. I've already promised to try and remember to call you Satan in formal settings, but no guarantees."

"Fine, fine," he said in irritation. "Now, what were you going to say?"

What was *I going to say?* I conjured up a ball of flame and began to toss it up and down. This was a habit of mine that often helped me think. "Oh, yes!" I said, squeezing my hand shut and extinguishing the fiery orb. "What if the Romans helped us spread Christianity to all the lands they've conquered?"

"Why would they do that? Rather than lionizing Christians, Romans prefer to feed them to the lions."

"Not bad, Nick. You'll grow a sense of humor yet."

"How dare you?" Nick thinks he has a wonderful sense of humor, and, in a way, he does, though it's very lowbrow.

Ignoring him, I closed my eyes and thought. When my vague idea turned into a plan, they popped open. "The Romans are going to have to give up their old gods, sooner or later, and when they do, they'll need to believe in somebody else." I looked at my old friend. "Have you been paying attention to this Constantine guy?"

"A little. Why?"

"Well, his father is the western Caesar, and it looks like he'll be promoted to Augustus someday."

"So what?"

I pursed my lips. "I think, with a little assistance from us, his son could follow a similar career path."

Satan conjured up a dart board and some tiny pitchforks and began tossing them at the board. "Why would we want to do that?"

"Do you know that Constantine's mom is a Christian?"

When he was young, Constantius had gotten involved with Helena, a Greek woman of low social status. He did it because, while his native tongue was Latin, he frequently needed to converse or correspond in Greek, and his Greek sucked. Constantius hired Helena to be his interpreter, and over time an office romance ensued, resulting in a kid: Constantine. Mom taught her boy all about Christianity.

"What? No. That's interesting. How do you know this, and I don't?"

I shrugged. "You've been focused on setting up Hell and ruling it. Me, after we got the Circles built out, well, I had some time on my hands. I've become a bit of a Romanophile. I've been hanging around the empire's corridors of power, both the western and the eastern, for some time. You hang around corridors, you hear gossip."

"Well this is interesting." I could see the wheels begin to turn in Nick's head. "Does Constantine share his mom's beliefs?"

"Probably not, though he's been exposed to them since childhood. Constantine strikes me as an opportunist. He probably believes in Jupiter, Jesus or whoever is in fashion at the time. One thing I'm sure of, though, is that in all this persecution of the Christians, he has stayed pretty hands off. I imagine he wouldn't want his own mom swept up into an ugly situation."

"No doubt."

"I think that's your in, Nick. Get Constantine to stop persecuting the Christians, so the new religion has a chance to get established."

Satan looked thoughtful. "That's a good idea, but I think I'll go one step further than that."

"What's that?"

"I'm going to convert him. Shouldn't be too hard. With his mom onboard, he's halfway in the boat himself."

And so began our campaign to make the Roman Empire a Christian one.

We laid out a four-pronged strategy. First, we would help Constantine move up the professional ranks. If we played our cards right, we could move him all the way to the top of the administration, at least in the western empire. Maybe even the eastern as well.

Step two would be to convert him to Christianity. Step three: have him formally end the persecution of the Christians, which if step two was successful would be easy. He wouldn't want to persecute himself. The final step would be making Christianity the official, that is, the *only* religion of the Roman Empire. We figured we could get all of this done in a reasonable amount of time. We just weren't sure we could do it all in one lifetime. You humans are such ephemeral creatures.

Since our plan depended upon Constantine's success in the Roman Empire, we felt it was time to meet him. We caught up with the man in Nicomedia. Nick and I disguised ourselves as military officers of the Western Empire, on a diplomatic mission to the court of Diocletian.

"This place is pretty big," Nick muttered, as we wandered the city, looking for clues to the whereabouts of Constantine.

"Don't worry, we'll find him. I just hope we don't get in trouble for interfering in things."

Nick stopped short. "You think that's possible?"

I shrugged. "We haven't really had a direct role in human events since before the Resurrection, and even then, our roles were heavily scripted."

"Well, better to seek forgiveness than ask permission, I suppose. Now, how was he described to us?"

We had first stopped by Diocletian's palace, looking for Constantine. "He's probably out by the stables," a servant had said. "Lord Constantine is a restless sort and can often be found there. Besides, uh, he really likes horses."

"How will we recognize him?"

"Let's see … He's about thirty. Big guy. Muscular, like he bench-presses large farm animals or something. Curly brown hair cut in a Page Boy. Strong nose. Cleft in his chin. Very impressive. Yes, indeed. He stands out. You'll know him when you see him."

And so we did. Sitting under a tree, by the stables, was a massively built young man, well, young to us, though fairly mature for a human back then, when people were lucky to live past twenty-five. He was dressed in the full military armor of a high-ranking Roman officer, which made sitting under a tree a bit of a trick. I wondered how he was going to stand up unaided.

"Excuse me," Nick said, after giving Constantine a proper salute, which involved slamming a fist with considerable force against the left side of the breast plate, making a ringing sound not unlike that of a cymbal. "Would I have the honor of addressing Lord Constantine?"

The man sighed then struggled to his feet and returned the salute. "Yes. What is it?"

I saluted too and got a proper return from Constantine. By this time, the horses in the stable were skittish, with all that clanging going on, but we were done with the introductions, and I was confident the animals would settle down in short order. "We have just arrived from the west and carry greetings from your father." Constantine's father, as the western Caesar, was the fourth most powerful man in the empire.

Constantine looked suddenly alert. "You have a message from my father?"

"Well ... no," I said. "He just told us to say 'hey.'"

"Hey? What is this hey?"

Nick gave me a dirty look. "My friend means your father extends his greetings and felicitations, hoping that we will find you well. Are you well, sir?"

"Yeah. I guess."

Satan looked at the Roman with skepticism. "Really? You seem kind of down to me."

Constantine buzzed his lips like one of the stable's occupants. "Neigh, I mean, nay." Then he paused, thoughtful. At last, he continued. "No, you're right. I *am* a bit depressed. Still, things could be worse, especially considering I've been a prisoner for nearly a decade."

"What do you mean?" Satan asked, curious. I knew all about Constantine's situation, but Nick didn't.

Constantine looked left and right quickly, as if searching for spies. "You say you are my father's men. You speak truly?"

"Certainly," Nick said, his fingers crossed behind his back.

The Roman hesitated. "I only ask, because if you were Diocletian's, my candor could get me in some trouble."

"Not to worry," I said. "Your secrets are safe with us. Besides, we're all Romans here. Intrigue is expected of us, I think."

"Yes," Constantine said, bitterly. "But so is assassination."

"I have some knowledge of your circumstances," I said, "but my friend does not. Go ahead."

Constantine wrapped his arms around his torso in a futile attempt to contain his frustration. "It's just that I've been held a virtual prisoner for so long. And Diocletian keeps dragging me around to the most boring cities: Nicomedia, Sirmium, Byzantium – well, Byzantium's okay, there are some pretty hot women there, and the wine is good too – then back here to Nicomedia. I *hate* Nicomedia," he ended bitterly.

"The Eastern Empire is vast, my lord," I said sagely. "At least you get to travel. And you *are* your father's heir presumptive."

"Big deal!" he said, bitterly. "That only means Diocletian holds me on a short leash so he can keep an eye on me. *Stercore!*"

"Uh, beg pardon?" Nick said.

"Stercore, stercore," Constantine said impatiently. "You know. The stuff that comes out of you when you go number two."

"We know what it means, my lord," I said. "Why did you say it just now?"

"I was swearing."

"That was swearing?" Satan looked at me, and we both burst out laughing.

Constantine frowned, "Quid tam ridiculam damn?"

By this point, we were howling with laughter. At last I explained. "What's so damn funny? Forgive me, my lord, but swearing in Latin, well, it just doesn't work."

"And why not?"

"Oh, you know, Latin is just too fancy. Swearing in Latin is almost as bad as doing it in Greek."

He sniffed. "And what language do you think I *should* swear in?"

"No question," Satan said. "The language of the Huns. Nothing is better for swearing than the old Hun-tongue."

"Give me an example. Stercore in Hun-speak is …?"

"Scheiss."

"Or better yet, shit," I said, trying to be helpful.

"Sheee-it," Constantine said by way of experiment. Then he said it again, rolling it around in his mouth, seeing how it felt. Not actual shit. The word, I mean. "Shit shit shit!" He grinned. "You're right. I like it. It conveys exactly how I feel. Ooh! Give me another one."

"Like what?"

"Pedicabo."

"Fuck," I said, chuckling.

"Fuck … Am I using the right verb form?"

"It's fine," Nick said.

"Oh, good. Fuck, fuu – uck. Shit … shit shit shit … fuck fuck fuck. This is great! Teach me some more!"

Nick rolled his eyes. "Another time."

"Promise?"

"Sure."

It's a little-known fact that for the rest of his life, Constantine only swore in the language of the Huns. His subjects, few of whom spoke Hun, marveled at the piety of their emperor. Though he swore all the time, his people thought he was speaking in tongues, which they considered a miracle of sorts. Constantine's supposed tongue-speak was, in fact, a major reason why he was made a saint.

Chapter 16

My lord," I said. "We have strayed from our subject. You were complaining about Diocletian keeping you on a short leash."

"Oh yes," he said, remembering. "When I saw you, I hoped my father had concocted some ruse to get me out of here."

This gave me an idea. "Have no fear. That's exactly what he is doing."

What the hell are you talking about? Satan said via telepathic connection, which was our communication method of choice whenever we were with humans and wanted a little privacy.

Patience. I'm making this up as I go along. "However," I continued aloud, "his plans are not yet ripe, so he, uh, he requests your forbearance. You will hear from us again, my lord. When next you see us, be prepared to fly to the west." We bowed and took our leave.

Two years passed before conditions were ripe to get Constantine out of Nicomedia. By then, Diocletian, suffering from a debilitating illness, had abdicated. Galerius succeeded Diocletian, and Constantius was made Augustus of the Western Empire, or number two in the empire's pecking order, but Constantine was passed over for the position of western Caesar. That job went to a fellow named Severus.

After Galerius took over, Constantine was watched more closely than ever, since he was now officially a malcontent with some claim of legitimacy for one of the top leadership positions in the empire. If Diocletian had Constantine in a white-collar prison, Galerius effectively had him in lockdown.

Constantius, recognizing his son's danger, sent two emissaries, who happened to be Nick and I, to the court of Galerius. Seems there had been difficulty with the Picts, and the western Augustus wanted his son to help him put down the insurrection in Britain. After some persuasion, Galerius agreed to let Constantine go.

"How did you two get in my chamber?" The young lord said, leaping from his divan.

"Your father sent us," Nick said. "We have convinced Galerius that your military prowess is needed on the western front. You are to leave immediately for Britain."

"And we do mean immediately," I said, checking for spies.

Constantine dressed quickly, packing a light travel bag. "I can't believe Galerius fell for this."

"This was the plan we told you about two years ago."

"Well, shit, it took you long enough to execute it."

I grimaced. "Oh, good. You've been practicing your swearing."

"How did you convince Galerius?"

"We got him drunk," Satan said mildly.

"Yes, and he's likely to regret his decision to let you go in the morning. Best to put some miles between you and the court."

A strange gleam came to Constantine's eyes. "Do I get to travel by horse?"

"Horse or ship, I suppose. Why do you care?"

He shrugged. "I really like horses. Always have."

"Well, then," Nick said, "you should grab the fastest horse you know and high-tail it for Byzantium."

By morning, when Galerius, head aching and more than a little nauseated, realized his blunder, he sent a squad of soldiers to retrieve Constantine. It was too late, however. Constantine was well out of reach.

Constantius had not been lying about the trouble in Britain. For more than a year, he and his son fought the Picts in the lands north of Hadrian's Wall, in what is now southern Scotland. Then, Constantius got ill. On the verge of death, he supported his son's advancement to the position of western Augustus. When Constantius died in 306, the troops, out of loyalty to the father, accepted Constantine by acclamation.

But Galerius was having none of it. He grudgingly offered Constantine the job of western Caesar, with responsibility for Britain, Gaul and Spain. However, the top spot in the west went to Severus, which made a certain amount of sense, since he had seniority. Times being what they were, Constantine accepted the demotion, knowing that at least it gave him claims to legitimacy, which back then was a certain amount of job security, that is, he was less likely to get assassinated.

For the next few years, Constantine gained a reputation as a military commander. Yet, since his mother had been a Greek of low social standing who had borne Constantine out of wedlock, he still struggled for credibility. And so arose a period of political instability and intrigue among the Roman elite, a time of arranged marriages, and a series of revolts by Maxentian, Maximius and others of the "Max" persuasion. This was still going on in 311, when Galerius died. Oh, Maximius had also died.

But then, that's what you humans do.

With the death of Galerius, the notion of a ruling Tetrarchy went by the boards. Of all the pretenders to the western throne, only Constantine and Maxentian were left.

It all came to a head in October of 312. Constantine was advancing on Rome, where Maxentian was holding court. The only way to end the conflict was for one side to win a decisive victory over the other. Unfortunately for Constantine, his army was half the size of the competition's. He had a couple of things going for him, though. Constantine was a military genius; he didn't often lose battles. And the people of the Italian Peninsula hated Maxentian's guts.

Satan and I once again involved ourselves. We were taking no chances.

The day before the decisive battle, we found Constantine with his army, about twenty-five miles north of Rome. They had been marching all morning and were on lunch break. The would-be ruler of the Roman empire was standing alone in a copse, his only companion his steed. Thinking that no one was watching, Constantine was taking the opportunity to French kiss his horse.

Satan looked at me with raised eyebrows. *Jeez. He really* does *have a thing about horses.*

Let's withdraw thirty or forty feet, give them some privacy then try again.

We approached a second time, making a great deal of noise before we got too close. By the time we reached Constantine, he was facing our direction, sword drawn.

"Hail, Augustus!" we exclaimed, slamming our respective chests so hard that we dented our breastplates.

"You guys? Where the fuck have you been? And it's Caesar Augustus." He frowned. "Or will be, soon enough. I hope."

Satan bowed deeply. "We come bearing tidings, my liege. Maxentius has crossed the Tiber with his army. They line the banks of the river, awaiting you."

"Old news. My spies reported this to me an hour ago."

"Uh, my lord," I said, "you do realize his forces outnumber yours two to one."

Constantine cursed. "I know that. He's an idiot for pinning himself against the river like he's doing, but he still has the advantage."

The would-be Caesar Augustus plopped down on the ground. His horse bent and lovingly nuzzled his master's ear. Constantine stroked its muzzle. "I hate this, Roman fighting Roman. Why it's almost impossible to tell who's who."

I looked to Nick. He was staring up at the sky, thinking hard. Then he brightened. "Perhaps, my liege, you should pray to the divine."

"Who would you recommend?" Constantine asked, his words edged with sarcasm. "Jupiter? Mars? Or perhaps that oldie-but-goodie, Mithras. Shit. We Romans worship everybody."

"I was thinking of Someone else," Nick said, pointing upward. "Look at those clouds there. What do they remind you of?"

Constantine stared at the sky, a look of rapture on his face. "A horsey?"

"No. How do you get a horsey out of that?"

"I like horseys."

No shit. I grumbled.

I'll handle it. Not to worry. "See how that long cloud is crossed almost exactly by that shorter one."

"A tall horsey with broad shoulders?"

Nick sighed. "No, my lord. Its not a horsey." He looked at me. *Help!*

I nodded, seeing where Nick was trying to lead Constantine. I cleared my throat. "Crossed? Did you say crossed? You know, I think you're right. That looks very much like a … a …"

We both looked in expectation at the Roman commander.

"A … a cross?" He looked again. "A cross! You know, you're right!"

"And what god is associated with a cross?" It was a leading question, but I didn't blame Nick for asking it.

"Why, the god of my mother. The Christian God."

"Who *is* God," I intoned breathlessly, knowing that a breathless intonation always impressed people.

"Are you two Christians?"

"No, not exactly. But we," Nick swallowed hard, as if choking on the words, "we believe in Him."

"So does Mom. Yes. This is a sign. I will pray to the Christian God for victory in battle."

"You might toss in a few kind thoughts about the meek and the sick." I suggested. "Couldn't hurt."

"Good idea. Are you two going to hang around for the battle?"

Nick smiled. "Wouldn't miss it."

That night, Constantine's army neared Rome. We were so close, we could see the campfires of the opposing forces.

Constantine summoned us to his pavilion. He was in his sleeping garments. They were, unsurprisingly, covered with images of horses. "My mom showed me how to do this, but it's been a long time. Seems I recall slaughtering a sheep or something."

"No, that's old school," Nick said. "Just start with something like, like …"

"Now I lay me down to sleep," I suggested.

"Yes," agreed Nick. "That's good. Then ad lib. I'm sure it will work out fine."

It worked out better than fine. The next morning, Constantine awoke refreshed and encouraged. He ran out to speak to his generals, though I noticed he'd taken time to change out of his horsey pajamas. "Today we will ride forth in battle, carrying the Greek letters Chi and Rho on our shields. These are the first two letters of the Christos name. We fight for him. And we will be victorious!"

"Might also help distinguish Roman from Roman," Nick whispered to me.

"Ah, right," I said, discreetly conjuring up a box of chalk. "Okay, now, we don't have a lot of time here, and I know many of you don't know Greek. Basically, lets do this. Take a stick of chalk … here you go … and make a capital P on your shields. Then on the bottom half of the P, cross it with a small x." I demonstrated on Constantine's shield.

"Very stylish," he said and turned back to his generals. "Make it so!"

Hurriedly, the army scrawled the P and the little x on their shields. Some of their penmanship was atrocious, but the shields now looked distinctively different from the other side's.

And then Constantine and his army marched to war. In the end, all he needed was a little self-confidence. Besides, he really was a terrific military commander. As the saying goes, "God helps those who help themselves."

In the ensuing battle, Maxentian drowned in the Tiber, just proving that he was an idiot for facing the opposing army with his back to the river. Constantine was victorious, the last man standing of the ruling elite, and so became the undisputed ruler of the western Roman Empire. A dozen years passed before he defeated Licinius, the eastern emperor, but then Constantine became undisputed ruler of the entire empire.

For the rest of his life, he considered himself a Christian, though he waited until he was on his deathbed before getting baptized. While emperor, he provided funding for Christianity and effectively eliminated the persecution of its believers.

Another fifty years elapsed before Nick and I could complete our plan to extend Christianity throughout the Roman Empire. By then, we were working with Theodosius I. He did his job though, decreeing that all citizens of the empire adopt the Christian faith. Right after his death, the empire finally split in two, but by then, we had millions of new converts.

Ironically, Rome, a key player in the Crucifixion, did more than any other force to spread the Gospel in those early centuries. Satan got a bonus the year Theodosius made Christianity the official religion of the empire. It looked like not long would pass before Nick's probationary period would end, and he would get tenured as the Adversary.

But Leviathan had other ideas.

Chapter 17

When you're dealing with a more or less eternal lifespan, "not long" is a relative thing.

Theodosius I issued his *Cunctos Populos*, in which he decreed that Nicene Christianity was the empire's only legitimate religion, in 380. Satan and I were still basking in our success in the early Six Hundreds, when we started to hear of a significant happening in the Middle East.

That part of the world was not just the cradle of many early civilizations. It was also the birthing ground for all three religions of the Book, the Abrahamic religions. Judaism started there, as did Christianity. And then came Islam.

I was just finishing up work on the Stairway to Paradise when I first got word of it.

I said earlier that I completed the Stairway at Peter's request, and that's true to a point, but the Stairs also met a need for Nick's workforce. While the Mouth of Hell worked fine for getting damned souls down to the various circles, getting them up was another matter, and there were times when we felt it advisable to move one of the Damned. For example, someone might have been damned for being both greedy and lustful. When that happened, we liked to leave the person a few centuries on Level Four, where most of the avaricious were punished, then boot them up to Two to be tormented by Sekhmet and her staff.

There were only a handful of devils who could teleport, and they often had to handle inter-circular relocations personally, at least when the direction involved was up. We also used BOOH, who had grown into a fine, strapping bat, but he wasn't always available, since Satan preferred to keep his precious pet close at hand. Belphegor suggested that we have some second-tier devils regrow their wings and fly these souls up through the Throat of Hell. That worked for a while, but as the ranks of the Demon Corps began to swell, we developed a need for interdepartmental demon transfers. Finally, I got fed up with this, so I made good on my promise to Peter and built a stairway connecting Gates level and the various Circles of Hell.

I was just finishing connecting my stairwell to the Gates-to-Limbo segment Peter and I had built in the first few years of Hell 2.0. (He used this segment to gently transport the unbaptized babies.) This was a ceremonial occasion, like the driving of the golden spike in Ogden, Utah, though in my case I used a ceremonial pitchfork nail. I hate those things, by the way. They're a bitch to drive – three tines and all, you know. I had to will it into place as I swung my hammer for dramatic effect. The attendees applauded, a marching band started to play, and we popped a bottle of champagne.

There weren't just devils and demons in attendance. A handful of heavenly representatives, including Peter, the impetus behind me building the Stairway in the first place, were there. One of them I hadn't seen in ages.

Gabriel was, and still is, a quiet, unassuming archangel. This is ironic to me, since he is often chosen by Management as a heavenly herald to Earth, bringing important news like the Annunciation to the faithful. About the only thing ostentatious about him is that big post horn he always carries with him.

There's no good way to carry a thing like that. Usually, Gabe balances it on his shoulder like a soldier's rifle. Occasionally, he rolls it up and sticks it in his garments, but it puts an unsightly bulge in his robe. "Is that a trumpet in your pocket, or are you just glad to see me?"

You know.

Yet, he feels he needs to keep it with him, despite the inconvenience of the thing. After all, he'll never know when he will be called upon to blow the damn thing. The Rapture could happen at any time. Or someone could request a fanfare, or even Leroy Anderson's "Bugler's Holiday."

"Gabe!" I said, going up to the archangel and shaking his hand. "What's up?" I looked at his attire. He appeared to be dressed for traveling. "Heading to Earth again?"

Gabriel flashed a brief smile. "Yes. I'm supposed to help establish a new religion." He shuffled his feet, looking uncomfortable. "I don't know why I always get these jobs. Michael or Uriel would be a better choice."

I frowned. I didn't know about Michael. Being an emissary didn't, in my mind, fit his, ah, skill set. He was a fighter, not a talker. Uriel, smart as a whip and smooth as a silken hankie, could do it, and he had recently been relieved of Garden guard duty. When Hell got transported from the mortal plane to the metaphysical one, management had moved Eden as well, eliminating the need for a watchman. The Garden was a popular spot with the Saved, who would frequently have picnics there.

So, why didn't Uriel get any of these courier duties? "Perhaps it's because both Michael and Uriel would be a bit overwhelming to humans. You, well, you're impressive in your own way, but more approachable. You wouldn't scare the shit out of a human."

Gabriel frowned. "Your language has certainly deteriorated since you became a devil. How's that working for you, by the way?"

I shrugged. "It's okay, I guess. I enjoyed my old job better."

"You mean as an angel or a false god?"

173

"False god." I sighed, thinking of the good old days. I slipped my hammer into my tool belt. "I've enjoyed building Hell, though."

Gabe whistled. "Big job."

I thought about digging the Circles, pouring the oceans, installing the torments. Then there was the HVAC system and all the troubles it gave me. "You got that right. Still, it was more interesting than torturing the Damned."

"Indeed." Gabriel looked at his watch. "Sorry. I'd love to chat longer, but I have to get down to a cave near Mecca."

"Why?"

"I have a prophet to meet. Name's Muhammed. See you." With that, Gabe teleported.

Over the next few years, Satan and I heard periodic reports about the new religion of Islam, but we didn't pay much attention. We were preoccupied with the spread of Christianity. Encouraging its progress into the Slavic regions was slow going. There were also those dratted Norse gods who were refusing to capitulate.

This inattention, in retrospect, was a mistake on our part. And it left an opening for the Leviathan faction.

I should note here that we devils are never allowed to interfere, in either positive or negative fashion, with the founding of a new religion. Not since the temptation of Adam and Eve have we been permitted to shape the narrative. At best, as with Job and Jesus, we have minor roles, and usually we don't even get any lines.

Once the religions are established, though, we're allowed to work our magic, though in only limited ways. Tempting individual humans off the Path, yes, that's allowed. We can also help spread the religion, as we did with Constantine and Theodosius and were trying to do with those hard-headed Slavs and Teutons. We'd even tried to expand into India, but that didn't work very well. With Hinduism, shit, they already had so many gods and goddesses, our religion got lost in the crowd. We eventually established a small presence in India, but Christians were only a drop in the bucket of that very large country.

While we were focused on growing Christianity, not to mention tormenting the Damned, Leviathan looked for ways to expand Islam's market share. Not that the Muslims needed much help. They were formidable warriors and, imbued with religious zeal, quickly spread to Africa and other parts of Asia. Islam reached Somalia in the Seventh Century, less than a century after Muhammed's death. In no time, virtually all Northern Africa was Muslim.

At least in terms of its rulers. The conquered peoples were generally allowed to continue with their own beliefs. In the early years of the Muslim empire, conversion wasn't required, or even necessarily encouraged. Muslims, which is to say in those early years, Arabs, were the elite. Conversion of the conquered would have diluted the social status of the conquerors.

But Satan and I – once we started to pay attention to Islam, that is – did not believe such religious tolerance would hold. History proved us right by the way. Now Islam is the second largest religion on the planet, not much smaller than Christianity, and in a few decades, first place will go to the younger religion.

Nick was particularly bothered when the Berbers of northwest Africa became Muslim. That put them just nine miles south of Gibraltar. Only two hundred years had elapsed since we had helped the Visigoths set up a mini-empire on the Iberian peninsula. The Visigoths were Christian, and we were concerned that at any moment, the Berbers would cross the Strait of Gibraltar and land in Spain. If they took Hispania, Europe would be next.

Sure, Muslims, Christians and Jews were/are all part of the same religious universe, but we had thrown our hat in with the Christians, and if Islam swept away all our hard work, Leviathan would look pretty good in the eyes of Management. To put it bluntly, Nick was afraid for his job.

He and I discussed it one beautiful spring day in Toledo. That's Spain, not Ohio, though I like the North American version of the town, especially their Triple A ball club, the Mudhens. We were sitting, disguised as a couple of traveling merchants, in an Eighth Century version of a tapas bar. I remember it like yesterday. Nick was sipping on a vino tinto while eating sausages. I had a flagon of beer and some pretzels, the latter having been invented barely a century earlier by an Italian monk.

I took to pretzels immediately, regularly popping by the monastery to filch some. Since the monks were making them for the kiddies who had learned their prayers, I suppose my theft was tacky, but hey, I'm a devil. Evil is my job.

"I tell you, Beezy," Nick said, as he downed another sausage, "if the Berbers cross into Hispania, the Visigoths will fall, and all Europe will be at risk."

I took another slug of my beer, a nice honey lager infused with narcotic herbs, then belched loudly, rattling the tables around me. Their occupants looked at me, wide-eyed, then retreated to the far end of the establishment. "You worry too much," I said.

He sniffed. "Easy for you to say. Your job isn't on the line."

"And you don't know that yours is either." I drained my flagon then signaled the barkeep to refill it. "Leviathan has done very little over the millennia that would justify promoting him over you."

"What I don't understand ..." Nick began, swishing his glass around so rapidly that the liquid threatened to become a scarlet waterspout. Or wine spout. This amused him, so he held his other hand a foot above the glass and drew the wine upward. I watched as the funnel of liquid licked at his palm.

There was a rumble from the far end of the bar. The other customers were hurrying for the exits. One even jumped through a window.

I guess they'd been watching as well.

"What I don't understand," Nick began again, "is why Leviathan, Ziz, Behemoth and the others can disobey me in the first place. They have no free will, and I'm the boss."

"We've discussed this, Nick," I said, bored with a conversation we'd had a thousand times. "It must be your probationary status as Satan. Once you're made permanent, they'll fall in line."

"And when will that be?" He opened his mouth and directed the funnel of wine to flow into it.

I sighed. "When we win."

"Exactly!" Then he faltered. "Whenever that is."

I shrugged then looked through the open door of the bar. I could spy a mule cart clattering along the cobbled road. I waved an index finger at the cart, and one wheel flew off. Then I signaled a horsefly that was buzzing around the mule's butt. It stung the animal repeatedly, and the creature took off, dragging the crippled wagon and its cursing master behind it. I chuckled. It wasn't exactly diabolical, but it was funny. Besides, I hadn't done anything evil since swiping the pretzels. At this rate, I wasn't going to hit the day's quota.

Then I turned back to my friend. "Look, I don't disagree with you. Leviathan and his gang are a problem." I frowned. "And you may be right about the Berbers and Hispania. In fact, something may happen even sooner than you think."

"What do you mean?"

"Well," I said, scratching my beard. "You know about this feud between Julian and Roderic?"

"Yes, a little. What of it?"

Satan and I make a good team. He is all about feeling and intuition. He comes up with some ideas that are absolutely inspired, but he pays little attention to details. Me, I'm all facts and figures. My good ideas are built on evidence, which is a delicate way of saying that I pay attention to what's going on around me, as opposed to Nick, who prefers creating his own reality.

Despite his concern over the Berbers, I doubted he knew much about the current political climate. "Well, it's turned into a civil war. I just heard through the grapevine that Julian has reached out to Tariq bin-Ziyad, requesting a little extra muscle to deploy against Roderic."

Satan crushed his glass in his hand and cursed. "Julian. What a numbskull. Who asks a people that has been looting along your shores to help you fight a war? And Roderic. He's even more of a chowderhead. Didn't he cause all this mess in the first place by raping Julian's daughter? Just you watch. Hispania will be under Muslim control in less than a generation."

I looked at my friend appraisingly. He had been paying more attention to current events than usual. More, Nick's intuitive side was so keen that I had learned over our long lifetime together to pay it close attention. If he was worried, so was I.

I got up from my chair. "Then we better see if we can stop this before things get out of hand."

We exited the bar. Standing in the center of the narrow street, we stared south toward Gibraltar. The distance, over two hundred miles, folded beneath our gaze, and we could see a number of merchant boats crossing over from Africa. "It may be too late," Nick said.

"Maybe we can sink their boats or something," I said, without much conviction.

My friend kicked at the stone beneath him and teleported. I was close on his heels.

I must have been in a hurry, for I skidded when landing atop Gibraltar, and it was only because Nick grabbed my arm that I didn't tumble into the water below. "Thanks."

He nodded then shot a blast of Hellfire at the boat closest to shore. We watched as a fist of water reached out from the sea and batted it aside. "Leviathan!" Nick hissed, as a towering incarnation of his rival rose from the water.

"More than that," I said, pointing out the cadre of devils that stood protectively on either side of the flotilla traveling from Africa to Hispania. We saw them plainly, though they were invisible to the soldiers in the boats.

If we'd had our own associates with us, we might have been able to stop the crossing, but we were outflanked and outnumbered. Leviathan must have been planning this for some time. Still, maybe we could stop the invasion. "Get the gang," Satan said. "We'll put an end to Leviathan's insurrection once and for all."

"No," said a voice above us. "Let them alone."

Gabriel landed gracefully next to us, his azure robe billowing around him.

"You!" Nick sputtered. "This is all your fault."

"What do you mean?" Gabriel was carrying his horn, as usual, and he set it, bell down, on the stone. Gabe sighed, relieved to disburden himself of the thing, if only for a moment.

"I think he's talking about that special assignment of yours to the Middle East last century."

"Oh, that." Gabriel shrugged. "All part of the Divine Plan. As is this," he added, waving his hand at the invading army.

Satan squinted at the angelic herald. "And we're just supposed to sit here and do nothing while Christians are being threatened by Muslims?"

"Both are His children. You should know that." He looked down at Leviathan, who was grinning and giving his associates the thumbs up. "Leviathan certainly does."

"You have been remarkably inattentive as the Islamic religion has taken shape. Management expects its Adversary to be a bit more attuned to current events, you know." Gabe pursed his lips. "This is not going to look good on your performance review."

Satan sputtered some more.

"Chill, Nick," I counseled. "So, Gabriel, you seem to know more about this aspect of the Plan than we do. Care to fill us in?"

"The Moors will take Hispania, at least for now. That much has been ordained."

"But what about the Visigoths?" Satan asked. Now, he didn't give a crap about the Visigoths, but they were Christian. His team, you know.

Gabe shrugged again. "They're history. If it's any consolation, you can encourage Navarre and Leon and a few of the surrounding areas to contain the invasion. If they can take back Hispania, they may." He looked severely at Satan. "But they have to do it on their own. You can't do it for them."

"And what will the Moors do?"

"Flourish," Gabriel said, picking up his horn and fluttering upward. "It's all part of a social experiment. You'll see."

And we did. For hundreds of years, we witnessed the blossoming of a culture that has seldom had an equal. We saw Muslims, Christians and Jews living in relative harmony together. We saw a flowering of the arts and sciences.

The Moors called their newly conquered land al-Andalus. But for me and Nick, it was nothing but trouble.

Chapter 18

Down in his office, Nick sat behind his desk, his head in his hands. "This is a disaster!" he wailed then yanked on his horns in frustration.

Score: Leviathan 1. Satan 0.

"You always say that when something goes wrong. Just calm down," I said soothingly, patting him on the back. "We'll get through this."

In truth, I wasn't much calmer than he was. For better or worse, I had signed on with Satan Incorporated. Nick's successes would be my own, as would his failures. Right now, this situation appeared very much like the beginnings of a hostile takeover.

Nick looked at me, the frustration plain on his face. He had another analogy in mind. "It's like Leviathan and I are playing a giant chess game, with Christians and Muslims as the board pieces."

I shrugged. "Except that we have been expressly prohibited from intervening in any significant ways."

Satan frowned. "If that's so, how did Leviathan get away with guarding the Moorish fleet when it crossed the straits of Gibraltar?"

"Well, first off, he and his crew were invisible, as you well know. Second, and more importantly, he wasn't interfering with anyone but you and me." I puckered my lips in thought. "I don't think that counts."

Satan's fingers tapped rapidly on his desktop. Smoke was rising from his forehead. He was pretty steamed. "We have to find a way to counter Leviathan. Any ideas?"

I plopped down on a sack of flour, Nick's new version of a guest chair in his office. It was comfortable enough, but awkward to get up from. Nick started to say something else, but I waved him silent. I needed time to think. He shot me a dirty look but held his tongue. Then he got bored and started tapping his fingers again. I tried to ignore him while working through the problem in my head. "Yes," I said at last.

"Yes what?"

I looked up at him. "If this really is a proxy war, we are definitely on the side of the Christians, right?"

"Well, I don't think we have officially chosen sides, but it looks that way. The Muslims have taken over Hispania, and if not checked, they will soon overrun all of Europe. They have already made incursions into Francia."

"Yes, I heard about the goings-on in Toulouse. And only ten years after the Moors invaded Hispania. If Odo – gotta love that name, right? – hadn't been there to stop them ..." I looked at my friend. "What do you think will happen if the Muslims take over Europe?"

Satan thought it through. "At the very least, they'll marginalize Christianity. Worst case scenario? They'll wipe out the religion in this part of the world. More, they'll have the rest of the Christian world in a pincer grasp, the Moors on the west of Constantinople, the remainder of the Islamic world on the east. If that happens, I can kiss my job goodbye."

"So, we need to stop them, and preferably sooner rather than later." With some difficulty, I got off my bag and gained my feet.

Nick looked at me quizzically. "What do you have in mind?"

I brushed some flour from my clothes. "Have you ever heard of Charles Martel?"

My friend scratched his mustache. At that time, he was trying one of the handlebar variety. It looked stupid on him, especially with his horns. "He's the Mayor of the Palace of Austrasia, isn't he? The power behind the throne in Francia."

"So I hear. Never actually met the gent. He's also apparently a hell of a soldier. What if we could nudge him into action against the Moors?"

Nick sat quietly, thinking about it for a while. At last he spoke. "Couldn't hurt. If we can influence the right person to take action, I don't think we'd get in trouble for that."

"Me neither. Just a minor act of devilry."

"Or maybe even part of the Divine Plan. Worth a shot, regardless. So, where to?" he asked, standing.

"The Palace at Quierzy."

"Let's go."

Quierzy was in the north, not far from what would one day be known as the English Channel. Calling Martel's stronghold a palace was an exercise in hyperbole. This was, after all, the Seven Hundreds, and Francia had nothing that compared with the villas in Rome or Constantinople. Still, by Dark Age standards, Martel had pretty good digs, with two large courtyards surrounded by a church, some outbuildings, including horse stables that were in major need of a flush, and the main residence.

We arrived in disguise, impersonating emissaries from Odo the Great. Apparently, the mayoral calendar had had a cancellation, and we only had to wait an hour to see the great man.

"Do you know why they call him Martel?" Nick asked. "That's not really his name, is it?"

184

I shook my head. "No, Martel means hammer. I assume it's because of his reputation as a warrior. You know, hits like a hammer. Stuff like that, and … Why are you chuckling."

"There could be another reason," he said, with a snicker.

The doors from some inner chamber had opened, and a man who I assumed was Charles Martel entered the room, surrounded by an entourage of sycophants, all laughing, apparently at something the great man had just said.

"Oh," I said.

Charles was a human of powerful build and noble bearing. He was dressed in battle armor with a dashing robe draped across his broad shoulders.

He also had the most unusual nose I'd ever seen. It had a long, narrow bridge, and two strangely shaped nostrils, one round as an acorn, the other cylindrical, like a short stack of pennies running parallel to his upper lip. In my view, his nose strongly resembled a ball peen hammer.

Satan snickered again.

I bit a knuckle, trying not to giggle myself. "Just don't laugh in his face as we talk with him, okay?"

"I'll do my best. My Lord Mayor," Nick said, bowing deeply to Charles.

The Mayor frowned at the two of us. There was no love lost between him and Odo. "What does the Duke of Aquitaine want? Another thrashing?"

Charles's proto-French accent — the French needing another few centuries to perfect that irritating tone of superiority for which they are so famous — was very difficult to understand at first. It didn't help that as Charles talked, his nose snorted and wheezed, like a bagpipe drone.

"No, no, my lord," I said hurriedly. "Odo bows to your superior battle skills."

Nick was doing something behind his back. Satisfied, he glanced up at Martel. "My Lord Mayor, Lord Odo has sent this humble offering as a gift." My friend produced a newly-conjured sword then knelt before Charles. Nick supported the blade with his palms as he offered the hilt to the Mayor. The sword, a popular weapon of the day called a spatha, was about two and a half feet long, with a blunt nose and a gold hilt. That hilt was special – rare and highly prized – making the weapon a suitable gift for the man who had humbled Odo in battle.

Charles accepted the spatha, waving it above his head then thrashing an imaginary opponent with a powerful yet controlled swipe in the air. "Good balance. Nice blade." He handed the sword to a courtier. "Add that to my collection. Other than giving me the sword, which I'm happy to accept – you can never have too many swords, I always say – what the hell do you two want?"

"We came to tell you about the battle of Toulouse."

The mayor looked down his very long nose at us. "What about it?"

Satan nodded deferentially to Charles. "As you know, a couple of years ago, the Moors invaded Narbonne from Hispania. Since that time, they have been amassing forces there, planning an attack on Aquitaine."

Charles yawned and took a seat on a large, uncomfortable looking chair. It wasn't quite a throne, but it might as well have been. He called for wine. Nick tried to continue his tale, but the great man held his hand up for silence. His courtiers shot Nick some dirty looks. Never the most patient of devils, Nick had to bite his lip to keep from blowing his cover with a long string of devilish obscenities. I think he must have poked a fang through the skin, judging from the look of pain on his face.

A servant brought a flagon of wine and a single glass. I thought this quite rude. After all, weren't we his guests?

Charles took a deep swallow from his glass, sighed, and waved a hand for Satan to continue.

Nick extracted the fang from his lip. "A few months ago, the invaders attacked Toulouse. Their goal was to conquer the entire valley of the Garonne River."

Charles took another sip of wine. "This I know. Odo came to me for help, but I sent him on his way. I wanted to see if he could handle this on his own. After all, this was his battle … to lose." He looked archly at his courtiers, who stared back in confusion.

Charles snorted through his schnoz. "Get it? Toulouse was his … to lose."

Slow comprehension came to his toadies. "To lose!" One of them said at last and began a forced laugh.

"Ah!" cried another. "A wonderful bon mots, my lord. Toulouse. Too lose. Too perfect!"

"Your wit knows no bounds, sire!"

Each of the lord's sycophants made similarly admiring statements.

Satan looked at me and rolled his eyes. "Bon mots," he whispered. "Must be French for bad pun."

"Something like that. Here, let me take over for a while. Looks like you could use a break."

"I'd like to break that monstrous honker of his," he grumbled.

The laughter died down. "My lord," I said. "Odo arrived back in Toulouse just before the city fell to the invaders. Only with great difficulty did he managed to repel them."

"In that, he was undoubtedly successful. I have always found Odo to be … repellent." There was more forced laughter from his courtiers. Charles nodded to them then returned his attention to us. "Seriously, Odo did better than I expected. So, why are you here? The battle is won."

"Because we fear the Moors are not finished with Francia. They have retreated for now, but they continue to amass their forces. It is only a matter of time before they try again. When that happens, without the support of the Hammer, Odo and Aquitaine will fall, the Muslims will overwhelm Francia, and eventually all of Europe."

"Hah. Inconceivable."

"With all due respect, I fear it is all too conceivable." Satan drove the point home. "In under a hundred years, the Muslims took control of the Middle East, northern Africa and Hispania. So far, they have proven unstoppable. Odo's victory at Toulouse was only a momentary check."

Charles looked into his wine goblet, frowning. "I have heard that the Moors use heavily armed cavalry as their chief attack forces."

"That is so, my lord," I said.

He looked at both of us. "I have never lost a battle, but my army has nothing that could stand up to such a force. At least not for long."

"Then build one, Lord Charles," I pressed. "We will help you."

"How?" he looked at the two of us with skepticism. The disguises we had adopted were those of two couriers, not great warriors. "How can you help?"

I thought quickly. "I came to you today as a messenger, but in truth I am a master armorer. In my youth, I studied under the great, ah, Yassir al-Bashya."

Martel frowned. "Who?"

"al-Bashya, al-Bashya! Surely you have heard of him. Very famous."

Nick rolled his eyes but came to my rescue. "Yes, very famous indeed."

I soldiered on. "And I know how to create the armor you would need for your own heavy cavalry."

"While I know how to train your men to fight in this new style," Nick added.

I look at him with surprise. He most certainly did not. Satan, always a quick learner, though, could figure it out before Martel's army would need such training. Nick, being a dirty fighter, would also probably teach them a few nefarious moves that would help the Frankish army defeat the invaders.

"This will take time. Do we have such time?"

Satan nodded. "We believe so, my lord. Odo's victory, while only temporary, should buy you, let's see ..." Nick stared upward, and I knew he was using his precognitive powers. "Ten or eleven years. Oh," he added, "and they're likely to attack at Tours."

"How do you know all this?" Charles asked skeptically.

Nick shrugged. "Just a guess, but it's an educated one."

"He's always been good at this sort of thing," I added, in a show of moral support.

Charles put down his glass forcefully. "Very well. I will see what kind of armor you can build," he said, looking at me, then turning to Nick said, "and I will see if you know anything about this method of fighting. If you do, I will build the heavy cavalry, and woe to the Moors when they try to invade again."

"You are dismissed," the Lord Mayor said to us then turned to one of his men. "Francois, have you heard the one about the friar, the ox and the chamber pot?"

The courtier's eyes scanned the room, desperately looking for an exit. Finding none, he swallowed hard and forced a smile. "No, my lord. Please tell us all, so we may be graced by your thrusting wit!"

Charles put his back to us and started his joke, so Nick and I slipped out of the room. We were satisfied with the arrangement we had made with the Hammer. Nick took off to study the fighting style of the Muslims and to add his own spin to it. I began to make armor.

And when the attack on Tours came in 1732, exactly as Satan predicted, the Hammer was ready. I had to build an extra-large nose guard for his helmet – took twice as much metal as usual – but Charles Martel was ready.

Chapter 19

Nick and I were hunkered down in the dirt, atop a hill on which centuries later the University of Tours would be built. We were watching the great battle of Tours unfold.

The Moors had been surprised by the brutal efficiency of the Frankish heavy cavalry, and they were losing the day. I nodded in satisfaction, but my friend was cursing.

"What's up with you?" I asked at last.

Satan spat in the dirt. A small patch of ground sizzled and melted away. "Ten years of my existence to train these morons!"

"So? A decade is nothing. I have T-shirts older than that."

"Yes, but I could have stopped the Muslim advance with a single thought." He sighed. "If I'd only been allowed."

"Rules are rules," I said philosophically.

"I don't like rules," Satan grumbled. "At least when they apply to me."

I looked at him, considering. Over the millennia, since he'd been named probationary Satan, Nick had become even more of a rebel. Most believe Nick had always been one, since he was the first to turn away from the Creator, but that wasn't really a considered act. More an impulse. This whole "Satan" thing had gone to his head, though. He was the Adversary. You said black; he said white.

Me, I was glad just to have a little autonomy. Not Satan, though. He was coming to want it all.

Since coming to Earth, Nick and I frequently had butted heads. His superior attitude toward me and the other devils was particularly irksome, but he was still my best pal, my favorite brother. I resolved to help him work through his frustration, if I could.

"Old friend," I said, consolingly, putting my hand on his shoulder. "As powerful as you are, there is One, or Three, depending upon how you look at things, more powerful than you. Everybody has a boss."

"Humph. Well, I don't like having one." Then he waved at the battle below. "Christian. Muslims. Who cares? They should all come to me after death, either way. Why, I'd like to go down there and flatten both sides then find Leviathan and his gang and beat them to a pulp."

I nodded. That last part at least I understood. "It may come to that, I suppose, but I believe Management is testing you. Beat Leviathan here, on the mortal plane, and I'm sure you'll get the Satan job on a permanent basis. And in Hell, you have pretty much free rein to do what you will, including, to use your own words, flattening anyone who gets in your way."

Satan picked up a handful of pebbles and began juggling them. Soon they looked like a ring, what you would see around Saturn, if you had a good telescope. "I just don't understand why we have to go through all of this."

I gave him a gentle punch to the shoulder. "To teach you patience … and guile," I added after a moment's thought.

He let the pebbles fall to the earth. "What do you mean?"

What *did* I mean? I tried to put it in words. "Well," I said slowly, "devils are not known for their subtlety. Possess the occasional mortal here, torment the Damned there. Be devilish, or evil, as you prefer to say."

He sniffed.

"We're predictable, and not particularly creative. But your destiny is to be the first among devils. The Devil, with a capital D. You are being held to a higher standard by the Boss."

"Well that doesn't seem fair to me."

"Fair, schmair. It is what it is."

I coined that expression, by the way. I'm a realist, and a pragmatist. Tell me the situation, and I'll make the best of it.

"Look Nick," I said after a pause, "I've known you forever. Literally. And since the dawn of humankind, I've watched you. You have real potential for this evil shit. Much more than the rest of us."

My friend teared up. "Do you," he sniffed, "do you really think so?"

"Absolutely! Why, over this past decade, dealing with Charles and his subjects, I've watched you manipulate them. You're a natural. These ten years were by no means wasted."

"Well, that's something, I suppose."

"There you two are!"

We looked up. Andre the Gross, so named for his tendency to pick his nose in public, stood above us. Andre was one of the Hammer's personal assistants.

"What is it?" Satan said, irritation in his voice. "We're having a conversation here."

"My lord Charles has need of the fat one's services."

He was talking about me. Over the centuries, I'd put on weight. It started back around 100 AD, when I discovered pork rinds at an early fast food restaurant in Rome. Pork rinds, by the way, were one of the earliest junk foods. The first time a morsel of something that had been fried hit my palate, I was hooked. That was my initial step toward becoming the Lord of Gluttony.

I got off the ground. "What does the Lord Mayor want with me?"

Andre was preoccupied with his right nostril. "Hmm? Oh. He didn't say. Best you come now, though."

We made our way to a pavilion, where Charles had set up his office. The crowd of hangers-on parted when we entered the tent.

"What do you mean, wrong hole?" Martel said to the crowd.

I glanced around the pavilion. The faces of the Hammer's men were white with shock; the few women servants there were blushing furiously. The joke must have been a very dirty one, and no one was laughing. Charles scowled at his entourage, and I wondered if heads would roll.

When all seemed hopeless, from the back of the tent, a valiant, if forced, laugh commenced. Soon the survival instincts of everyone else kicked in, and all began to laugh.

Satisfied at last, Martel turned to us. "Sir Barnabe, Captain Nicolas," Charles said, nodding in recognition. "My son has come to join in the fighting."

"Carloman?" I'd never met either of the sons, but Carloman was the elder, so I assumed it was he.

Charles snorted. "Non. Carloman is a devout man," he said with mild disgust, "and prefers not to raise his hand against another. Thou shalt not kill, and all that, you know. No, I'm talking about my second son, Pippin."

"Isn't he a little young to be fighting?" Nick asked.

Another snort. "He is eighteen, and a man, ah, full grown. He is fierce and skilled with a blade. He will prove himself a mighty warrior. However," Charles paused. He thought for a moment, then shook his head. "However, you will need to modify some armor to fit him."

"Not necessary," I said dismissively. "It's one size fits all. I designed the armor that way."

"We shall see. Pippin! Attend me."

The crowds parted, and out stepped Pippin.

Pippin the Short, history has named him. Hah, Pippin the Pipsqueak would have been better. Before me stood a young man, perfectly proportioned, well-muscled. And under four feet high.

In fact, Pippin was three feet six inches. Since, in my normal incarnation, I'm seven feet, I considered the young man half my size. So, Pippin the Halfling might have been appropriate as well.

"I see the problem," I said with a frown. "He is a bit of a shrimp."

Pippin turned red then pulled his sword with remarkable grace, considering it probably weighed a third of what he did. "You insult me sir! I will have my satisfaction." He rushed me.

With a sigh, I sidestepped the attack and plucked the sword from his grasp. Not to be gainsaid, Pippin jumped on me, wrapping arms and legs around my right thigh. Then he bit me.

"Pippin!" His father said sternly. "Down! Down boy!"

With a growl, Pippin stopped chewing on my thigh and released his grip, falling with a thud on the ground. Then he got up and backed away from me, an angry look in his eyes.

"I apologize, young lord." There was no point antagonizing the little guy. Besides, there was a fire in him that I appreciated. "Lord Mayor," I said to Charles. "I can quickly modify some armor to fit him, but he may have difficulty in the saddle."

"Not to worry," said the mayor. "Pippin has been riding since before he could walk and has developed his own unique style. Just fix the armor for him, leave the horse's own gear as it is, and my son will be fine."

I bowed. "as you wish, my lord."

I fitted Pippin that afternoon. Small as he was, he cut a dashing figure. I even downsized a robe that he could wear over the armor between battles.

We made our peace that afternoon. For as long as he lived, Pippin and I were friends. And he was indeed a mighty warrior, with his own unique fighting style.

You should have seen it. Nick and I were back in our spot on the hill, watching a new foray beneath us. The Franks surged forward with an odd horseman at their front.

It was Pippin. He was standing on the back of the horse. He wore no shoes, and his toes were tucked beneath the sides of the saddle. Looked pretty weird, but he seemed stable enough. In his hands was an unusually long sword. How he could wield it was a mystery to me, but wield it he did, slicing through the enemy ranks as if they were sticks of Parkay left on the counter too long.

Though the history books claim that Pippin did not fight at Tours, I know better. He led the Franks to a victory that day.

In the end, Charles Martel and his army, with a little help from his second son, won the battle of Tours, stopping the Muslims from conquering Francia and the rest of Europe. Years later, when Pippin succeeded his father, he grew tired of being the power behind the throne, abandoning the fiction that the Lord Mayor served the Merovingian King. With some help from the Pope, Pippin usurped the throne and became the first Carolingian King. He solidified the Frankish position against the Moors from Iberia, and the rest of Europe was saved from invasion.

His son, Charlemagne, continued the fight against the Muslims, part of the Reconquista, an almost eight-hundred-year conflict that was the longest war the world has ever known.

Charlemagne was most noted for being the first Holy Roman Emperor, reuniting much of Europe – for the first time in over three hundred years – under a single sovereign.

All in all, we got a good return on our ten-year investment arming and training Charles Martel's army. Even Nick admitted to me that it had been worth it. And now, the score was:

Leviathan 1. Satan 1.

Tie game. But it wasn't over yet.

Leviathan filed a formal protest against our interference in Francia. I felt we were on firm ground but dreaded the prospect of a hearing. You never knew who you might get as the judge. Usually it would be an archangel, like Gabriel. Sometimes, though, a saint would be chosen. When that happened, I had to put up with Satan's temper.

Nick always felt that the Creator loved his flawed human creations better than his angels. This made no sense to my friend. After all, we were created first. We were more powerful. We had better hair. Wings too.

As far as Satan was concerned, the only thing humans had going for them was free will, and that was a questionable virtue at best. Free will, more often than not, was a huge weakness, easy to exploit. That was the crack in the door that any devilish salesman, a false god, a temptress or what have you, could squeeze through. Humans had a choice about how to act, and four times out of five, they chose wrong.

But then there was that fifth time when they'd surprise you. Though Satan generally liked chaos, he didn't like it in humans. Their unpredictability made them difficult to manipulate, so Nick never wanted one of them as the arbiter of any Celestial dispute.

Fortunately, Leviathan's protest arrived at a busy time for the Heavenly Host. Some sort of festival was in the works, and all the likely candidates to convene a hearing were already busy with the planning committee. In the end, we handled the whole thing through the mail, each side sending in written depositions and arguments.

Our position was simple. Any devil, and especially the Satan pro tem, was allowed to influence individual humans. By way of proof, Nick noted his filing cabinet of contracts for human souls.

I only had a small accordion file. I found that kind of work – tempting humans into selling their souls – tedious. I also wasn't very good at tempting humans.

Want to sell your soul?

No. Why would I want to do that? Is there anything in it for me?

Well, I can make your life on Earth pretty sweet.

What about after I die?

You'll go to Hell and be tormented for Eternity.

Ah, I think I'll pass.

Nick was much better at this. He didn't exactly lie to his prospects, but he was much better at talking around the whole damnation issue. He made selling one's soul seem like a sweet deal, like your modern long-term care insurance. Sure, the cost is high, but look at all you get?

I was much better at selling myself as a false god. That was more straightforward than trolling for souls the way Satan did it. And, as a false god, I got to do lots of smiting, which was fun.

Sigh. I miss that.

In the end, Leviathan's protest was denied. Heaven pointed out that even he had executed a few contracts for individual souls. Management ruled that helping Charles Martel develop the Frankish version of heavy cavalry was no worse than that.

Though we didn't bargain for it, we got Martel's soul in the end, his and Charlemagne's. Curious, though, that we didn't get Pippin. He was such a rabid dog. I thought for sure he'd get damned for Wrath. Ends up, Pippin was one of those marginal cases, and he beat Peter at rock-paper-scissors.

Getting Charlemagne was a boon. Especially for me.

Chapter 20

Even though Nick and I only spent about a decade of quality time with Charles Martel, we both found him and the other two generations of alpha males who were his descendants fascinating, so even after our gigs as armorer and trainer to the Frankish army were at an end, we periodically checked up on them. After the Hammer's death, we adopted new personas. It would not do to have two ageless advisors hanging around the Frankish nobility. That's a good way to get yourself burned at the stake.

Not that I mind a good stake on occasion, but being torched for witchcraft is a quick way of blowing your cover. Coming up with new disguises was easy enough, though.

Pippin lived and died in the shadow of his father. The little shrimp was a great warrior and a fine king, but Martel was the greater man. And Charlemagne, well, we all know about Charlemagne. I felt sorry for Pippin, doomed to be the least of three great men. Still, he was the only one who made it into Heaven, so I suppose he had the last laugh.

I had my eye on Charlemagne from the time he was a child, though it wasn't for his promise of greatness. Charlemagne enjoyed puttering. He liked to fix things, fancying himself a great handyman. A little-known fact: he was the person who coined the expression "do it yourself." You know: "Ours not to reason why. Ours but to do and DIY."

With apologies to Alfred Lord Tennyson.

I had often seen Chuckie attempt to make repairs to his own armor. You know, like when a leather strap broke on a breast plate and needed to be replaced or when a sword snapped because you sat on it just the wrong way.

There really is no right way to sit on a sword. At least, it's an unpleasant surprise. At worst, you can impale your butt. And at just the right angle, you can snap it in two. The sword, not the butt.

For some reason, Charlemagne thought he had the makings of a great handyman. I will give him credit for one thing: his fixit attempts were creative. Once I saw him try to repair a snapped sword by using pitch, a bit of twine and a bunch of sticks. It didn't work, falling apart the first time he tried to hack down a Moor. In disgust, he threw the two shards into a bog.

It didn't help that Charlemagne had almost no fine motor skills. Gross motor skills, sure, he had those aplenty. He could leap on the back of a horse, throw a spear with the best of them, wield a blade. But try to lace his own boots, not so good. He had fingers like massive sausages, making precision jobs beyond him.

Over time, Charlemagne admitted to himself that he was terrible at fixing things. Being a king and, eventually, the Holy Roman Emperor, he was used to success, so this frustrated him. After repeatedly trying and failing at almost every home improvement project you can imagine, from leveling the legs on his throne to sticking a ruby back into his scepter to mending a tear in that blue cape he was so fond of wearing, he developed an antipathy to DIY that has not been equaled to this day.

And this gave me an idea.

For almost a thousand years, I had served as Hell's Mr. Fixit. For millennia before that, I'd done the same for Gehenna, despite all those damned bugs. And I was bloody tired of the work.

After some persuasion, I convinced Nick that the job would be a perfect eternal punishment for some doofus.

Besides, if anything important needed to be done, I was still around to handle it.

Charlemagne was the perfect candidate. I was also pretty confident he'd end up in Hell. If I'd known that three hundred years later, he would be canonized by the antipope Paschal III, I'd have been sure of it. (For political reasons, none of those canonized by antipopes got into Heaven.)

I was with Charlemagne when he died in 814 at the age of seventy-one. He was old for someone who had lived his life in the Dark Ages. I was impersonating his personal physician, whom I'd locked up in a closet. The emperor had always hated doctors, and it galled him that he had to have one there at the end, but well, you know, when you're dying you simply can't keep away the medical profession. The family insists upon it, though back then, a good bleeding – which was the preferred therapy for the sick and dying – did more to hasten the end of life than prolong it.

In fact, mine was the last face Charlemagne saw before he passed. I watched his eyes glaze over, his lids droop, his breath fail. His heart stop. I felt a chill in the air, and looked up to see a figure cloaked in black, holding a scythe, materialize.

"Hey, Morty," I said, giving him a little wave.

Mortimer, the Angel of Death, is all business when he's on the clock. He returned my wave with a dignified nod, then turned to his charge.

I released a befuddled physician from his imprisonment then hightailed it to Gates Level. When I got there, I dropped my disguise, hiding behind a cloud to watch the show.

Mortimer and Charlemagne floated above Gates Level in dramatic fashion then descended to the cloudy surface before Saint Peter's station. The Angel of Death and his charge made a perfect landing in front of Petey's desk. Then Morty

202

released the hand of the first Holy Roman Emperor and disappeared.

Heaven's Concierge looked anxious. He was still fairly new at his job, but I don't think it was a case of nerves. More likely, he'd been expecting the emperor and had already checked the Book of Life. He was about to dispense some very bad news.

"I regret to inform you that you have been damned for all Eternity."

Charlemagne looked a tad confused, as most people do right after their deaths, and especially if they have the bony specter of DEATH escort them personally to the afterlife. On hearing the judgment of Saint Peter, though, his eyes swiftly came back into focus. "Wait a minute!" he cried. "Do you know who I am?"

Peter winced. Yes, he knew. It was his job to know. However, Petey showed great restraint, and answered politely, which I thought was classy, since Chuckie was now a soul beyond redemption. "Yes. You are Charles the First, King of the Franks, King of the Lombards and ..."

"And Holy Roman Emperor, you twit!" Charles roared.

From my vantage point, I chuckled. I'd never heard anyone call Peter a twit before, though I'd thought it myself on more than one occasion. Peter frowned at the man. "And I am Saint Peter, the Apostle, the Rock on which the Church was built, Keeper of the Book of Life, which I hold in my hands here." Peter was clasping the Book to his chest. "It's my job to separate the lambs from the goats, and you, sir, are a goat!"

Charles was in shock, as much for being addressed without deference as for being damned. "Abadah abadah ..." he began.

Peter ignored his incoherent protests. "You have your choice of how you'd like to descend. You can jump into the Mouth of Hell," he said, indicating the nearby black chasm, "or you can walk down the Stairway."

I glanced over to the new Gates of Hell, which provided a classy entrance for the stairs I had completed only a couple of centuries earlier. I smiled. Some of my better work. The Iron Gates, the giant rat astride the stone arch above said gates: they looked scary as Hell. Charlemagne looked slowly at his choices, dismay on his face.

"That's okay, Saint Peter," I said, stepping out from behind my cloud. I had resumed my normal appearance, horns, fangs, claws, etc., and my preferred seven-foot height. "I'll handle this one personally."

"Beelzebub?" Peter said with surprise. "I didn't see you come in. No matter, he is one of your own now. You can do with him as you will." With that, he dismissed Charlemagne from his mind and signaled for the next soul in line to step forward.

Charlemagne looked at me in fear. And then puzzlement. "Don't, uh, don't I know you?"

I grinned, flashing my black canines at him. He shuddered. "Yes, you do," I said, taking his arm. Then we teleported to the Fifth Circle of Hell.

The great man was more than a little startled by the abrupt change in scenery, from a domain of white clouds to the muted yellow sky and drab landscape of the Fifth Circle, in the company of a seven-foot prince of Hell, yet he tried not to show it. This was an emperor, tested in battle. In life, he had borne a continent on his shoulders, and he wasn't going to let a little thing like being damned to Hell get to him.

I smiled evilly. *We'll see how long his brave façade holds up.*

At that moment, a dozen or so of the Damned began to scream. This was staged. I had arranged for a dozen demons to skewer their charges with pitchforks at the precise moment of our arrival. Worked, too. Charlemagne did an involuntary hop. "What was that?"

"Colleagues. Yours."

"Humph. I have no colleagues. I am emperor."

"We'll see."

Charles and I stood before a small shack, not unlike one of the cottages he might have found on the lands of his many manses in Francia. The walls of the structure were made of daub: soil, clay, straw and animal dung. In Hell, we used an extra measure of dung to enhance the olfactory effect. Nothing done by half measures, I always said.

With a firm push, I sent Charlemagne stumbling through the shack's open door. "Gaah! What a terrible smell."

"What did you expect? It's made of shit."

In life, the Holy Roman Emperor cut a large and robust figure, especially among the men of his age, who tended to be on the puny side. Please remember who his dad was. Now, summoning what dignity he could manage, Charles raised up to his full six-foot height, which would have impressed most people back then, though I still towered over him by a foot. "Why am I here?"

I cocked my head to one side, listening. "Just a second."

"SKREE!" Thump. The building rocked slightly, and a turd fell out of the tattered straw that formed the roof, impaling itself on one of the prongs of Charlemagne's crown.

"Merde!"

"Indeed."

"SKREE!" A monstrous claw ripped a hole in the roof. Charlemagne looked up through the opening. Then the onetime ruler of Europe cowered in fear. It was a first for him, I think, but then he'd never seen anything like BOOH before. The monstrous bat hissed at Chuckie then dropped a tied bundle through the hole. It landed with a whomp before us. BOOH released a final skree and, with a flap of his monstrous wings, shot into the air. In seconds, he was only a black dot zooming across the yellow sky.

"What ... what was that?"

"The Bat out of Hell."

"I thought that was just an expression."

"Most expressions have their groundings in fact. You'll be seeing a lot of BOOH ..."

"BOOH?"

"What are you, slow or something? It's what we call an acronym."

I watched as Charles sounded out the letters. A small "oh" popped from his lips.

"BOOH will be delivering your work orders."

"Work orders? What are these work orders?"

"Open the package and find out."

Charlemagne dropped to the ground. The twine was difficult to untie. "Do you have a knife or something I can use? I've never been very good with my hands."

I shook my head.

He shrugged and began working on the knot. Five minutes elapsed before he got it loose.

Brother. This is going to be painful to watch.

Fun, though, said a voice in my head.

Nick, have you been reading my mind again?

You said I could watch was the petulant reply.

The contents of the package were wrapped in a bright yellow bit of burlap. Inside the burlap was sheet after sheet of vellum. "What are these?" Charles asked, flipping through the sheets.

"Work orders. Good thing you learned to read in life. Most people of your station can't, you know."

"There are no people of my station."

"Oh really? Remind me to introduce you to Constantine sometime."

"Constantine is here? In Hell?" This seemed a revelation to the great man.

"You're here, aren't you?"

"But why is he here?"

"Same as you. Sin of Pride. You both also killed a bunch of people."

"But they were the enemy! I was only fulfilling my destiny."

"Enough!" I said sternly. "I don't judge 'em. I just torment 'em."

"But …"

I was losing my patience with this guy, so I blasted him with some Hellfire. It incinerated his blue robe, and …

"Ow, ow, ow!" Charlemagne screamed, tossing his crown from him and struggling to get off his breastplate before he cooked inside it. With an Herculean effort, he broke the leather straps holding his armor in place then threw the metal to the far corner of the shack. He stood before me in his small clothes. I looked appraisingly at him, shook my head, then burned even those off him, until all that remained was a shriveled old man.

Of course, there may have been shrinkage.

Just for fun, I dropped the temperature of the air around him to about zero degrees.

More shrinkage. And a lot of shivering.

"Here. Put this on." I threw the yellow burlap at him.

Charlemagne recoiled when he caught it. "Faugh! It smells foul!"

"No one ever said Hell was a stroll through the tulips. Now, would you stop being so contrary? You *do* realize who I am, don't you?"

"Some devil!" he said, spitting into the dirt at my feet.

That was too much. I wrapped a hand around his neck and lifted him up to my eye level. "Did you catch what Saint Peter called me?" I said in a soft voice.

Now, the newly-dead tend to be a bit befuddled when standing before Saint Peter's desk. Charlemagne was no different, but he took a second to run what he remembered of the conversation through his head. As realization dawned on him, he looked at me and gasped. "Beelzebub! The Lord of the Flies!"

He was turning purple. Thinking perhaps I was squeezing his neck too hard, I dropped Charlemagne to the ground. "That's right. Also, a prince of Hell ..."

Second only to me.

I sighed. "Second in Hell's hierarchy only to Satan himself."

He cowered beneath me. *Finally*. Got to hand it to him, though. He had guts. "What do you want of me?" he whimpered.

"First, do as I say, and put on that tunic."

Charlemagne lifted the yellow burlap from where it had fallen in a heap when I grabbed him by the throat. He turned it around. "What are these red markings here? And is this blood?"

"Yes, you twit, it's blood. We're in Hell, get it? Blood, pain, eternal damnation. Jeez, how did you ever get to be emperor?"

208

"Well," he said, shuffling his feet in embarrassment. "There was my dad, and my granddad. A bit of nepotism, I guess. Still, I was talented with a sword and good buddies with the pope." He looked at the two letters on his burlap tunic. "So? So what?"

I rolled my eyes. "Not So. It's another acronym. S O. Stands for Sustentationem officium."

As he slipped on the tunic, he looked puzzled.

"Letters go on the back."

He flipped it around. "Maintenance office?"

Now we were getting somewhere. "Right you are. Maintenance office. You are the new superintendent of plant maintenance for all of Hell. You now report to me, and it is your job to fix everything that breaks down here."

"Aggh! But I'm all thumbs! I can't even tie my own shoelaces."

"Exactly!" I said with satisfaction. "Welcome to your eternal damnation."

For a minute he continued wailing. Then the gnashing of teeth started. It was very satisfying.

"Can't I just be boiled in oil for eternity?" he said with some desperation.

"No. On each of these pages of vellum," I explained, "you will find details about something that's broken. Fix it, get whoever submitted the work order to sign off on the job, then file the paperwork over there." I indicated a hole in the ground next to a bench.

He looked at his sausage fingers. "How can I fix what is broken? I have no tools."

"Oh, right." I walked over to the bench, on which sat a wooden chest, and lifted it. "Here. Catch."

Charlemagne trapped the chest between his arms and torso. He gasped, the wind knocked out of him, and staggered from the weight, nearly falling. "What is in here? It weighs a ton."

"The tools of your trade. You must carry it with you wherever you go. Part of your punishment, you understand. Go ahead. Open it."

He kneeled to place the chest on the dirt floor, almost losing his balance in the process, popped the latches and lifted the lid.

Inside were four items: a large rock, a stick, a two-foot stretch of thick rope, and a tiny dagger.

"What's the rock for?"

"Weight mostly."

"This is it? These are my tools? What can I fix with these?"

I shrugged. "Probably nothing. This is Hell, you know. It's *supposed* to be inconvenient."

"And I alone must fix everything what breaks here?"

"Alone? Hell no. In fact, here comes your assistant now."

"Assistant?"

Through the door walked a twisted excuse for a human being. He looked to be a well-worn thirty-year old, which was about the age he was when he committed suicide. This wretched creature was dressed in a yellow tunic, like that which Charlemagne now wore. On the man's head was a crown of laurels. "Lord Beelzebub?" He said, eyeing me warily. "I'm here as ordered."

"Excellent!" I said in a hearty voice. "Emperor Charlemagne, meet your new assistant, Emperor Nero."

Nero was in Hell for lots of reasons. First off, he was batshit crazy. Heaven wouldn't touch him with a ten-foot pole. Second, he burned down a good chunk of Rome so he could have it rebuilt to his specifications. Nero killed tons of Christians, including, rumor has it, Peter and Paul. Oh, he also murdered his own mother. And there was that suicide thing too.

"But wasn't Nero a pagan?"

"No," I said, watching Nero writhe in place. "Once, to get himself out of a jam, he converted to Judaism. That didn't work out too well, did it, Mr. Assistant?"

The former emperor of the Roman Empire winced.

"Nero, meet your new boss, Charlemagne. He was an emperor also."

Charlemagne and Nero regarded each other with suspicion. Then Chuckie walked over to his now-cooled crown, slammed it against the side of his new office wall, knocking the shit off the metal, and placed the diadem on his brow. "Just remember," he said to Nero, "you report to me."

"Bwahahahahahaha! I think you'll find that won't make much difference. Oh, look at the time. Gotta go! Now, you two. Get to work!"

And then I disappeared.

Charlemagne was Hell's Super for even longer than I was: almost twelve hundred years. He was a terrible Mr. Fixit, but in time he learned how to do the job. Since it's no fun having a competent handyman, I promoted him to demon and replaced him with someone equally inept.

Chapter 21

The Muslim army may have lost the Battle of Tours and a series of other encounters that effectively confined the Islamic threat to the Iberian Peninsula, but Leviathan wasn't done. Nick and I knew the competition would strike again.

We didn't think it would take so long, though. Almost five hundred years. Leviathan was subtle about it too, which was out of character for him. As a result, we didn't even see it coming.

This is how the story goes:

Far to the east, in the country westerners now call China, there lived a family of vagabond fleas. For many generations, which in flea parlance is about a year, they traveled from village to village. This was the early Fourteenth Century, and it was a great time to be a flea. Tons of food and drink, mainly because China during that period was a hotbed of disease, thanks to a perfect storm of misfortune: a series of natural disasters, the Mongol invasion and a decline in farming and trade. All the vermin, including rats and fleas and other disease-ridden nasties, left the desiccated grasslands of the countryside and moved to the more populated areas of the country. People got sick. Many died, which makes for good eating when you're a flea.

But, as I said, these were vagabond fleas. Every once in a while, they'd get itchy feet, six per flea, and want to explore new parts of the world. But they needed a ride.

They soon found one. A kindly black rat offered to carry them on his back. He was a bit of a wanderer himself, and this rodent hoped to travel with the Mongol army, which was heading west, along the Silk Road. These being Oriental rat fleas, the plan had appeal, so the entire family hopped aboard.

Now, fleas travel light. No suitcases. Not even a toothbrush. They were carrying something, though, something special, a gift from China to the rest of the world. The Plague.

The rodent knew this. Ratty was Leviathan in disguise.

The rat and his fleas hid under a pile of hay on a wagon that carried supplies for the army as it pillaged its way westward. No one seemed to notice that not all the dead bodies left in the wake of the Mongols were the results of slaughter. Many just got sick and died. Plague, you know.

Numerous generations of the flea family lived on Leviathan's back. They were happy to have such a dependable ride, and none of them gave much thought to the fact that Ratty seemed immune to harm. For example, one time, or so the story goes, a Mongol soldier – we'll call him Cookie, since he was one of the many responsible for cooking up grains and game for the army – spied that rat in the wagon. The man grabbed a pitchfork and attempted to skewer the rodent. Funny how the tines bent around the body of the rat, who just scrabbled away, unharmed.

Oh, Cookie died of acute jock itch three days later.

In 1347, the Mongols reached the Crimea, where they besieged the port city of Kaffa. The horde was beginning to succumb to the effects of the Plague that had been traveling with them. There were many disease-riddled corpses among the Mongols, so their leader, an enterprising fellow named Jani Beg, got the idea of catapulting the infected bodies over the walls of the city. Infected and infectious bodies, raining from the sky: this scared the crap out of the besieged people, including a group of traders from Genoa who'd just stopped by Kaffa for a little R and R. Plague and an invading Mongol army being a bit more excitement than bargained for, they high-tailed it out of there, landing in Sicily and then heading to other parts of southern Europe.

The first mate was a little under the weather during the voyage. At first, he thought he had the sniffles or, worst case, the flu. He was not quite dead when the other crewmen tossed him over the side. Too little, too late.

A certain rat had managed to slip aboard the fleeing vessel. He wanted to witness with his own rodent eyes the arrival of the Plague in Europe. From Italy, the disease spread north. Soon all the continent, even the Muslim-occupied lands of Hispania, was living [and dying] with the stench of dead bodies. By the time the worst of the Plague had passed, about half the population of Europe was dead.

As I said, the Black Death sort of snuck up on us. Satan and the princes of Hell were out of pocket at the time, attending a management retreat in the Tau Ceti star system.

Yes, it's true. Satan invented the planning retreat. Why are you surprised?

There, on a water world called Klmpfh, a race of highly advanced cephalopods operated a posh spa that catered to immortals from across the universe. That's where I met Odin, by the way, though that's another story.

The damnation of Charlemagne and Nero had been a revelation to me and Nick. Up until that time, we had relied on our standard forms of torment: fire, ice, pitchforks, body odor, etc. These were things that assaulted our charges in physical ways. Charlemagne's damnation, though, was of the psychological variety, and in our view, it was much more effective than a poke in the eye. We had been limiting ourselves to the five senses, but by getting into the psyches of our charges, an almost infinite set of possibilities opened to us.

The planning retreat was to explore what this meant. We intended to expand our definition of torment, to enrich Hell in ways we would not have imagined a thousand years earlier, when we were just getting the enterprise off the ground.

While it had been my idea to have Charlemagne replace me as Hell's handyman, Nick was the one who saw the potential for making damned souls do in death what they most hated in life. Or to take what they loved to do and spoil it for them, so that it was no longer any pleasure at all.

Me, I had just wanted to get out of a job that had grown tiresome over the centuries.

Satan was facilitating the discussion, assisted by a demon named Lars, whom Nick had brought along to do scut work. "Here," he said, handing Lars some pieces of charcoal, the Fourteenth Century equivalent of a number two pencil, and some birch bark. "Distribute these to the group."

Astaroth stared in bemusement at his piece of charcoal then popped it in his mouth.

"Stop that!" Satan snapped. "These aren't snacks, you idiot."

Astaroth shrugged. "I dunno. Tasted pretty good to me. I've always liked charcoal."

Nick rolled his eyes. "Well, at least wait until after this exercise is over. Beezy, give him some of your pig's knuckles." With reluctance, I relinquished to Astaroth the bowl of snacks I'd been monopolizing, though not before scooping out a large handful of knuckles. Satan motioned to Lars, who handed Astaroth another piece of charcoal. Then the probational Lord of Hell looked around the room.

Sekhmet, who was sitting to my left, was giving him a dirty look. "What's your problem?" he asked her.

"You know I hate exercise." She crossed her arms under her breasts, which made them stand out prettily. This distracted Satan – and the rest of us – for a moment. Then he shook his head.

"Not that kind of exercise. I'm just going to take you through a brainstorming exercise, uh, session. No actual exertion is required."

She unfolded her arms, to everyone's general disappointment. "Promise?"

"I promise." He sighed then looked at the rest of us. "May I continue now? Good. Ahem. The six of us, aside from being Hell's elite, are the patron devils of the Seven Deadly Sins. For over a thousand years now, we have been punishing the Damned, whether they be lustful, greedy, gluttonous or whatever, in pretty much the same ways. A stab with a pitchfork, a blast of Hellfire, time in one of the seas of thorns, drowning, mutilation, etc. All good stuff, but not very creative."

Belphegor yawned. "I agree with you there. It's as dull for us as it is for them."

Astaroth stared at his associate. "I would think you'd prefer dull, Belphegor."

"Well, yes, it's true that I'm the patron devil of Sloth, and I hate to put myself to any unnecessary physical effort, but, well, I've always been of an active mind, and I believe with a little thought, I could come up with punishments that fit the crimes of my charges."

"Capital, Belphegor!" Satan said heartily. "Just what I had in mind."

Except I did it first.

Nick shot me a dirty look, and I blushed. I hadn't been guarding my thoughts.

216

As a general rule, we devils don't read each other's minds without first getting permission. Satan, however, feels he's exempt from this stricture. In his defense, well heck, he *is* Satan. I expect this sort of behavior from him, more than even from other devils. However, I don't always appreciate him doing it, so my habit is to guard my thoughts when I want privacy. As long as I stay alert, his telepathic intrusions are not a problem.

"Can you give us an example of a punishment that fits the crime?" Astaroth asked.

"Beezy has a report on his experiment with Charlemagne and Nero." By now, all the devils had had some experience with the new handymen. "Those two both ended up in Hell because of Pride."

"Well, Nero was also a maniac," Sekhmet added.

Astaroth nodded. "True, true, though that doesn't usually get you damned. But damned they both are, and having them fix broken things around Hell doesn't seem like much of a punishment, or even a punishment that fits their crime, as Belphegor suggested." Astaroth cursed. "And those two couldn't fix a pig sty."

Sekhmet looked puzzled. "How do you fix a pig sty? I mean, they're just mud puddles, aren't they? Wouldn't seem to require the skills of a craftsman, in my view."

"That was my point."

"Oh."

"The punishment, in a way, does fit the sin of Pride," I explained. "In life, they were each the boss. Now they're flunkies. They service all of Hell."

"I like it better when *you* service me," Sekhmet said, running her hand up my leg and resting it on my Johnson.

"Ah, right. So, their punishment provides constant blows to their egos. But it's more than that. I chose these two, especially Charlemagne, to replace me because they possess no mechanical skills at all. Zero. Nada."

At a motion from Satan, Lars dropped a screen and lowered the lights. "If you will observe this video, you will see what Beezy means." We were treated to a fifteen-minute comedy routine, where Chuckie and his assistant attempted to use a torch to light the pilot of Pretty Dependable, one of Hell's numerous volcanoes. Nero, the assistant, was doing assistant-like work, in this case carrying the torch. Charlemagne stared into the dark space beneath the volcano, where the pilot normally burned, then gestured to his assistant for the torch. Nero, who wasn't thinking things through, gave it to his boss, burning end first. Charlemagne screamed as the flames licked his hand and batted away the torch. This knocked it into Nero's laurel crown, singeing his hair. A fist fight ensued, two butts got burned, but they worked things out, meaning Charlemagne pounded his assistant into submission. Thus chastened, Nero picked up the torch, handed it over to his boss in proper fashion, and Hell's Super reignited the volcano.

When the video ended, the devils erupted in laughter, applauding. "Well," Astaroth said, wiping a tear from one eye, "I have to admit that's a lot more fun to watch than someone screaming in a lava pit."

Sekhmet chuckled then looked thoughtful. "You're right, Lord Satan. They're suffering much more than the other Damned, especially those who have been here a while. They look bored more than anything else. As bored as we are."

"Exactly!" Satan agreed. "Ladies and/or gentlemen, it's time we upped our game. Please take five minutes to brainstorm torments in your respective areas of expertise, punishments that screw with your charges' brains instead of or in addition to their bodies. You can jot your ideas down on the birch bark."

"Then what?" Belphegor asked.

Satan snapped his fingers, and a dozen scraped cowhides, sewn together to form a large pad, appeared on the wall. "Then I'll have each of you read out your suggestions. Lars here," Lars gave a little wave, "will record them."

"Then what?" Belphegor persisted.

"We'll vet, rank and prioritize them, and ..."

Chapter 22

Boss?" said a voice in the air.

"What is it, Belial?" We had left Belial in charge of Hell during the retreat.

"I think you and the others need to get back here ASAP. Something's happened."

"What? We're in the middle of a planning exercise here."

"Sorry. I hate to interrupt, but I think you need to see this for yourself. I'm on Five, near the Stairway."

Nick sighed. "Very well. I guess this concludes our retreat, folks. Just write your ideas down and send them to me. I'll have Lars compile them and we can meet again later to discuss."

"Good," Belphegor said in a soft voice. "I could use a nap."

"I could use something else," Sekhmet said, giving my privates a final squeeze before releasing them.

"Raincheck?" I said, with a small smile.

"Oh, quit flirting and come with me," Satan said, laying his hand on my shoulder. We disappeared ...

... and landed on Five, where we found a very troubled Belial staring at a long flow of damned souls exiting the Stairway.

"What's wrong?" Nick asked.

Belial indicated the crush of humanity coming out the door. "It's been like this for days. Nonstop. On every level of Hell. And you should see the Stairwell itself. It's a safety hazard."

I snorted. "They're dead, Belial. They're beyond safety."

"You know what I mean."

I nodded then looked at our boss. "I think we should pay a visit to Saint Peter."

We had never seen Gates Level so crowded. Peter, who back then wasn't as fast as he is now, couldn't keep up with all the incoming souls. He had his brother Andrew directing traffic.

When Peter saw me, he motioned to Andrew, who pulled out a whistle and blew a loud tweet then held up one hand in the universal gesture signaling halt. The horde of dead humans that had been pushing toward the desk froze in their tracks. Those behind them, having nowhere else to go, flowed around the others. Soon, the desk, the two saints and Nick and I were surrounded.

"What the hell's going on?" Nick shouted over the masses.

"Plague," Peter answered. He took a kerchief from a pocket in his robe and wiped saintly sweat from his brow. "It started shortly after you left on your retreat. By the way, thanks for giving me a heads up that you were going to be unavailable."

"What are you talking about? I didn't tell you that we were going on retreat."

Andrew who had been standing behind his brother, poked his head over Petey's shoulder. "Simon was being sarcastic," he said, trying to be helpful.

Peter shoved his brother's head backward then gave us an angry look. "Next time, let me know, okay?"

"Fine, fine," Satan responded with impatience. "Don't know what all the fuss is about. We were only gone a few years."

The passage of time is insignificant to immortal beings, as I've said before. "Tell us more," I said, trying to get us back on topic.

"They're calling it the Black Death, at least they are in Europe. It started in China, which is out of my jurisdiction, as you know, but I'd heard about it from some colleagues in Nirvana and Diyu. Didn't give it much thought until the disease spread into Muslim and Christian Lands." Peter frowned. "Funny, the Plague hit the Middle East and Europe at almost exactly the same time, as if it had been planned or something."

"What's been the effect on the Jews?" I asked.

Andrew answered. "Well, being the chosen people and all, they're a pretty small group compared to the souls arriving from the two larger religions. Yet the Plague seems not to be hitting Jewish communities as hard. The Black Death thrives on unsanitary conditions, and the Jews have always been big on personal hygiene, you know."

"Interesting." I looked at the humans piling up around us. If this kept up, we'd soon need an expanded Gates Level to hold them all. "I don't know about 'Black,' but the 'Death' part of this plague seems on target. Has Mortimer chimed in?"

"Yes," Andrew replied. "Morty says at this rate, the population of Europe may be cut in half, with comparable casualties across the other areas over which our religions have sway."

A lot of dead folks. I whistled.

The crowd, thinking my tweet meant that break time was over, began to surge forward again. Andrew hurriedly pulled out his whistle and gave another toot, along with the accompanying hand sign. The signal was a little different this time, though, and it generated some indignant looks from the humans.

Funny, I didn't think a saint would make my signature gesture. It seemed out of character for him, but perhaps I was mistaken in what I saw.

That's when I noticed all the small children, especially the infants. They were carried by the adults, and while some of them may have been parents to the children, the rest of them had probably just been given the duty to help transport the dead who had never learned to walk.

Morty's work, no doubt. He's always been efficient.

I shook my head. "This is going to strain our infrastructure. The Stairway is bursting at the seams already. We don't have nearly enough lava pits for all of these souls. And our sulfur reserves are already in short supply." I was less worried about Heaven's capacity to absorb its share of these newly arrived souls. First off, it was not my job. Besides, Heaven always managed. In any event, it only got one or two souls out of ten. Hell, on the other hand, would take the brunt of this uptick.

"Not to mention the strain on our staff." Satan frowned. "The Demon Corps isn't up to full strength yet. It will be a mess handling all of this traffic down in Hell."

"Your problem, not mine," Peter said, eyeing the crowds. "I've got my own issues. How am I going to process all these people? Especially the unbaptized infants. I've never had so many, and I don't know how I'll get them down to Limbo. I guess I'm going to have to get some more saints to help out." He looked thoughtful, then swallowed hard, a sour look forming on his face. "Maybe even Paul."

Paul and Simon Peter didn't get along. Yet, with a shrug, he dispelled that unhappy thought and again began dispensing judgment from the Book of Life.

I leaned over to whisper in his ear. He flinched.

It wasn't my fault he didn't like the smell of garlic. Or perhaps it was the proximity of my devilish personage. I wasn't offended though. It's part of the fun, creeping out the good guys.

"Well," I said, ignoring his look of revulsion, "I think I can help you out with the babies, if you'd like. What?"

Satan looked as if I'd slapped him. "Why would you help him? He's on the other side."

I sighed. As smart as Satan was – he always had been the smartest of the devil crowd, except perhaps me and Belphegor – sometimes he could miss the obvious. "Nick, Limbo is part of Hell. It's our responsibility."

He pursed his lips then nodded. "Oh, very well. Just be quick about it. I want to get to Earth and see this Plague thing for myself, and I want you to come with me."

"Okay. This won't take long. Perhaps while I'm doing my thing, you can devise some triage system that the devils and demons can employ while we're gone."

He frowned. "Whatever I come up with will require a bunch of overtime. Meet me at the Pantheon in Rome in, let's say, an hour." With that he disappeared.

I didn't need an hour. In no time, I constructed a mile-long slide that ran from Gates Level to Limbo/Level One. "There," I said, brushing some sawdust from my hands. "Peter, can you station someone at the bottom to catch the babies?"

"I'll go." A saint in Fourth Century garb shoved his way through the crowds. It was Saint Augustine. The one from Hippo. You know, *Confessions* and *The City of God*. Good books both, though I wouldn't have minded some pictures.

He was a bit of a rake in his youth, but I guess he redeemed himself in the end. Heck, he made "Saint," didn't he?

"Thanks, Gus," Peter said. Augustine just nodded, then hopped on the slide and let it carry him down to Limbo. Andrew started loading the babies on the slide. Some of the kiddos screamed in fright, even more screamed in delight – most kids love slides, you know, even mile-long ones – but they all made it without incident to Augustine's waiting arms.

With an easy solution for the babies in place, dealing with the crowds became more manageable. Peter nodded at me. "Thanks," he said, in a rare expression of saint-to-devil gratitude.

"No problem."

I materialized before the Pantheon. Seconds later, Nick stood beside me.

"Ugh, what a stench!" he said, coughing. "It's even worse than the Forest of Flatulence in the Sixth Circle."

"Well, dead bodies will do that," I opined, indicating the scene before us.

Anyone who has visited the Pantheon will recall that in front of the building is an open square, the Piazza della Rotonda. In the middle of the Piazza is a stately fountain, capped by an impressive obelisk.

This was not the case in the Fourteenth Century. Back then, the space was filled with ramshackle buildings, shops and dwellings and work sheds. I looked at them with distaste; I always hated poor construction. Between and among these structures ran a spiderweb of walkways. Said walkways were at present choked with the bodies of dead Romans.

The Black Death had taken a terrible toll on the city, though not as much as in Siena, where eighty thousand died, or Florence, where three out of five perished. Still, Rome looked a bloody mess to us.

There were many approaches to combatting the disease. There were those who prayed to their Creator to intervene. They were called dead people. Some tried more active solutions, like strapping live chickens to lymph nodes swollen to bursting by the plague. They and the people who helped them strap on the chickens were also called dead people. (The birds didn't fare very well either.) And then there were those who just ran like hell. They fled to the countryside, away from the steady accumulation of carcasses within the city walls. Not all, but many of these fleet-footed mortals got to call themselves survivors.

The rulers of Rome – those who remained – had enough sense to know that they needed to get all the dead bodies out of town. They conscripted a bunch of schmucks to drag the dead from houses, out of the streets, stacking them in wagons and carting them as far away from the living as they could. Most of the workers in the doom patrol were themselves doomed, but they did save some lives in the city, I suppose.

While the Piazza della Rotonda had not yet been created, there existed a small grassy area surrounded by shops and eateries. We walked from the steps of the Pantheon to this open space. The restaurant business wasn't very brisk that day. That probably had something to do with the exceptionally large pile of dead bodies that had been dragged to this undeveloped bit of land to await pickup and transport out of town. The patrol was hard at work when we got there, scurrying around, getting their business done, as fast as possible, so they could get the hell out of there.

Above the pile of carcasses flew a swarm of flies. On seeing me, they darted over to pay their respects, but even the Lord of the Flies wasn't as interesting to them as an odoriferous mountain of rotting flesh, and they soon hurried back to the dead.

Rodents were everywhere, for this was Feast Day for them. Satan and I watched as a large, black rat skirted through the partially open door of a nearby brothel, scampered up the pile and stood on the head of the top body. Then the creature raised up on its hind legs.

"Bwahahahahahaha! Look what I have wrought!"

Satan and I regarded the rat. My friend rolled his eyes. "Hello, Leviathan. Enjoying yourself?"

"I always enjoy besting you, Lucifer. Bwahahahahahaha!"

"Stop that!" I yelled. "That laugh is copyrighted. By me. You can't use it without my permission."

The rat looked at me haughtily, assuming a rat can look haughty, that is. "I'm a devil, and I get to use it. Metatron told me so himself."

That set me to grumbling, but I figured he was right. A rival or not, he was still a devil, and that was the official devil laugh. "Well, I ..." I began. "Look, could you transform into some different form? Talking to a rat is ..."

"Is what?" he squeaked.

"Well, it's undignified. For one thing. And I'm getting a neck ache staring down at you."

Leviathan grinned at me with his little rat teeth. "Would you like me to pile up a few more bodies? Wouldn't be hard, you know. There are plenty available."

Our conversation with Leviathan had drawn a small crowd of humans. Nick and I had assumed human guise and were thus unremarkable. A talking, grinning rat, though, scared the crap out of them, and they took off running.

Leviathan transformed into a creature roughly our size. A talking corpse. Now he sat atop the pile, swinging his legs idly.

Satan, who had kept quiet while I'd argued with Leviathan, at last spoke. "What's your game here?"

Leviathan spat out a loose tooth, then grinned again. "As I said, besting you."

"And how would killing millions upon millions of Jews, Christians and Muslims be besting me?"

"Why that should be obvious even to a weak mind such as your own."

Satan's eyes narrowed, but he kept his temper. "So, why don't you explain it to me and my weak mind?"

The corpse laughed. "Happy to, and I'll use short words, so you can understand me."

At that point, Satan's hands clenched into a couple of fists. I grabbed my friend's arm and shook my head. He frowned but nodded.

"For some time, I and my crack team of devils have been transporting fleas from China, along the Silk Road, across the Middle East to Constantinople, ports on the Black Sea, Alexandria. We came to Sicily and Italy, even traveling to Genoa. My plague has raced across Northern Africa and all of Europe, even crossing the Channel to England."

"To what end?" I asked.

He looked at me in astonishment. "Beelzebub, I thought you were smarter than this. Smarter than your buddy here."

I could feel the muscles in Nick's arm tighten. Another insult like that and the two would be brawling. "I guess I'm not. You're going to have to spell it out."

He shrugged. "Very well. The reason is simple: souls. I'm harvesting them, and most will go to Hell. And when Management sees how much better I am at getting souls for

228

Hell, I'll be given your job. I'll be Satan, and you, Nicky, will be a has-been."

A small smile crept onto Satan's face. "You did this all to get souls into Hell?" Nick and I stared at each other. Then we chuckled.

That was the one thing Leviathan hadn't expected. This was supposed to be his moment of triumph, and we were laughing at him. "What? What?!"

Satan was laughing so hard he almost fell over. "You're right that there's an idiot here, but it's not Beezy, and it's certainly not me. It's you, you numbskull. You're not much of a forward thinker, are you?"

"What do you mean?"

"If you were," Nick said, chuckling some more, "you would have realized that we would have gotten these souls regardless, when they died a natural death. More, in fact, because they would have had more opportunities to sin."

"And don't forget the babies," I added. "Millions of them have died from the Plague and are in Limbo. Did you know we don't get full point value for unbaptized babies?"

For the first time, Leviathan looked uncertain. "I didn't think of that."

"Apparently not," I continued. "If those who wouldn't have died in infancy had been allowed to live, we would have gotten, let's see, eighty-five percent of them into one of the main Circles of Hell. Also, those who had reached adulthood would have produced babies of their own, and most of those would in time also have gone to Hell."

Nick shook his head. "You really are an idiot, Leviathan. It will take at least two hundred years before the world's population is back to its pre-Plague level. Far from garnering more souls for Hell, you have permanently deprived us of millions."

"That's the way I see it, too." I could feel the muscles in Nick's arm relax. He knew he'd won this round, without even taking a swing. Leviathan had punched himself in the face.

"You took your profits out of the market of souls prematurely," Satan concluded. "I doubt this will impress Management. If anything, all you will have shown them is that you lack vision."

Leviathan's mouth started to spasm, like that of a freshly caught perch that finds itself on the ground beside a fishing hole.

"Ah. Look, Nick. There's Leviathan's fish face, the one we've come to know and love."

"Bwahahahahahaha!" we laughed in unison. Then Nick and I teleported.

Chapter 23

After checking out the Plague, we returned to Hell. The huge uptick in newly damned souls kept us all hopping for about five years. During this period, the Stairway was inadequate for all the traffic, so during peak periods, we went back to using the Mouth of Hell as well. Peter hated that, but there was no other choice. It did cause a problem for me. I had to remove the slide I'd built between Gates Level and Limbo, replacing it with hundreds of dumbwaiters that traveled between the two levels. The kiddos were small enough to fit in these mini-precursors of elevators, and they descended quickly, so the trip wasn't much of a hardship for the tots.

With the flood of new souls under control, Nick and I returned to the initiative we'd begun discussing with the Management Team at the planning retreat. He and I sat down with each of the other devil princes to see what ideas they had for new ways to torment souls condemned for the sins of lust, gluttony, greed, pride, sloth, envy and wrath.

Over the centuries, it had become apparent that Sekhmet, Abaddon and Astaroth disliked their roles. Oh, don't get me wrong, they were all excellent devils, and Sekhmet was particularly well-suited for her role as devil prince for Lust. It's just that she'd rather have been the object of someone's lust than the punisher of a human who had the same proclivities she had. Astaroth and Abaddon, while competent in many ways, weren't any good as supervisors. They were often overwhelmed by their responsibilities. Only Belphegor showed the combination of interest, creativity, intelligence and managerial skills appropriate for the job. Ironic, I suppose, since he was the patron devil of Sloth.

But at least for the nonce, those four were what we had.

To her credit, Sekhmet had some good ideas for her area. "Doling out punishments that fit the crime is pretty straightforward for those guilty of Lust," she said, as she stretched luxuriously on a chaise lounge. We were sitting beside her in two comfortable winged back chairs. Sekhmet was dressed in a Seven Veil special, though five of them were currently discarded, so not much was covered up. At her feet were two damned humans looking up at her in erotic adoration. As she talked, she absently whipped them with a cat-o-nine-tails.

"Impotence is one of the biggest fears of any male, but particularly one of the lustful."

"So?" Nick said.

"So, we take the starch out of their willies. They won't be able to get it up, no matter how hard they try. Oh, we'll give them erection aids, and they'll be so desperate, they'll try them."

"Like what?" Nick was intrigued.

She whacked her human charges a few more times then signaled some demons to take the damned souls out of the room. When they were gone, she turned her attention back to us. "Metal or glass rods, or daggers or javelins, that we can surgically implant in them. It'll hurt like hell." She grinned at him.

"But then they'll be able to do the deed, right?"

"Well, yes, they'll be able to 'do the deed,' as you so quaintly put it, but they won't want to. All that friction will aggravate the wounds of their surgeries. Also, we'll pair them up with the most hideous demons-in-drag that we can find."

I stroked my beard. "Makes sense. What about the women?"

Sekhmet frowned. "Women are more complicated, but I think extreme vaginal dryness should do the trick."

"Excellent, excellent," Nick said, rubbing his hands in anticipation.

Belphegor also had a good notion of what he wanted to do. "I envision a town, no, a city, where the slothful work round the clock, trying to meet impossible deadlines. They'll build walls, tear them down, then do it all over again. Wells will be dug, then the dirt shoveled back in, back and forth, ad infinitum. I'll call it Sloth City. The name's not very creative, I suppose, but I like the irony, since the inhabitants will be kept quite active."

"Your demons won't like this," I pointed out to him. "They usually knock off around four." In the past, at the end of the day, we would just throw all the Damned in one of the numerous seas of thorns scattered throughout Hell. It would take them all night to extricate themselves from the bushes. That way, the devils and demons could have some down time.

Belphegor shrugged, then lay back on the large bed on which he spent almost all his time these days. The slight motion seemed to exhaust him, though it may have been only an act. When he regained his breath, he started again. "We'll set up three shifts, just to keep an eye on the slothful, to make certain they don't slack off. It should be fine. What?" he asked, looking at Satan, who seemed to have something on his mind.

"Perhaps we should run three shifts all over Hell and keep everyone's new punishments going non-stop.

"That's no good," I said, shaking my head. "We don't have the staff to do that. For now, I think we'll have to stick with the stickers – the seas of thorns."

Belphegor got quiet, as if he were thinking through an idea he'd just had. Then he nodded, satisfied. "If I might suggest something. There could be some benefits for some of the Damned, not the slothful, but the rest of them, to have their nights off."

"Why in Hell would we want to do that?" said our boss.

Belphegor snickered. "Haven't you noticed that humans are their own most effective tormentors? Give them some time to think, and they can come up with all sorts of worries."

"Nah," I said. "They'll just sleep through it, waking up refreshed."

Belphegor shook his head. "I don't think so. Hell instills a profound sense of anxiety in all the Damned, and it will really be driven home as they toss and turn in their beds at night, dreading the beginning of each day. I doubt that many of them will sleep at all. If they do, it will be fitful, and during those times, their dreams will be the stuff of nightmares."

"You mean they will be actual nightmares. That's all I'll allow," Satan said, a stern look across his brow.

Belphegor again shook his head. "You might consider an occasional good dream, Nick, so that when the human awakes, it will be like being damned to Hell all over again."

I laughed. "Instant replay. That's very good, Belly. The moment of damnation results in more torment in a second than we can create in a decade down here. This way, they can experience it over and over." I had to admire my friend's subtlety of mind. He was really a great devil prince.

"Well, crap," Satan says. "I agree it's a good idea, but that means we're going to have to build places for the humans to go at night."

I snorted. "You mean *I'll* have to. Not a problem, though. I've been looking for a new project."

"I thought you didn't want to do manual labor anymore," Belphegor commented.

"Oh, I don't like fixing things that break, but I enjoy creating new things, just as Nick likes making demons." Constructing the giant slide between Gates Level and Limbo and then installing the dumbwaiters between the same two levels made me realize I'd missed building stuff. I smiled. "I'm looking forward to it. In fact, it's an interesting exercise. Every lodging will itself be part of the damnation experience. They will be hovels, I promise, vermin-infested, uncomfortable, etc." I pulled out a roll of parchment, which I kept up my sleeve for just such occasions, and began writing down ideas.

Astaroth and Abaddon were not nearly as creative as their two colleagues.

For the greedy, all Astaroth could think of was taking their lunch money or picking their pockets. The basic concept was correct, but it needed elaboration. Satan and I would later come up with the concept of New Rome and the theme, "Render unto Caesar that which is Caesar's." We realized that different people valued different things, so the currency of the greedy would be as individual as their souls.

Abaddon had been practicing sulky expressions in the mirror. Satan looked at me and rolled his eyes. "Thank you for your input," he said. "We'll get back to you."

Ignoring Abaddon's meager contribution, Nick and I came up with the concept of Covet Town, later shortened to Coveton. It was loosely based on Belphegor's notion of Sloth City, except that frantic activity wasn't the point of the town. Envy required someone to be envious of, so you needed to put people together, establish communities, create a family of Smith and another of Jones, so they could be envious of each other.

And so it went with each of the Circles of Hell.

Chapter 24

A cold wind blew across the Mediterranean Sea, making me shiver. I pulled the cloak more tightly around my body and took another draught of beer.

I was in a seaside tavern in Valencia, eating paella, and waiting for Nick to finish. That evening was amateur night, and Satan had decided to sing. He was onstage now, or what passed for a stage in this modest establishment. At least the floor on which his stool wobbled was made of wood. My feet were resting on stone, which wasn't as resonant.

Nick had adopted the "blind bard" look. His eyes were a milky white, his long cloak tattered. In his hand was a harp, which I thought was funny, given his fallen angel status. Satan is often associated with a fiddle, but that hadn't been invented yet. Yet Nick could play harp well enough.

With his gnarled fingers, he struck a chord. The sweet sound of the harp cut through the din of the tavern, and all fell silent. Then, in a fine baritone, my friend began to sing.

The tune was catchy, and I found myself humming along. Centuries later, the melody would resurface in the form of another popular war ditty, "When Johnny Comes Marching Home."

Hear now my song
From times of old,
Of knights so strong
And pretty bold.

Spain they had lost
To Moorish might,
Without much cost,
Without much fight.

Hasta la vista,
Sweet señorita.
I'm off to see to
The Reconquista.
We'll all be there when
Ferdinand wins the war.

Seven short years
The conquest spanned,
Moors boxed our ears.
Our knights got canned.

A hundred times that
We'd have to pay,
Send millions to Hell
To win the day.

Hasta la vista,
My fine señor.
I'm off to see to
The Spanish war.
And we'll all be there when
Ferdinand wins the war.

And so on.

The lyrics were funny, if interminable. In typical blind bard fashion, Satan had written an epic poem. I tuned it out, yet Nick had succeeded in getting me to think about the war.

Ever since the Moors began their conquest of the Iberian Peninsula in 711, the Christians in the rest of Europe had been trying to take it back. First, the Muslim aggression had to be stopped from proceeding further. As I've already told you, Charles Martel and Pippin the Short accomplished that, with a little help from me and Nick.

238

But while the Conquest of Hispania by the Moors took only about seven years, the Reconquista, which is the official name for the reclamation of the Peninsula, took almost seven hundred. (As Nick said in his song, "a hundred times" paid.) The Christians started small, toilet papering a few trees on the fringes of al-Andalus. But no one noticed that, so they decided to get more aggressive.

In 778, Charlemagne tried, unsuccessfully, to capture the city of Zaragoza, which for the geographically-challenged among you is in northeastern Spain, a bit west of Barcelona. His siege stalled, so he left in a huff, heading back over the Pyrenees. On his way home, his rearguard was ambushed. Nothing like having your tail cut off. All in all, not one of Chuckie's better efforts, though a good poem came out of it, "The Song of Roland."

He did, however, control the main passes across the Pyrenees, and there he established toeholds in the three vassal regions of Pamplona, Aragon and Catalonia. Barcelona came back in the Christian fold in 801, thanks to Charlemagne's twenty-three-year-old son, Louis.

After that, it was back and forth, back and forth. Yet slowly, the Christian forces were retaking the peninsula. Though the Reconquista was a long slog, it was much more successful than all those silly Crusades in the Middle East, where the Christian armies more often than not got their butts kicked.

Nick and I pretty much stayed out of both efforts, though we kept a close eye on the action. We wanted to make certain Europe, at least, held against the Muslim advance, not because we particularly disliked the people of Islam, but because Leviathan was cheering them on, and anyone or thing he supported we opposed on principle.

There were other distractions during this period that threatened Europe. The Vikings were a headache for two or three hundred years. And that Black Death thing was a major downer, as I've already told you.

The Reconquista. Ah, the storied places, where the war for the Christian reoccupation took place! There was Barcelona, Castile, Leon. There was Aragon − not to be confused with Aragorn, that fellow in the *Lord of the Rings*. And Navarre, and Portugal. These all fell to the Christians. Then the Caliphate of Cordoba collapsed, triggering a time of military rivalry among the Muslims themselves. Seville was reclaimed. When that happened, all that remained of al-Andalus, of Moorish Spain, was Granada.

Granada! I'm falling under your spell.

Sorry. Another favorite song of mine, even better than "When Johnny Comes Marching Home."

Granada became a vassal state of Castile.

The actors in this centuries' long conflict were also names out of legend. On the Muslim team were many great figures, but their names weren't very funny, so no point listing them here. Yet many of them were called "Al." A number of hyphens were also involved, Muslims being very fond of them.

On the Christian side, though, well. There was Odo of Aquitaine, Charles the Hammer, Pippin the Short, Charles the Great (that's what Charlemagne means, folks). There was Ferdinand III who united Castile and Leon; he was a major figure in the Reconquista. And who can forget El Cid, noteworthy for fighting on both sides? There was Denis the Menace, who fought with his own Christian allies to finalize the borders of Portugal, essentially unchanged even into modern times. There was Alfonso the Brave, Sancho the Great − not to be confused with Sancho the Panza − along with James the Conqueror and

Theobald, who was also called the Conqueror, because after half a millennium they had finally run out of catchy nicknames. For our part, Nick and I called him Baldie, just because we could. Last but by no means least were the two who would end almost eight hundred years of Moorish occupation of Spain: Isabella I and Ferdinand II. The so-called Catholic Monarchs.

And we'll all be there when
Ferdinand wins the war!

The applause was loud and, for the most part, heartfelt, though the people of Valencia, like almost everyone in Europe, were by this time bloody tired of the Reconquista. And interminable epic poems. Still, Nick had always been a fine performer. He rose from his stool, bowed to his audience and made toward the door. I dropped some coins on my table and followed.

"Pretty good, don't you think?" he said, as he tossed his harp over a stone wall. We heard a "kerplop" when it hit the water.

"I guess so. Do you really think Ferdinand will win the war?"

My friend nodded. "That's what I've foreseen. Well, he and Isabella together. She's even more formidable than he is."

"Then why didn't you mention her in your song?"

"Too many syllables."

"Oh. So, shall we go?"

"Yes, let's." The only person who saw us disappear was an ostler from the nearby stable, but he was drunk as a skunk and paid us no mind.

We met the king and queen when they were still young, in their late twenties. Ferdinand had just inherited the crown of

Aragon upon the death of his father in 1479. Shortly thereafter, Isabella secured her own kingdom: Castile.

Ferdinand's path to monarchy was an easy one. By comparison, Isabella practically had to use a machete, hacking away at the political vines and thorn bushes, to get to hers. This was owing to a rather duplicitous older half-brother. The fellow died though, and his thirteen-year old daughter, who otherwise would have been his heir, was no match for her aunt.

Nick was certain that these two, who had worked so effectively together over their ten-year marriage, would bring an end to the Reconquista, and in the process piss off Leviathan, which was always a good thing. Moreover, Nick was convinced that in the Reconquista, somehow, the end game with the rebellious devils would be played. So, we paid attention.

Meeting the monarchs would be easy to do. These two were the power couple of their age, like Beyonce and Jay-Z are today. Or perhaps, Spain's early reality stars, the Kim and Kanye of late Medieval Spain. They went out of their way to meet and greet people.

The new monarchs had united two large kingdoms, which formed the nucleus of what is now modern Spain. To secure their power with the people, and most especially with the feudal lords upon whom they depended to keep the peace and fill the royal coffers, the court of the king and the queen operated Bedouin-style, traveling from town to town. This was the Fifteenth Century equivalent of the weekly press conference, I suppose. Or the whistle-stop tour. Or a series of tweets, but without the character limit.

A few days after Nick's performance, he and I transported ourselves to the outskirts of Zaragoza. We were disguised as feudal lords. There was a crowd nearby, lining the road on the far side of the main bridge across the Ebro, the great river that passed through the city. We folded into the group. Word had gotten around that the two monarchs, who had wintered in Aragon, were to begin a trek to Toledo that day, and we intended to join the entourage.

The morning air had a crispness to it that sent another chill up my spine. Over the centuries, I had begun to spend less and less time on Earth, preferring instead my own little corner of Hell, the Eighth Circle. In fact, except for attending Nick's performance in Valencia, I hadn't been on the mortal plane since the Black Death affair a hundred years earlier. As a result, I'd gotten used to the superheated air of Hell.

Still, except for the chill, it was a nice day. The sky was a clear, cheerful blue. This was a rarity for me, cerulean not being a common hue in the Netherworld.

I was wearing a somber if well-tailored garment, with one of those high ruffled collars so popular back then. It itched. Nick's outfit was of a similar style, but more outlandishly hued. It was bright red. He looked like a cardinal, the bird kind.

I shook my head. Over the centuries, Nick had become completely stuck on himself. Always prideful, he had descended to the lowest form of that sin; he was vain.

There was the bleat of an out-of-tune post horn. Then another, and another. When they attempted to honk in unison, I winced. The same note played simultaneously by three different people is hard to get in tune, and when the listener is a devil like me, possessing perfect pitch, the result is often painful. I looked at Satan, who had his fingers in his ears.

The screeching stopped, and we felt a rumble beneath our feet. On the other side of the bridge, the Zaragoza side, the royal entourage was beginning to cross, hundreds of servants, dozens of courtiers, horses, livestock, dry goods. It was a moveable feast. Or a moveable capital.

In a few minutes, the vanguard reached us. I was craning my neck trying to see the king and queen. Finally, I spotted them, in the center of the train. The king rode on a fine black charger, the queen atop a white palfrey.

I had heard that the two were very compatible, and they looked it. Ferdinand seemed to be the brawn and Isabella the brains. The king, who wore his crown resting on the visor of a war helmet, was dressed in armor. Looked uncomfortable, though dignified. His complexion was dark and his bearing proud. He might have been more impressive, though, if he'd had just a bit more chin. And his eyes were rheumy, as if he'd drunk one too many glasses of sangria the night before. Ferdinand had a puzzled look, an expression of perpetual befuddlement, as if surprised by his good fortune. At once, I dubbed him the Simpleton. Not out loud. Being the king meant he could kill a smart-mouthed subject.

Isabella was a stark contrast to her mate. Where he was dark, almost swarthy, she was pale, like porcelain, with hair a light strawberry blonde. She had an enormous crown on her head, encrusted with rubies, sapphires and diamonds.

When I say it was enormous, I'm not kidding. Her crown was the diameter of a large Frisbee. By necessity.

Isabella I, Queen of Castile, Queen Consort of Aragon and Sicily and Majorica and a bunch of other places, was afflicted with a condition modern medicine calls macrocephaly. She had a very big head, and so, being a devil, in my mind I began referring to her as the Fathead, or simply Fathead.

Nick chuckled.

"You're not supposed to read my thoughts," I whispered, but when I looked at him and saw his grin, I started chuckling as well. "Must be all those brains of hers."

If you modern folks were to take a trip to Granada, you could go to the Capilla Real, the Royal Chapel, which is next to the city cathedral, and see the tombs of the Catholic Monarchs. Atop the tombs are life-sized statues of Isabella and Ferdinand, in repose. One thing you would notice is that Isabella has one more pillow than Ferdinand. The guides in the Chapel will tell you that's because she was considered the smarter of the two.

So, maybe that very large cranium did in fact contain more brains. Or maybe it was nothing more than a damn big skull.

Like me, Isabella wore one of those oh-so-stylish ruffled collars. With my devil vision, I saw that the collar was more than mere ornamentation. The fabric hid a massive structure of iron bars that supported her head.

Chapter 25

While I was engaged in ogling the queen's odd appearance, Nick stuck out a foot and tripped a horse. The animal fell sideways, knocking over another horse, which in turn destabilized a third. In domino fashion, an entire row of steeds and their riders tumbled to the earth. This brought the moving royal court to a halt.

As the knights, grumbling, got themselves and their mounts back on their feet, Nick stepped up to the monarchs. I followed.

"Your royal Majesties," Nick said smoothly, as he bowed to the king and queen. "We are two feudal lords, come to swear our fealty to you, and to request a boon."

Isabella, who despite her disability, was no fool, looked at us with suspicion. "I don't recognize you. You are ...?"

I cleared my throat. "Feudal Lords, my liege. That's good, right?" I looked at the two, uncertain.

"She wants your names," Ferdinand clarified. I decided he wasn't as dumb as he looked.

"Ah," Nick said. "My friend here is Sancho the Fat. And I am," he paused for a moment, "I am Alonso the ..."

"The Popinjay," I said, without missing a beat. I may have been fat, but I didn't appreciate the label, especially when being introduced to nobility. And if I was fat, then he was a strutting peacock. Or parrot.

Our audience snickered.

"Ah, yes," Nick continued, giving me a dirty look. "I am Alonso the, ah, the Popinjay, of Illescas, near Toledo. My friend, here, is from ... Chattanooga."

"I know Illescas," said the queen, "but I have never heard of Chattanooga."

"Small town," I said hurriedly. "Very small town."

"I have not heard of it," she repeated. "Where is it?"

"Far to the south," Nick supplied.

"For that matter, I have not heard of either of you." Ferdinand eyed us with suspicion, his hand resting on the hilt of his sword. "Are you in fact lords and, say, is that silk you're wearing?"

Nick smiled. "Why yes, it is, my lord. All the way way from China it came, along the Silk Road, to Genoa. I find it very comfortable."

Isabella frowned then scratched at the woolen garment she wore.

"Okay," said Ferdinand. "If you're rich enough to wear silk, I guess you must be somebody. So, what is this boon you wish?"

Nick, I mean, Alonso, shrugged. "The road is long, and prithee we would like to travel in the security of your company."

Isabella frowned. "If you are nobility, then where are your servants? Where are your horses?"

Nick leaned over to me and said, *sotto voce*, "Servants! We forgot the damned servants! And the horses. Shit."

"Got it," I whispered back, waving my hand behind me.

I'm sure Simon Magus and his platoon of demon trainees were more than surprised to find themselves standing on Earth on a bright spring day, looking like humans and dressed in itchy wool garments, with two of them (the demons, not the garments) holding the traces of a couple of fine stallions. But then they spotted the two of us. Simon, always the sharp cookie, gestured to the others to be still. He bowed to me.

"There they are, your Majesties. We are ready to ride with you, if you will allow us."

"What's in it for us?" Isabella asked suddenly.

Satan considered this, then smiling, reached into a pouch at his waist. "I have other treasures from the far east, your Majesty, and I would be honored to offer you this." From the pouch, he extracted a glorious pearl necklace then handed it to the queen.

Sold. We were accepted into the monarchs' entourage without further ado.

As we began our travels, Satan cozied up to the king and queen, while I pulled Faust to one side and explained what I wanted of them. "Simon, just tell the gang to stay together and keep their mouths shut. In a day or two, we'll find some excuse to send you ahead of the train and zap you back to boot camp."

Faust looked around in wonder at the lush greenery of northern Spain. He whistled. "I never thought I'd see Earth again. It's even more beautiful than I remember."

"That's because you spent your life in the desert. Most people prefer trees to sand, though I'd take the Sahara over this any day."

Simon looked up to the crown of a tall conifer jabbing at the brilliant blue sky. "If you say so, boss. Looks pretty nice to me."

"Well, don't get used to it. Take care of your men. I want to see what Nick is up to." My friend was deep in conversation with the royal personages, who rode along the path some thirty yards ahead of me. I nudged my horse forward and joined them.

"Ah, Lord Sancho," Nick said, as I sidled up to the entourage. "There you are. Her Majesty was just telling me of the terrible headaches that frequently afflict her."

I nodded to the queen. *Neckaches too, no doubt.* I looked at her colossal cranium. *And backaches.* "I wonder what causes them," I said innocently.

Nick looked at me with skepticism. "As I was telling her Majesty, I believe I can help. In my travels, I have learned many secrets for curing pain. I am a well-known physician. Why, I even studied with Maimonedes."

"What?" Isabella said in astonishment. "Why, Maimonedes died almost three hundred years ago!" She looked at Nick with suspicion.

"Not that Maimonedes!" he almost shouted, realizing his error.

Jeez, Nick. Do the math.

Maimonedes had died in the early Thirteenth Century.

"I'm talking about his descendant, Maimonedes the, ah, Twelfth, who was also a great physician. Sadly, he has passed from this earth, but not before he trained me. I would be honored to help you."

"How?" Ferdinand asked, curious. "No one has ever been able to relieve these headaches of hers. Why, at nighttime, when I knock on her door to perform my husbandly duties, her Royal Majesty often tells me that she has a headache, and ..."

"Never mind that!" Isabella said in a shrill voice. Then she returned her attention to Nick. "What would I have to do?"

My friend shrugged. "Just submit to a cranial massage, perhaps drink a potion, that's all."

"And how long would all of this take? I'm a busy woman, you know."

"Without doubt, my liege," Nick said. "I think a single treatment would do it. In fact, I believe I can cure you of these headaches tonight, after we encamp."

She looked at her husband with trepidation. "Surely not *all* of my headaches."

Nick looked to Ferdinand, who was busy adjusting his codpiece.

Then my trickster pal looked back at Isabella and winked. It was a very cheeky thing to do, but if anyone could get away with winking at a monarch, it would be Satan. "No, not all of your headaches." He leaned over and whispered. "Just the inconvenient ones."

Isabella seemed much relieved. "This evening then, after dinner and the evening's entertainment."

Dinner was cured pig, hamón ibérico. The chef went on and on about it as if pork from the Iberian Peninsula was the greatest delicacy the world had ever tasted. It was okay, I guess, though I preferred pork rinds and pig knuckles. And bacon, of course.

Then there was a short game of shovelboard, which was the predecessor of shuffleboard, except rather than pushing a hard, flat disc across a wooden floor with a cue stick, you flung cow patties across the grass with a shovel. The turds tended to crack apart after a few impacts with the ground, but fortunately we had turd boys who would rush in, scoop up the damaged patty and replace it with a spare.

Smelly job, turd boy, but back then scooping up shit for the king and queen was considered a highly respected form of employment. And there were promotional opportunities too. Do a good job, and you could get promoted to Royal Fool, or at least Under-Fool, or Substitute Fool, or something.

But all this activity caused the queen's headache to return, and so the monarchs retired to their pavilion, Nick and I in tow.

Nick had the queen sit in a comfortable chair then persuaded her to remove her crown. This was harder than it sounds. Seems she never took it off, even slept in it. I had an image in my head of the monarchs doing the nasty while still wearing their crowns. Must have been awkward as hell, and I bet the two royal headgears would sometimes get locked together like a pair of teenagers' braces could when they were sucking face. Yet they must have managed somehow. After all, they had seven kids together. Five of them even survived to adulthood, which was a very good percentage in those days.

With the crown removed, Nick was able to give Isabella a good massage. Just the top of her. Nothing below shoulder level; Ferdinand made certain of that. Just as well. Satan is not above copping a feel, and I could imagine the Prince of Darkness groping Her Royal Majesty for his own amusement. How outlandish would that have been? Nick would have loved it. Yet beneath Ferdinand's and my watchful gaze, my friend managed to control himself.

After the massage, Isabella said she felt much refreshed. Even the pain in her back and neck was greatly reduced. Nick gave her a potion to drink, but first he had to drink some of it himself in order to demonstrate that this wasn't some elaborate plot to poison the queen. Then he told her to see him in the morning.

Ferdinand looked thoughtful. "Your friend appears to be a fine doctor. What can *you* do?"

I shrugged. "I'm good with my hands. I'm a builder. In fact, I just did some work on the Pantheon." I didn't tell him which Pantheon. He would not have believed that there was an all-gold facsimile of the original or that the replica was in Hell.

Everyone knows the Pantheon, though, so Ferdinand was impressed by my experience. "Well, then, perhaps you can help me as your friend is helping my queen."

"How would I do that?"

"We are traveling to Toledo …"

"Holy Toledo!" I said, not wanting to pass up an opportunity for a bad joke.

"Yes, of course," he responded. "We are going to consult with the archbishop there about some needed renovations to the cathedral. Perhaps you could take a look at the structure and offer some recommendations."

"I would be honored, your Majesty."

"Why are you smiling?" he asked.

"Do you know what the word 'irony' means?"

"No. I'm afraid not."

"No matter. Let me send our entourage ahead of us, telling our vassals in Illescas and … Chattanooga that we will be detained a while."

I summoned Simon and told him to get his cadets and scram. He had been awaiting my signal and was able to leave in short order. Once they were out of sight, I sent them back to Hell.

"You know," Nick said to me later that evening, as we were sitting alone by a campfire, out of earshot from the mortals, "these humans sure know how to grovel. Look there."

Each royal was surrounded by half a dozen courtiers, pouring wine, fluffing pillows, laughing at royal jokes. And all of this was accompanied by plenty of "my lieges" and "Your Royal Majesties" and the like.

Satan looked thoughtful. "I think you should start calling me my lord Satan."

I snorted. "Oh, come on! After all we've been through together? You can't be serious!" I looked at him and saw that he wasn't joking. He was, instead, staring at me imperiously, waiting for me to acknowledge him as lord and master.

Despite myself, I cringed. This was a showdown I had seen coming, and dreaded, for millennia, ever since Nick got promoted to Satan. Who would have thought things would come to a head on a quiet night, in such an unassuming place?

Now, you know I don't have free will. None of us devils, demons or angels do. It's true that Nick, though he was the Satan, was still in his probationary period. Leviathan and his crowd might still have been able to resist this Satan pro tem, but I had long ago given him my allegiance, and I could feel the compulsion to obey. I swallowed hard. "Nick," I said with difficulty. "I will, if you order me to. I find that I must. But for the sake of our friendship, for all our years together, please don't make me do this." I looked mournfully at him.

For a long time, Satan looked at me in silence, with a severity that he'd never displayed toward me, but then he softened. And sighed. "Very well, Beezy. I always have been and ever shall be your friend. How about only during formal occasions, down in Hell or on Gates Level, open houses, that kind of thing?"

Breathing a sigh of relief, I nodded. "Yes, that would make sense, and it's really not that different from what we've discussed before. The public needs to see you as the supreme ruler of Hell. Okay, you've got a deal ... my lord Satan," I added.

Satan laughed. "You're right, Beezy. It just doesn't feel right, having you talk to me that way, with all the deference and crap."

But I was the single exception. Lucifer had always been prideful, and the kind of public acknowledgment he craved was a logical outcome of his personal self-regard. From that day forward, he demanded that all other inhabitants of Hell treat him with the deference reserved for a head of state.

Chapter 26

The encampment woke to the sounds of chirping birds and the delighted shrieks of the queen.

"It's gone, it's gone!" she said, running out of her tent. "After all these years, my headache is gone!"

The king exited his own pavilion. "Wonderful news, my love, but, uh, why is your crown looped around your neck?"

"What?" she said, puzzled, then slipped it back to its proper position, only to have it fall back around her neck, stopping when it hit her shoulders.

I looked over at Nick, who was trying with minimal success to suppress a grin. "You shrank her head."

He shrugged. "It was the easiest way to relieve the pain."

"But now I can't call her Fathead," I said, disappointed.

"Sure you can," he said, patting me on the back, in an attempt to console me. "She'll always be Fathead to you."

I nodded then looked back to the queen, who kept trying to prop her crown at different angles atop her slimmed-down skull, to no avail. I approached her and bowed. "Your Majesty, it appears your crown has, ah, stretched a bit. Allow me." I slipped it off her neck.

"I have a tool in my saddlebag with which I can fix this in a trice." With that, I walked over to my mount.

"Be careful with that!" she called after me. "It's my favorite crown!"

I stepped around to the far side of my horse, willed the diadem down three full hat sizes and, without slowing my pace, came around the other side. "There! All fixed," I said, handing the crown back to her.

She placed it on her head. As expected, the crown fit again, and I was rewarded with a royal smile.

"That was fast!" Ferdinand marveled.

I shrugged. "Like I said, I've always been good with my hands."

Satan's bit of doctoring and the demonstration of my considerable handyman skills earned us respect among the entire assembly that day. And when some weeks later, I came up with the plans for the vaults above the central nave of the cathedral in Toledo, our place as favorites in the court of the Spanish Monarchs was secured.

For years, we'd come and go, visiting the royals wherever we found them. Frankly, I liked the two, as did Nick. And, though Isabella's head was no longer fat, and Ferdinand no longer struck me as a fool, my friend had been right. To me, they would always be Fathead and the Simpleton.

The year was 1485, and the royal court had moved to Cordoba. Spring came early that year. Even in March, the weather was balmy, not surprising, since Spain is a hot country, particularly the southern part.

We had shown up that morning to check with the monarchs on the progress of the Reconquista. Oh, and to pick up some olives. I had developed a taste for the Spanish varieties. As always, we were welcomed at court, but we had just missed their Royal Majesties. They were at church.

Standing outside the Alcazar, another name for "castle" on the Iberian Peninsula, Nick scratched his chin in thought. Then he gave me a perverse grin. "Care to see how the other half lives?"

"You mean go to church? Why not?"

That was a surreal experience. Well, going to church at all was a little weird for a couple of incognito devils, but it was made doubly bizarre in that we "worshipped" in what had originally been a mosque. A very big mosque. One might even have called it great.

The Great Mosque of Cordoba had its beginnings in the late Eighth Century, when its first phase was begun. After Cordoba was recaptured by the Christians in 1236, the mosque was consecrated as a Catholic church. In the Sixteenth Century, Isabella and Ferdinand's grandson, Charles I of Spain – who by the by also reigned as Holy Roman Emperor Charles V – consented to having a Renaissance cathedral plopped into the middle of the mosque. The results were hideous. Take it from me; I think by now you understand I know a bit about architecture. Even Charles regretted his decision, once he saw the results, saying to the Christian rehab team, "You have destroyed something unique to build something commonplace."

But back in 1485, the Christians had only added a few ugly touches to this magnificent mosque. Though a chapel had been built here, a cross hung there, the Great Mosque still lived up to its name. It was (and still is) fucking huge. And most of it still maintained the original character of the Muslim structure.

Seems like every time we encountered Ferdinand and Isabella, they were either in church or going to church or just having come from church. By these few clues, we gathered that they were extremely religious. In fact, just nine years later, they would be named by Pope Alexander VI the "Catholic Monarchs." This was in honor of their successful completion of the Reconquista, bringing the last piece of the Iberian Peninsula back into the Christian fold.

Oh, fun fact. Pope Alexander was a Borgia. He was, also, the father of Lucretia and Cesare. Weird, huh? He was a pope, yet he had at least six kids, and those kids went down in history as poisoners and pricks. Back then, though, being a pope wasn't the same thing as it is now. But I digress.

During the service, we had no opportunity to approach the monarchs, so we decided to catch up with them later, when they returned to the Alcazar. After church, Nick and I spent a little time admiring the exquisite architectural touches of the Great Mosque. As we were wandering beneath the many arches of alternating red and white brick, we spied a stranger, dressed in traveling clothes still dusty from the road. He was arguing with a priest. The stranger spoke perfect Spanish, though with an Italian accent.

"But really, Padre, I must see the king and queen. I have a wonderful business proposition for them and ..."

"My son," the patient priest said, "you have just missed them. They have already returned to the Alcazar. But I must tell you, you won't get in without an appointment."

"But I just got into town and haven't had time to ..."

"Go with God, my son," the priest said and turned his back on the stranger, who was biting his lip in frustration.

I recognized his type. In fact, I'd been much like him, back in my false god days. This fellow was a traveling salesman. I turned to Nick to say something snide, but never got out the words.

Nick was staring at the man with a curious intensity.

"What is it, Nick, I mean, Alonso? Do you recognize him?"

My friend grinned. "Yes," he said, excitement in his voice. "I believe I do. Unless I'm mistaken, he's what I've been looking for for a very long time."

"What?"

"He's the Catalyst."

I looked at him, puzzled, but all he said was, "Later."

The stranger was asking for directions to the Alcazar but getting the brushoff from everyone. I could see his exasperation grow.

"Young man," Nick said, "allow ..."

"I'm thirty-four years old, my lords, surely as old as you." The man seemed to have a bit of a chip on his shoulder.

"Not even close," I responded, with a snicker.

"Never mind that," Nick said, impatient to give destiny a jumpstart. "The Alcazar is only a few blocks from here. Let us show you the way."

As a rule, when Satan offers to show someone the way, said someone is usually the worse for the information. I'm sure you understand. In this rare instance, though, my friend was being helpful.

"What's your name, sir?" I asked, as we led him outside.

"Columbus. Christopher Columbus."

Sancho the Fat and Alonso the Popinjay introduced themselves to Columbus. Then we led him a quarter mile to the west, where the king and queen held court.

At the entrance to the royal castle stood Lothar, the doorman. Since he could read, he also doubled as a secretary of sorts. Lothar nodded to us – we were regulars at the Alcazar – but looked with suspicion at our companion. "State your business, sir."

"I'm here to see the Majesties," Columbus said.

"Do you have an appointment?"

Columbus, who did not strike me as a patient character, tried to control his temper, with small success. "No, I don't have an appointment! How could I? I just got in town."

"Well I'm sorry, but no one sees the king and queen without an appointment. Would you care to make one?"

Columbus sagged. "I guess so. What's the wait time?"

"I think I can get you in on Thursday. Ooh, sorry. My mistake. The queen is being fitted for a new horse that day. But," Lothar said brightly, "I can schedule you for the following Thursday. Will the following Thursday work for you?"

"No." Columbus scowled at the doorman, who took a step backward. He knew an implied threat when he saw one.

"Never mind, Lothar," Nick said. "Señor Columbus is here with us."

The doorman's tune changed at once. "Oh well, my lords. That's different. Please see yourselves in. You know the way." He shot a warning glance at Columbus, to whom he had taken a dislike. The feeling appeared to be mutual.

"Thank you, my lords," Columbus said, bowing deeply to the two of us. Anyone who was a regular at the palace was worth treating with respect.

Only centuries later did people like Chris, that is, salesmen types, begin to realize the importance of being polite to the person who controls the appointment book. Assistants such as Lothar and Radar O'Reilly rule the world. They are gatekeepers, and you antagonize them at your peril. Fortunately for Columbus, he had us on his side. At least for the nonce.

As we escorted Columbus through the halls of the castle, I wondered what was on Nick's mind. I dropped my mental shields and reached out to Satan with a thought. *You said he was the Catalyst. The Catalyst for what?*

Satan arched an eyebrow. *For ending this tedious competition with Leviathan.*

How?

My friend looked puzzled. *I'm not sure, but I have foreseen it.*

I nodded. That was good enough for me.

"Will I have to deal with another character like the doorman?" Columbus asked.

"No. You're with us now, and time is wasting." Nick grabbed Columbus by one elbow, gesturing for me to grab the other. "We're going to have an audience with the king and queen right now." We whisked him away, toward the throne room.

He looked down at his feet, which were about half an inch above the pavement. And then he looked at us, eyes wide, astonished that two lords could carry him along without even breaking a sweat. "Do you two work out?"

"We maintain a healthy lifestyle," I replied.

"Except for your pork rinds."

"Yes. Except for those. Now, are you ready for your audience with the Majesties?"

"Right now? But I haven't made myself presentable."

"You're fine," I said, willing away the perspiration and dirt from his clothes. "Just run a comb through your hair."

"I have no comb."

"Your fingers then."

We stood before the entrance to the throne room.

"Why are you helping me?" Columbus asked, as he ran his fingers through sweaty hair. Nick wiggled a pinkie behind his back, and the greasy mop styled itself into a becoming coif.

"Why, Señor Columbus, we like you. We are your new best friends."

"You do? You are?"

"Yes." Nick saw the king and queen, who had not had much of a head start on us leaving the cathedral/mosque, settle into their thrones. "Let me soften up the Royal Majesties – they're friends of mine, you know – and then you can try to sell them on whatever it is you have in mind."

261

For the first time, Columbus looked humble. "Thank you, my lords. I will be eternally at your service."

"That you will," Nick said, with a wry grin, then the three of us stepped inside.

Chapter 27

My lords Alonso and Sancho!" the queen squealed with delight. "It has been months since you have graced us with your presence."

Ferdinand got out of his throne and came down to shake our hands. "It is good to see you, my friends."

Back then, royalty didn't always stand on ceremony.

"How goes the war, your Majesty?" Alonso asked.

Ferdinand grimaced. "Oh, you know. We kill some of theirs; they kill some of ours. Faugh!" He said, which was the medieval equivalent of an obscenity. "Granada has been a vassal state of Castile for over two hundred years, but they've decided to stop paying tribute to us. Can you imagine? The nerve of the Emir! So, we decided to just take the whole shebang. Make Granada part of Castile."

He frowned. "Yet they haven't made it easy. We've been at it three years now, but the Emir refuses to yield. You'd think these Muslims would just give up, but they're remarkably stubborn."

"And doughty warriors," I added.

"You have that right," grumbled the king.

"Enough shop talk, you three!" Isabella said, not having risen from her chair. "Come talk to me about happier things. Alonso, have you traveled anywhere recently?"

I suppressed a smile. *To Hell and back, if that counts.*

"Nowhere of consequence, your Majesty," Alonso/Nick said, bowing to the queen and kissing her offered hand.

While we'd been saying our hellos to the monarchs, Columbus had been standing to one side in silence. Isabella noticed him. "And who is this?"

"A new friend of ours." Nick motioned to Columbus to join us before the two thrones, as Ferdinand regained his seat. "Your Majesties, may I present Señor Christopher Columbus."

Chris put on his best manners, bowing deeply.

"Señor Columbus has a wonderful opportunity he'd like to present to you."

Ferdinand looked suspicious. I guess, like me, he had an eye for spotting salesmen. "What?"

"I think it best that our new friend explains it himself."

Good. I'd been trying to read the young man's mind for some time, with no luck. I wasn't surprised. While devils and angels can communicate across the cosmos with just a thought, reading the minds of humans is much harder. Still, it was habit for me. Once we got them down to Hell, picking the thoughts from the brains of the Damned was a cinch, but a living human's brain was a closed book to us. Yet their actions almost always revealed their inner desires. Since all mortals were susceptible to one or more of the Seven Deadly Sins, they were easily manipulated.

"Your Majesties," Columbus said with a bow. "I am an explorer, a sailor from Genoa. I have an exciting business opportunity for Aragon and Castile."

"Castile and Aragon," Isabella corrected.

Ferdinand looked with displeasure at his wife. He was well aware that Castile was larger than Aragon, but he didn't like having his nose rubbed into the fact. "A business opportunity," he said, turning back to Columbus. "What is it?"

"It may surprise you to know that the Earth is not flat but round, like a pomegranate."

"Most assuredly it is round," Isabella huffed. "Everyone knows that."

"Only an idiot or commoner would think otherwise," her husband added.

"Ah, yes, well, I propose to use this fact to enrich you beyond your wildest imaginings."

"I don't know," Ferdinand said. "I can imagine quite a lot."

Columbus wasn't faring well. A little encouragement was in order. I patted him on the shoulder, gave him a smile. "Why don't you just tell us what you have in mind?"

He looked at me in gratitude then turned back to the monarchs. "The Silk Road between Europe and the Far East is a thing of the past. It soon will be replaced by sea routes, traversed by great ships that can transport vast amounts of goods in both directions, at far greater speeds than possible by land travel."

"Your Majesties, the age of exploration is upon us. Henry the Navigator of Portugal started his country on its path to finding a sea route to India, and his nephew, John II, has continued his work."

Isabella scowled at the mention of John's name.

"I predict a Portuguese ship will reach the tip of Africa before the decade is out. From there, it will be an easy matter to sail to India, where the goods and treasures of the Orient will be Portugal's. Yet, as I said earlier, the Earth is round."

"We heard you," the Royals said in unison.

Columbus, undeterred, continued. "Why sail so far south and then east, when a few stout ships could sail west, directly to India, saving thousands of miles?"

Despite myself, I snorted. *Because there are a couple of continents in the way.*

He doesn't know that, Satan commented.

Well, he should know at least that the distance is far greater than a short hop. The math proving this has been around since the ancient Greeks. He hasn't done his homework. Idiot!

"I don't know," Ferdinand said, scratching his beard in thought. "On the one hand, it finesses the Portugal problem ..."

A little background here. In the 1470s, Portugal and Castile had fought a war. The upshot: Castile won on the land and Portugal on the sea. Through four separate treaties, Portugal renounced any rights to the throne of Castile. In return, Castile gave up claim to many disputed territories in the Atlantic. This gave Portugal a huge advantage in exploring the western edge of Africa, which at the time was the only possible way of getting to India and the Orient by sea.

As Ferdinand said, a western route to India, assuming such a thing were possible, would finesse this problem, but ...

"... it's never been done. Dangerous, expensive and highly speculative, or so it seems to me." He looked over at his wife. "What do you think?"

Isabella frowned again then nodded. "Non terrae plus ultra."

I understood. "Non terrae plus ultra" or "No land further beyond" or colloquially "That's all she wrote" had been the unofficial motto of the Iberian Peninsula since ancient times. Gibraltar, the European side of the Pillars of Hercules was, by tradition, the end of the known world. Other than a few islands, there was no land beyond it, according to conventional wisdom.

Nick and I knew otherwise, but Isabella and Ferdinand did not, even if they intellectually grasped that the world was round. Sending ships west instead of east would require a major act of faith. And a ton of money.

To his credit, Columbus understood that. Seeing he was losing his prospective customers, he made an intuitive leap. In what was perhaps the most inspired moment of his life, he followed his hunch. "Your Majesties are known throughout Europe as the most devout of rulers."

"Well," Ferdinand conceded, "we do go to church a lot ..."

"In this voyage," Columbus continued, without skipping a beat, "we will come upon unknown people in unknown lands. Think of the opportunity we will have to spread the world of our Lord and Savior, to bring new souls into the fold of the Church."

Nick looked at me in triumph. *This is it! This is what we've been waiting for.*

A mental lightbulb switched to the on position. There were at least fifty million people in the two continents that lay to the west. At present, they were perfectly happy worshipping their own deities, but if, through an aggressive missionary campaign, a few threats and some bribes, even a quarter of that number were converted to Christianity, then ...

Then I'd win! They'd have to give me my job on a permanent basis.

And Leviathan and his cronies would be shut down once and for all. I nodded. Nick was right.

Chris now had the full attention of the monarchs. "You know," said Isabella, beginning to look enthusiastic, "this is quite a good idea."

"Yes, my queen, it is," Ferdinand agreed. Yet he looked troubled.

"What's wrong, your Majesty?" Alonso asked.

"Oh, it's just those blasted Muslims in Granada. They're keeping us awfully busy. It's hard to think about anything else right now, with the back and forth looting and killing and all."

267

Then the king brightened. "Why don't we put Señor Columbus's idea in the parking lot?"

He hopped off his throne and went to a nearby roll of vellum, the Fifteenth Century version of a flip chart. He wrote on the animal skin "Parking Lot," and then beneath the phrase the words, "Sail west. Find new lands and new peoples. Get riches. Convert the locals."

"There!" he said, pleased with himself. "Now we won't forget."

Columbus groaned.

Many people think that modern meeting techniques were all devised by management consultants over the past fifty years, but it's not true. The Parking Lot, for instance, is an ancient method for dismissing a good if inconvenient idea without appearing to do so. Julius Caesar himself came up with the parking lot tactic after he saw how putting a chariot in one neutralized said chariot, mainly because it was so hard for the horses to back out the damned thing.

Parking lots were bad news. I feared Columbus's idea would go nowhere.

"Perhaps you could create a committee to study the idea instead," Alonso suggested.

It was my turn to groan. Nick had always loved committees. For example, after we built Gehenna, he established a social committee to come up with diversions for off-duty devils. That group created the rock-paper-scissors game. They also invented tic-tac-toe. In Hell's early years, Nick set up a Wellness Committee, charged with helping newly made demons cope with "horn head," a debilitating condition not dissimilar to a migraine, tail spasms, and the carpal tunnel syndrome that many developed through overuse of their pitchforks.

Committees, planning retreats, strategic plans: Nick got off on all that stuff. Eventually, he would take his entire managerial toolbox to the mortal realm, establishing the field of management consulting in the late Nineteenth Century.

You're welcome.

Though Nick adored committees, I hated them. Usually, they were a bloody waste of time. Still, I had to agree that sending the idea to committee was better than putting it in the parking lot. That was, pardon the pun, a dead end.

And so, it was agreed. A commission would be established to study the idea. This would give the king and queen time to wage their war with the emir.

We left the castle that day with Columbus in tow. We found a local eatery that also served a quite passable red wine. It took two bottles to loosen the tongue of our new friend.

"I'm really discouraged," Columbus admitted. "First King John and now Queen Isabella and King Ferdinand."

"Oh," I said, pouring myself another goblet of wine, "so you asked John first. Turned you down flat, did he?"

"Not exactly. He was intrigued and referred the matter to some of his navigators. Not unlike," Columbus said with distaste, "what the Royal Majesties are doing now."

"Never mind that," Nick said. "At least they didn't leave the idea in the parking lot."

"Verily," Chris said, slamming back another goblet's worth of wine.

"What did John's experts say?" I asked, curious.

He grimaced. "That I underestimated the distance that would be required to get to India."

"Which was?"

"About twenty-four hundred miles."

"They're right. That estimate is way too low."

Columbus looked offended. "And how, Sir Sancho, would you know that? Are you a navigator too?"

I shrugged. "I dabble."

"But your idea is still sound," Nick said with a rush. "Even if the distance is greater, there may be undiscovered lands between here and India that would be worth exploring. Maybe untold riches await you and the Spanish Monarchs."

"Well, BURP, that would be nice, but I'm not sure we'll ever find out. My idea could be stuck in committee for years." Columbus stood. "Maybe I'll just go back to Portugal and try again with John. Besides, my wife is expecting me."

"You married a Portuguese woman?"

"Yeah. We have a kid. I think." With that, Columbus staggered out of the tavern and toward some nearby stables, where he'd told us he'd stashed his mule. He would soon be snoring away in a stall shared with his mount.

"He doesn't even know if he has a kid, so he can't be much of a family man." I looked at Nick. "We need to find a way to keep him in Cordoba for a while. Think we can find a way to distract him?"

Nick stroked his chin in thought then nodded. "Shouldn't be hard. I have a young woman in mind."

The next day, we caught Columbus on his way out of town. We offered to buy him a farewell drink, which is almost always a successful delaying tactic.

We were on our second bottle, when Nick excused himself. In moments he approached us with a raven-haired beauty. The young woman's name was Beatriz Enríquez de Arana. She was quite a charmer, due to some tutoring by Satan. Before long, she and Columbus left, headed for the sack.

"Well, that was easy," I said, pouring my friend some more wine.

"Yes, I've had my eye on her for some time. Beatriz loves the Genoese. They should have fun together."

"You think it's love?" I said, making mock moony eyes at him.

"Or lust. In the case of Columbus, he probably doesn't know the difference."

"No doubt. Do you think we can keep him here?"

Nick shook his head. "Not forever. In time, he'll go back to Portugal to see that wife and kid of his. When he does, he may approach John again with his idea. Let's hope not. Beatriz, though, should continue to draw him back to Cordoba."

As usual, Nick's prediction proved correct. When Beatriz had a child, whom Chris named Fernando, Columbus had even more reason to return to Cordoba.

Yet Nick and I knew that Ferdinand and Isabella had to win a war before they would be ready to even consider funding a sailing expedition beyond the ends of the Earth. And winning that war would take six more years.

It was a long time to have to stall.

Chapter 28

Unbelievable!" Ferdinand fumed.

"Now, dear, you know wars are expensive."

The king was sitting at a long table, a stack of paperwork in front of him. Isabella, on the other hand, was on her throne, knitting a new hauberk for her husband. Working with metal rings was a little harder than knitting with wool, but the queen was an expert at it. "Besides," she told me once, "it's something to do with my hands."

She was humming. Her husband was grumbling. "Look at this bill for hay! Unbelievable! How can horses eat so much hay?"

"It's better than wagon wheels, your Majesty," I said. I was at his side, trying to help with the paperwork. "You know, when horses get hungry enough, they'll eat wagon wheels. I've seen it happen."

He looked at me in desperation. "Why can't they just graze, like they're supposed to?"

I shrugged. "All the grazing lands around Baza have been stripped clean – by grazing horses. I think you'll find, though, that here is your biggest expense."

I handed him a stack of vellum. "What's this?" he asked.

"It's a report I've compiled on the cost of hiring mercenaries from the rest of Europe. Having all these fighters has been great for waging the war, but it's a good deal more expensive than using the locals."

"We're running out of locals," he moaned. "And no time to make more."

"Certainly true," I agreed. "We need at least sixteen or eighteen years for that, and if our estimations are correct, the war will soon be over."

"How can you be so sure?" Ferdinand wrapped his hands around his head. "I feel like my brain is going to explode."

"Here's a potion. Take two draughts and see me in the morning."

He eyed the vial with skepticism.

"Don't worry. Alonso prepared it for you. It's safe." This was not true. Well, the safe part was, but Nick hadn't prepared it at all. I'd just conjured it up on the spot. Ferdinand, though, after Nick's miraculous cure of the queen's macrocephaly, considered the faux-Alonso to be a great doctor. I played into that.

Ferdinand swallowed the contents. I could see the tension drain from his face. "I do feel better. Thank Alonso for me."

I tried not to roll my eyes. "To answer your question, Baza will fall any day to your forces. When it does, you will control the entire eastern province and be ready to lay siege to Granada. The endgame is near."

Isabella smiled. She and I had had a similar conversation the previous day in her garden, while she worked on her own hauberk. The king and queen of what would soon be a united Spain were partners in all things, even war.

Ferdinand sagged. "You're right, I know. We'll just have to find a way to keep paying these mercenaries. I'll increase everyone's taxes, but it will take a while to collect them." He looked at me. "Do you think I should get a payday loan?"

I shook my head. "Better not. Those things are dangerous."

"Perhaps a bake sale," Isabella offered, as she put the finishing touches to Ferdinand's chain mail shirt. Then she tossed it to him, knocking him out of his chair.

"Ow!" He said, holding his forehead as he climbed back into his seat.

She reddened. "Sorry about that."

"Hello everyone," Alonso said from the doorway. He and I were coming and going so often these days that the courtiers had long since stopped announcing us. "Look who is back in town."

At Nick's side was Christopher Columbus. "Your Majesties," he said, bowing low.

"Not him again," Ferdinand grumbled.

"Dear," Isabella chided, then bowed regally to the would-be explorer. "To what do we owe the pleasure of your visit?"

"I come with news from Portugal. Bartolomeu Dias has sailed past the southern tip of Africa."

"Well, bully for him," the king said with mock enthusiasm.

At a nod from Alonso, Chris continued. "Now that King John knows it can be done, the sea route to India will soon be complete, and controlling the major means of transporting goods from the East will make Portugal enormously rich."

Isabella frowned. The ongoing competition with Portugal was a distraction that Castile and Aragon could do without. "And what would you have us do?"

"Yeah," Ferdinand huffed. My, he was in a sour mood. "A little busy here, ya know."

"I was," Columbus hesitated, "I was wondering what the committee studying my idea for a western voyage has decided."

The king prepared to make another acid retort, but Isabella spoke first. "The idea is stuck in committee. Understand, the Royal We love, absolutely love this idea, but, well, we are in the middle of a war right now, and waging wars is expensive. I am afraid we are a little short of cash."

"You got *that* right."

"Ferdinand, please. Señor Columbus, until we can bring an end to the Nasrad dynasty, all of our resources must by necessity go to the war effort!"

The king was staring at a bill for saddle repair. "This is outrageous! Four gold ducats to mend a saddle. No way I'm paying that!" He crushed the bill in his fist and threw it over his shoulder.

The queen showed her empty palms to Columbus. Inwardly, I cursed. Chris couldn't have picked a worse time to touch bases with the monarchs.

Ferdinand looked up at Columbus. The king had the look of defeat in his eyes. He was a good general, but he was losing the war of the pocketbook. "Maybe you should just go back to John and see if he'd like two routes to India."

"Oh, no!" Isabella said in a hurry. "Don't do that. Just give us a little more time. The war will soon be over, the committee will finish its work, and we should be able to move forward."

Columbus hung his head. This back and forth between the courts of Portugal and Castile/Aragon had been going on for four years. "You needn't worry, your Majesty," he said, in a rare moment of candor, a bad quality for any salesman to have. "I've already approached King John, but now that he has his southern and eastern route, he's no longer interested."

Columbus did not see the look that passed between Ferdinand and Isabella. Nor did the young Genoese hear the queen's sigh of relief.

For all the expense and risk posed by the prospect of a western voyage, the Spanish royals were keenly interested in the idea. They weren't ready to do anything with the proposal, but they didn't want any other maritime power to steal what they saw as Spain's best chance to be a global player.

With a verbal pat on the back, and a cookie from a batch that had just arrived from the royal kitchens, they sent Columbus on his way.

The siege of Baza lasted seven long months. As Christian killed Muslim, and vice versa, Nick and I once again felt helpless, and indeed we were.

We were sitting on a high hill overlooking the action. This had become one of our favorite vantage points for watching the follies of mankind, which generally included a lot of slaughter and a fair number of wars.

"This is ridiculous!" my friend raged. "I could end this with a flick of my pinkie!"

"You said much the same, some seven hundred years ago, when Martel fought the Battle of Tours." I shook my head. "Talk about déjà vu."

"Things are worse, now."

"Yes. With the ratification of the Accords, our actions are even more circumscribed."

Nick's response was to spit on the ground.

The Heavenly Accords, which had been drawn up in the wake of Leviathan's little stunt with the Bubonic Plague, prohibited us from any significant involvement in the affairs of humans. We were still allowed to hustle for an individual soul or two, but a major show of power was forbidden.

Instead, we advised. We counseled, yet we did not directly interfere. On no account did we ride into battle, slaying the enemy. One thing the Accords codified was that devils don't kill people.

People kill people.

We got things done by tricking humans whenever we could, for that is the devil way. Take Columbus, for example. I'm sure Satan could have gotten his soul in exchange for a royal commission to the New World, but we decided not to bother. We were confident he would be ours in the Afterlife, whether he realized it or not, so confident, in fact, that we didn't deem it necessary.

Why did we feel this way? Well, there was the polygamy thing. Or was it adultery? Hard to tell, really, since he was equally devoted to his Portuguese and Cordoban families, though Chris's level of familial commitment left a bit to be desired.

No, we were sure what would condemn Columbus for eternity to Hell was his cruel nature. We saw examples of it all the time: stiffing a waiter in a tavern, beating up people weaker than he was, flogging a horse than was moving slower than he'd like. He was guilty of Wrath, one of Satan's signature sins. And we were confident Chris was just getting started.

Besides, he was easy to manipulate. We tricked him all the time, for he was a major chump.

Isabella and Ferdinand were another matter. Frankly, we would have loved to get them under contract, but they were so stiff-neckedly pious there was no chance of that. Can you imagine Alonso revealing himself to them as Satan? They would have clapped him in irons before he'd even had a chance to work his magic.

Not that irons could have held him. Still, it would have been undignified.

Even years later, when the Catholic Monarchs intensified their efforts with the Spanish Inquisition – which resulted in the persecution of Muslims, Jews and even the Roma people, who had recently emigrated to Spain – we were not confident Hell would get Isabella and Ferdinand. And indeed, we were right; they ended up in Heaven.

Back to Baza. We sat on the hill, watching the Castilian and Aragonese cannons pummel the city. The Muslims had little heavy artillery of their own. They were getting the worst of the exchange, and Nick predicted the town would be taken by week's end. "At least, I hope so. This is getting boring, and I've got stuff to do back in Hell."

"Me too. I just hope, if they capture Boabdil, they don't let him go again."

At this time, Boabdil, aka Abu Abdallah, aka Muhammed XII, was the Emir of Granada. He had been captured in 1483 and again in 1486, back when his father, Abu Hasan, was still in charge. Both times, Isabella and Ferdinand released him. This seemed strange to me. If I were in their shoes, I would have just killed him, but well, I *am* a devil and my respect for human life is perhaps suspect. Nick said it was all politics, but I'd never been a political animal. I had to trust him on that one.

Turns out Nick was right. The Spanish royals had cut a deal with Boabdil to start a civil war, with the promise of making him a duke with some limited autonomy in Granada after the war. Boabdil fought against his own father and later against his uncle, one of those guys named Al that I was telling you about earlier, in this case al-Zagal. Al caused problems for a long time. Only years later did we find out why he'd been so effective.

Turns out, his chief adviser was a fellow we liked to called Leviathan. When we weren't calling him asshole, that is.

Al and Leviathan were doing pretty well until they miscalculated and lost Malaga, the main seaport of the emirate. Mohammed shoved his humbled uncle to one side and became the undisputed Emir in 1487, ending the civil war in Granada.

Yet al-Zagal, deposed from power though he was, was not through. It was he, egged on by Leviathan, who was defending Baza against the siege. They held out a long time but were forced to surrender the town in 1489.

After the fall of Baza, the Spanish Monarchs took a break. Victory was in sight, yet they were tired, and they were broke.

The last act of the Reconquista, the siege of Granada, began in 1491, in the springtime. By then, the outcome of the war was hardly in doubt, yet it still took the rest of the year before Mohammed XII surrendered his emirate. Seems he felt the monarchs had not sufficiently rewarded him for his acts of treachery against his own family. Boabdil finally grew a pair and led the final defense of his all-but-extinguished emirate.

During this time, Christopher Columbus returned from Portugal to make one final pitch to their Royal Majesties. We helped broker yet another meeting between Chris and Isabella and Ferdinand, which took place in Santa Fe. Not the one in New Mexico; it hadn't been founded yet. No, this Santa Fe was on the western outskirts of Granada.

At that time, there wasn't much to Santa Fe. Most of the town had been torched, either by the enemy or an unattended campfire of the Spanish armies. Most people suspected the latter. In fact, this is where the expression "friendly fire" was first coined.

So, not only did the monarchs have a war to finish, they also had a town to rebuild. Suffice it to say they were busy.

Columbus had just returned from Portugal and headed to Cordoba. Nick was anxious to wrap things up, both the war, the Columbus proposal, and most especially Leviathan and his goons, so we dropped by Cordoba, waylaying Chris before he'd even had a chance for a connubial visit with Beatriz. Then we headed for Santa Fe, which was a little over a hundred miles to the southeast of Chris's second home.

I said we brokered the meeting, but that's not quite how things went. The guards had strict orders not to let Columbus, should he show, get within two hundred yards of the king and queen. So … we snuck him past Security. It was easy to do. Nick cast an invisibility spell over Chris. He didn't even know we'd done it and was surprised that Lothar didn't say hi to him. This was good; we didn't want to get in trouble for violating the Accords. Oh, we didn't mind violating them. We just didn't want to get caught.

Since Alonso and Sancho were still in the good graces of their Majesties, we were directed to the royal pavilion with little fanfare. Once out of Lothar's sight, we removed the spell. Easy-peasy.

We found the monarchs hunched over a table on which a detailed map of Granada and environs was spread. Ferdinand looked up as we came in the door. He sighed when he saw Columbus. "You again."

"How did you get in, sir?" Isabella looked at us severely. "Alonso, Sancho, this must be your doing. Be careful. Do not risk our royal displeasure."

Nick bowed deeply. "Your Majesties, we know this is a bad time, but your war is all but won. Don't you think it's time to consider what comes next?"

The king thumped his fist on the table. "What comes next is a vacation in Sicily. I'm king there too, you know."

"Yes," Isabella said, leaving the map and table and taking a seat on the porta-throne she used when away from court. She rubbed her forehead. I'd never seen her so tired. "Once this war is over, Ferdinand and I intend to take a nice vacation, maybe hit the beach. I can't really sunbathe – too fair for that, you know – but my clothiers have designed a truly marvelous sunbonnet that can handle the weight of my crown. We'll have the servants hunt for crabs along the shore, which we'll eat, along with lots of pasta, washing it all down with plenty of red wine. It will be glorious!" She closed her eyes and smiled, as I tried with limited success to picture the monarchs frolicking on the sand.

"That sounds, er, wonderful, your Majesty," I said, "but then what? Big plans take a long lead time. We should at least see what the committee has decided about Señor Columbus's proposal."

"The committee, the committee," Ferdinand said, looking puzzled. "What committee are you talking about?"

"The one you set up six years ago to study my proposal!" Columbus responded, an edge to his voice.

"Watch your tone, sir!" Isabella chided. "You wouldn't want your next trip to be to the dungeon."

The Genoan bit his lip, trying to hold back a retort that almost surely would have gotten him imprisoned. Fortunately, at that moment Ferdinand interrupted. "He's right about the committee, though. Damn. I'd forgotten about it. Rodrigo!" he shouted.

A small fellow in armor that was far too large for him came clanking into the room "You called, sire?"

"Do you remember what ever became of the Committee on Non Poo Poo?"

"What?" said Columbus.

"What?" said Rodrigo.

"You remember. The Committee on Turning Non Plus Ultra into Plus Ultra. Non Poo Poo." Reddening, he looked over at Columbus. "Sorry about that. The guys were just having a little fun."

Rodrigo brightened. "Oh. You mean the Committee to Examine the Merits of Sailing Westward to Discover a New Route to the Indies."

"That's the one."

"Last I heard, they couldn't convince anyone to be recording secretary. I fear they haven't met in years."

"What?" Isabella got out of her seat. "His Majesty and I established that committee, and we expect them to complete their assignment."

"That's right," huffed the king. Their Majesties may not have liked Columbus's semi-regular hounding, but they expected their subjects to obey commands. "Get them back to work immediately. We expect a report and recommendation in ..." He looked at his queen.

"One week," she said without hesitation.

"You heard her Majesty," Ferdinand said. "One week, and we expect charts. Lots of charts."

"We like charts," Isabella explained to me. Nick smiled. He was very fond of charts himself.

Ferdinand turned to Columbus. "Come back to us in a week, and we will have your answer." Then the king looked down at his map. Isabella rejoined him, and the three of us were forgotten. We stood around, feeling awkward, for a minute then left the room.

Columbus led the way through the encampment. Boy, was he steamed! "Six years of my life, and that crap committee didn't even finish its work."

I patted him on the back to console him. "This often happens with committees. They don't finish or fail to produce a product anyone wants."

"Well, they'd better come up with an answer soon, and it better be an answer I like or, or …"

"Or what?" I asked, curious. It was clear Portugal wasn't going to back him in his proposed expedition. What would he do if Spain wouldn't either?

"I'll go north to France and see if Charles is interested."

Charles VIII, known as Charles the Affable, was not known as a seafaring man. He was more interested in conquering lands on the Italian peninsula. If asked, he would almost certainly say no to Columbus. But at least he'd be affable about it.

Just as well it never came to that. Charles inadvertently killed himself only a few years later, at the tender age of twenty-eight. He wasn't paying attention to what he was doing and slammed his head against the lintel of a door in his own chateau.

I'm not kidding. Look it up. He died young, clumsy … but affable.

"So," I said, trying to keep up with Columbus, who had reached the outskirts of the encampment. "You would give up all your years of cultivating the Spanish Monarchs."

"Why not? I can't see it's done me any good, except for waste a lot of time."

"I think that's a very good idea, you going to France," said Nick, a thoughtful look on his face.

What? I thought at him. *Have you lost your mind? What about all the time we've put into this little venture?*

Nick smiled. *Listen and learn.* Then he spoke. "If Isabella and Ferdinand tell you no, you should proceed with your plan. And make sure you tell them what you're going to do, that you're going to France. They'll hate that."

Ah. Competition among the European royals. I looked in admiration at my friend. Nick had become a master at manipulating humans.

Columbus had reached the banks of the river Genil, where he took a seat on a large rock situated near the water's edge. "I, I don't really want to go to France."

"We know you don't, my boy," Nick said heartily. "You just need to tell them that you're going and then head out, preferably in a huff. But only if they say no to your proposal, got it?"

I thought that last part pretty obvious.

"Then what? I don't understand."

"Leave the rest to me," Nick said.

Chapter 29

The week crawled. Columbus hated sitting around with nothing to do, so we kept him drunk most of the time. That worked okay.

On the day we were to meet with the king and queen, the three of us stopped by the stables, saddled up Chris's mule, and led it to the edge of the army encampment. He tied the beast's reins to a nearby tree.

"I still don't know why I needed to bring Daffodil."

"Appearances and dramatic effect," Nick replied. "If the news from the committee is bad, and you indeed need to ride off in a huff, best you do so immediately. Trust me on this. It will make more of an impression on the monarchs."

Lothar had been expecting us. He waved us through.

The royal pavilion was crowded when we got there. Along with the king, queen and Rodrigo, seven gray-haired eminences filled the space. Some sort of disagreement must have been underway. The faces of the eminences were pale, ashen even. The queen's was beet-red. Ferdinand's, though, was a rich purple, like an eggplant. He looked as if he soon would be an exploding eggplant.

The king was preparing to shout something at the men, when we entered the tent. With an effort, he held his tongue.

Isabella, as angry as her husband, demonstrated great control and grace when she greeted us. "Ah, Alonso and Sancho, how good to see you. And Señor Columbus. We were, ah, just discussing the recommendation of the committee."

"Well," Nick said in a cheery voice, "how wonderful. What has the group decided?"

A very tall and thin old man – he must have been the chair of the group – stepped forward. Nick and I were shocked when we saw him. It was Ziz. A small smile bent the corners of his mouth.

That explained why the committee hadn't done anything in six years.

Ziz was very good at emulating the movements of an old man. As he walked, he swayed back and forth, like a willow branch in a strong breeze. He feigned concern as he glanced at His Royal Majesty, who appeared to be hunting for a paper weight to throw at the gent. Ziz cleared his throat. "It is the considered opinion of this committee that the proposed voyage is fraught with risk. Aside from the dangers to captain and crew, there's the capital investment of the Crown to consider. We deem the voyage a bad investment and advise the king and queen to save their money for safer projects."

"What?" roared Columbus. "You can't be serious!"

Confident that the committee would reject the idea, we had given Chris a script to follow. Nick felt that showing a little outrage, provided it was directed at the committee and not the monarchs, would play well.

"I am afraid, sir, that we are very serious," the chair continued. "In addition to the cost and the dangers, we feel that you have grossly underestimated the distance you would have to travel to reach India by sailing west."

Columbus closed his eyes for a moment. Script or no script, he was very upset, and he tried to calm himself. When he opened them, he spoke in a quiet voice. "For six years, I have been patient, waiting for this committee to make its recommendation. A lengthy sailing voyage is always risky, but it would not be the committee members facing the dangers. It would be me and my crew. And the costs? Pfaugh! Nothing compared to the benefits."

Chris regarded the king and queen. They both seemed distraught. It was clear they wanted the benefits such a venture might garner without taking the risks. Now, any good salesman could have taken those looks as a sign that his prospective customers were waffling. He could have turned it into a sale.

But Chris was *not* a good salesman. Never had been, not in the six years we'd known him. Besides, Nick had instructed him to accept the committee's recommendation as final. As he was coached, he bowed to the king and queen. "I thank you for considering my proposal, but it seems clear now that you will not sponsor me. It is my intention to ride to France and offer the project and my services to Charles the Affable. He has already expressed interest."

That last part was not true. We only told Chris to say that, thinking it might ratchet up the tension.

"In fact, I shall leave at once." With a bow, and before anyone could say another word, he left.

Ferdinand had been speechless for the entire scene, but at last his tongue was loosened. "You idiots!" he yelled at the committee. "Now you've gone and driven him off."

"But sire ..." said the vice chair.

"Shut up and let us think!" Isabella snapped.

"Oh dear, oh dear," Nick dithered. "This is terrible! It's such a good idea. I just know it is. Quick, Sancho! Go after Señor Columbus and see if you can convince him not to leave."

This was scripted as well. Flashing a look of worry at the group, I hurried from the tent. It didn't take long to catch up with Columbus. He was twenty feet beyond the pavilion, a hand cupped to one ear as he attempted to hear what was being said.

"Now, none of that, my friend. Stick with the plan. Here, I'll walk you to your mule." Then I took off at a brisk clip.

"I still don't know why we have to go through with this charade," he said, panting a little, in his effort to keep up with me. "Why are you so sure this will spur them to action, when six years of pleading haven't?"

"It's human nature, my boy. Up until now, the king and queen knew your idea was theirs for the taking."

"But the King of Portugal ..."

"Is no longer interested, and you know it. He has mapped his own route to India."

"But it's longer!" Columbus protested.

"So you say," I responded evenly, not mentioning the two inconvenient continents that were placed between Spain and India — or that I knew, like everyone else who had studied this, that his math was way off. He had no idea about the Pacific Ocean and how vast it was. There were more than fifteen thousand miles separating Spain from India, as the westward-wending devil flies, and said devil could hop over those continents I just mentioned. "And your proposal *is* risky. John doesn't need to take that risk, since he controls most of the traffic in the Atlantic, especially along the African coast."

We passed Lothar, whose nose was buried in his appointment book; he didn't even notice us. I loosened Daffodil's reins and handed them to Columbus. "But Charles, well, they have no idea what he'll say."

Columbus bit his lip. "I feel kind of bad about lying to them."

I patted him on the back. "Don't worry about it. They'll never find out, and if they did, you can always plead plausible deniability."

"What?"

"Skip it. Get on your mule and ride, Chris. Head north, and don't travel too fast. I wager you won't get twenty miles before you're asked to return."

Columbus climbed into the saddle. "This seems like a lot of trouble but, as you say, sir." With that, he put his heels to Daffodil and trotted off.

No one was looking, so I teleported to a grove of trees just outside the pavilion. There was some yelling coming from inside, most of it being generated by Ferdinand. I ran into the tent.

"Too late, your Majesties," I puffed, as if winded. "Columbus has already left Santa Fe."

Isabella looked to her husband. "I feel we are letting an opportunity slip through our fingers."

"Oh, my Queen, I fear you are correct," Nick said, shooting Ziz a look filled with venom. "And it's not just the treasures made possible by the western route you will be losing. There is something far more important at stake."

"What do you mean, Alonso?" Ferdinand asked. "What could be more important than money, especially now when the royal coffers are nearly depleted?"

Nick, playing his role for all it was worth, raised his eyes to the clouds and assumed a look of piety. "All of those souls, thousands upon thousands of people who have not heard the words of our lord and savior. For did He not say, "Be fruitful and multiply?"

"Uh, I think the Queen and I already did that," Ferdinand said.

I rolled my eyes. "I think, in his distress, Alonso quoted the wrong passage of the Bible. He meant the Great Commission, as found in Matthew twenty-eight, verse nineteen." I cleared my throat. "Ahem. Go ye therefore, and teach all nations, baptizing them in the name of the Father, and of the Son, and of the Holy Ghost."

Nick frowned at me. "Yes, yes. That's what I meant."

Isabella and Ferdinand turned their gaze upward, looking for the spot in the heavens Nick had been staring at a few seconds before. Their faces were rapturous, and they crossed themselves.

"Yes," Isabella exhaled. "For this is our true destiny. To spread the word of the Lord. To bring new souls into his House."

"Amen." Ferdinand bowed his head. "Rodrigo!"

The smirk Ziz had been wearing since I reentered the room dropped from his lips, and his eyes widened. At that moment, he realized what Nick and I had been doing all along. *This was never about reconquering Hispania!*

I grinned. *Oh, that was just gravy. But the new Christian souls: that was the main goal all along.*

You'll … you'll never get away away with this!

Nick glared at him. *We already have.*

Rodrigo entered the room and rattled his way to the king's side. "Yes, my liege?"

"Send riders to bring Señor Columbus back here. And tell them to treat him with respect."

"Yes, my king!" The rapid clanking of a running knight faded into the distance.

Ferdinand turned toward his committee. "And as for you! Your committee is dissolved."

The chair of the group was silent.

"But," said the vice chair. "Our recommendation?"

The queen looked severely at him. "Is not accepted."

"Get out of our royal sights!" Ferdinand snarled.

Eyes wide, the committee members bowed to the monarchs then backed out of the room. Ziz was frowning. As he stepped through the door, he glanced at us. *Well played, you jerks.*

At Nick's signal, I followed the committee out of the room. Then I teleported to where Daffodil and his rider were trudging along the road north. I guarded them until the riders caught up with Columbus fifteen minutes later. A direct attack on Chris would have been against the Accords, but we were taking no chances.

When Columbus returned, he was treated with all the respect he'd always wanted. The king and queen agreed to sponsor, that is, fund his voyage. Following our advice, Columbus negotiated a good deal for himself. He wanted ten percent of any profits. He also wanted to join the ranks of nobility, and to be made governor of any newly discovered territories.

At first, the royals balked at the terms, but Alonso pointed out that if Columbus succeeded, the gains would far outweigh the cost of these concessions. If he failed, he'd most likely be dead, and then Spain would only be out of pocket for the ships, supplies – oh, and the lives of a few Spanish sailors.

On January 2, 1492, Isabella and Ferdinand rode into Granada and received the keys to the city. They at once converted the town mosque into a Catholic church. This, by the way, was a tradition for both religions. Forty years earlier, the Muslims made a mosque out of the Greek Orthodox Hagia Sophia when they took Constantinople in 1453. And I already told you about the insertion of a Catholic Cathedral right in the middle of the Great Mosque of Cordoba.

One of the nice pieces of real estate the Spanish Monarchs acquired as part of the defeat of the Emir was the Alhambra. Beautiful place. It sits on a small mountain overlooking Granada. Great views. Because the Muslims built

291

such magnificent buildings and designed breathtakingly gorgeous gardens, Isabella wanted to take occupancy at once.

"Well, dear," said Ferdinand, "we can certainly spend some time here, but the royal traveling show must go on."

"Don't ruin my flush of victory, okay?" She looked through an ornately carved window on the second floor and saw an exquisite fountain in the courtyard below.

"Yes, dear."

Isabella moved to one side of the window so Ferdinand could look out as well. "Besides, I'm tired of all this travel. Why don't we just make this our royal court?"

Ferdinand looked thoughtful. "This is certainly a step up from our other homes. What do you think, Sancho?"

I was admiring a horseshoe arch separating two rooms. "I think you could do much worse. The craftsmanship here is impeccable, and some of the filigree exquisite. This place is both lovely and sturdy. It's built to last."

"See?" Isabella said. "Even the royal architect approves."

I wasn't the official royal architect, but with the improvements to the cathedral in Toledo and other small building projects with which I'd helped the Royals over the years, they thought of me that way.

The king smiled. "Then I approve as well. And if it's going to be the Royal Court, we might as well conclude some business."

"What do you mean?" his wife asked.

"Look who's here."

Up the stairway came Alonso, Columbus in tow.

"So, Señor Columbus," said the queen. "Are you ready to sign our agreement? I assume the terms are to your liking?"

"Yes, your Majesty," Chris said, with a huge grin. "When do I get to be called *Sir* Columbus?"

"When you make it back alive," Ferdinand said evenly. "Until you do, you're just a sailor with three of our ships and a lot of our money. See you make good on our investment."

"I will, your Majesty. Where do I sign?"

The queen made a motion, and Rodrigo set out the royal commission on a nearby table. The document was duly signed, witnessed and certified. The date was April 17, 1492.

From the moment of the signing, Nick posted a squad of devils to guard Columbus. They were invisible and did not interfere with anything, yet they stayed with Chris through all his adventures, making certain he, his ships and his men encountered no trouble from Leviathan's thugs.

Columbus left Granada in May, making a stop in Cordoba to see his Spanish squeeze and their son, Fernando. Despite the intrepid explorer's bravado, I imagine he wondered if he would survive his journey and see his loved ones – both sets of them, the Spanish and the Portuguese – again.

On August 3, Columbus set sail from Palos. The Pinta, the Niña, the Santa Maria, the commander and their crews sailed west and, while not discovering a better route to India, they did find country hitherto unknown to Europe, which Columbus claimed for the Spanish crown. The lands, combined with the new foods and spices he discovered there, turned Spain, for a time, into the greatest and richest empire in the world.

And the souls! All the glorious souls, ripe for conversion. Not that they particularly wanted to convert. They were very happy with their own pantheon of gods, but Columbus and later Spanish explorers gave them little choice. They either played ball with the conquistadors or got slaughtered. Or enslaved, if they were lucky.

I always felt bad about this, but as Nick often points out, religion is a zero-sum game. One belief system seems to win only at the expense of another. Unless you're Buddhist. Then you can be a Christian Buddhist, a Jewish Buddhist or ... well, you get the idea.

Alonso the Popinjay and Sancho the Fat were never seen again by the king and queen, much to the disappointment of the monarchs, who had grown fond of their faux courtiers over the years. "I wonder where they've gone off to," Isabella would sometimes say.

"As do I," agreed her husband, but they were too busy to worry for long. There was power to consolidate on the Iberian Peninsula, riches to plunder from the New World, an Inquisition to run. Busy times indeed.

Yet by all accounts, or at least the Eurocentric ones, the victory of the Catholic Monarchs was complete. And so was ours.

"Game over," Nick announced to me with a grin.

Chapter 30

Imagine Columbus's surprise, after dying, at being received into Hell by Satan himself. Columbus, owing to his acts of extreme cruelty to the native population in the Americas, was not allowed to take the Stairway down to the Underworld. Instead, after Saint Peter gave Chris the bad news, he was pitched into the Mouth of Hell by some demons we'd stationed there to perform the task. He fell all the way down to the Ninth Circle.

For five minutes, he lay groaning on the Persian carpet that Nick had recently installed in his office waiting area. During that time, the bones of the newly-damned's ectoplasmic frame, which had shattered on impact, reknit themselves, which is what they do in Hell, mainly so that we devils or our demons can break them all over again, if we so choose. When the pain receded, Columbus looked up. There, standing before him, a quizzical look on his face, was the form of a man Chris had known in life.

"Alonso!" he cried, still lying on the carpet. "You're in Hell too?"

"So it would seem," Nick said, barely suppressing a chuckle.

"And Sir Sancho! Is that you over there?"

I was installing a desk in the front office. If this had been a normal job, I would have had Charlemagne and Nero handle it, but Satan wanted it done right, and they would have just botched things. "Present and accounted for."

Columbus got to his knees, then to his feet. "Oh, the horror, that we three should be consigned to this fiery Inferno. Uh … where's the fire?"

"Different floor," I said.

"Oh."

"And we're not really consigned here," Nick added, "not like you are."

"But, but you're here, just like me."

"Yeah," I said, brushing some dirt off my hands and walking over to join the two. "But that's by choice."

"By choice? But only a devil or demon would ..."

"Bingo," I said, with a grin. "Oh, by the way, my name isn't Sancho. It's Beelzebub."

"Beelzebub? The great lord of the flies?"

"Yep."

"And, you," he said to Nick in fear. "Your name isn't Alonso, is it?"

"'fraid not." There was a puff of smoke, obscuring Chris's view of Nick. When it cleared, Satan stood before Columbus in full devil regalia, horns, tail, pitchfork, cloven hooves, the works.

Columbus, hands before his face, cringed. "Il diavolo!" Chris said in his native tongue.

"With a capital D, yes. I am Satan, Earl of Hell, and you have been damned for all eternity. Bwahahahahahaha!" It was a pretty good laugh, though everyone knows I do it best.

Columbus looked to me. Somehow the Lord of the Flies was less intimidating to him than the Prince of Darkness. "But why?"

"Probably had something to do with all those natives you killed."

"That makes no sense. I was just doing my job."

Satan no longer looked amused by the situation. "Yes, but you were unnecessarily savage about it. You enjoyed all the pain you caused. Even Isabella was troubled by it. Told me so

296

herself, when I ran into her near the Pearly Gates a couple of years ago. You were a cruel governor, a wrathful man, and as you may know, Wrath is one of the two cardinal sins in which I take a particular interest."

"You are mine, Columbus, and I will see that you are in agony forever."

Chris swallowed hard, then nodded. "I am ready for the fire and brimstone. I shall steel myself."

Nick shook his head. "No fire and brimstone for you, at least not on a regular basis. That's passé. I have something better in mind."

"Like what?"

Satan flashed his most diabolical smile. "I'm making you my personal secretary," he said, pointing at the desk.

A great load seemed to lift from the great explorer. "Well, that doesn't seem too ba ..."

"You will be responsible for scheduling all of my appointments, doing the office filing. Oh, and writing all the status reports. We do lots of status reports down here."

"Arggh!" Chris screamed, his fingers clutching at the air before him, as if he could in that way steady himself. "But I *hate* writing reports!"

"Don't I know it! Isabella commented on that too." The Earl of Hell pointed imperiously at the desk. "Now, get to work, and don't forget to sign up for new employee orientation."

Columbus wailed in agony. Some teeth may also have been gnashed.

The so-called discoverer of the New World served as Satan's personal secretary for almost five hundred years. Then we decided to take advantage of his penchant for cruelty by making him a demon. We replaced him with Bruce, a former martial artist and movie star, when he came to us in the 1970s.

Chris may have ended up in Hell, but he did us quite the favor. His actions led to the end of a multi-billion-year pissing match between Nick and Leviathan.

Two new continents came into the world view, and Columbus and the conquistadors who came after him converted, mostly through force, many natives to Christianity. The discovery and exploitation of the New World was the finale of the competition between Satan and Leviathan.

I remember when the memo came, ending Nick's probationary period and granting him career status as Satan. I was in the Eighth Circle, sitting on a mountain top, enjoying some alone time, when Nick materialized at my side. "Look at what I have." He handed me the memo.

I read it then handed it back. "Very nice. You should have the memo framed and hang it in your office."

Satan stared thoughtfully at the note, then folded and placed it in his pocket. "Either that, or stuff it down Leviathan's throat."

"Don't you think it's time to call in the rebels?"

"Yes, they've been revolting long enough."

"Har, har. Ziz used that same line on you when you first became Satan, remember?"

"Yes. A lot of water under the bridge since then." My friend sat in quiet thought for a few minutes then turned to me. "Do you mind if we do it here?" Without waiting for an answer, he waved his hand, and the other princes of Hell materialized on my mesa.

"I guess not. Hi, Sekhmet. Hi guys."

Sekhmet gave me a kiss, her whiskers tickling my nose. "Is this the day I get to stop being a prince of Hell?"

"I think so." I looked at Nick. "Clemency?"

Satan frowned. "Yes. It will make this a lot easier on everyone, though I'd really rather have the rebels cleaning latrines in New Rome."

"Then why not do that instead?" I asked. I was a bit peeved at the others myself.

"Management upstairs asked me to take this different route." Satan snapped his fingers, and hundreds of devils that I hadn't seen in many years appeared on the mesa with us. In the front were Leviathan and his two chief lieutenants, Ziz and Behemoth.

Leviathan stared at us wide-eyed. "How did we get here?"

"I summoned you." Nick stood before them like a king. "A ruler can do that with his subjects, you know."

"And what makes you think you're our ruler?" Ziz hissed.

"My probationary period just ended. I got the Satan job permanently. Which means," he said, staring at all the newcomers on the mountain top, "that you no longer have any choice but to obey me."

Mammoth looked at Satan with a measure of skepticism. "And why's that?"

"Because you have no free will."

"Oh."

"That means nothing!" Leviathan roared, advancing on Nick. "And now that I'm here, I'll …"

"Silence!" And, wonder of wonders, Leviathan shut up. No free will, indeed. All those years we'd fought: at times it didn't seem worth it, but seeing Leviathan at last come to heel was very satisfying.

Nick was transcendent. "I am Satan, the Earl of Hell. Bow before me!" And we did. Me, I just nodded my head in acknowledgment, but the others, well, they prostrated themselves in direct proportion to the degree in which they had resisted Nick's authority.

Leviathan was on his belly, using his tongue to scoop up ash from the ground.

Nick winked at me, a private gesture that only I saw.

"Princes of Hell, please rise and accept my thanks for your years of service. You have your jobs for as long as you want them, but if any of you would like to go back to being regular devils, now is the time to tell me."

"I'm out," Abaddon said. "I was never any good at being a boss."

Thank badness. He's been a disaster. Satan picked up on my thought and nodded.

"Me too," Astaroth said. "I did my best, but I don't think I was ever cut out for management."

Sekhsie was next. "I've never made any secret of my dislike of being a 'Prince of Hell.' I'm out too."

Nick nodded. "Very well. And again, you have my thanks. What about you, Belphegor?"

"I think I'll stay." Belphegor had assumed his new appearance, that of a giant slug. "I've gotten the hang of the job."

"Indeed, you have. We're glad that you've chosen a career in management."

"Thanks. May I go now?"

Nick smiled. He was always fond of Belphegor, and the fine work the Prince of Sloth had done over the ages was not lost on Satan. "Certainly, old friend."

"Good. It's nap time. It's *always* nap time for me." With that, Belphegor disappeared.

Satan nodded. "That means I have three open slots for princes of Hell. You three who have led the rebellion against me, step forward. Oh, that's right. You're still prostrate on the ground. Everybody! Get up, then Leviathan, Behemoth and Ziz step forward."

"Now, I could just order you to do this, but I'm going to be nice about it. Would you three like to be princes of Hell?"

They looked at him in astonishment. Then, one by one they nodded.

"Ziz, you're a randy one. You will be the prince of lust. And your name shall be ... Zizmodeus ... no, that just sounds stupid. Asmodeus you shall be called. Sekhmet, that was your job. Will you show him the ropes?"

"Gladly," she said, eyeing her replacement with a small grin. My face reddened, knowing how Sekhsie would begin training her successor. Sekhmet always did like variety, and Ziz, I mean Asmodeus, had been unavailable for a long time. She winked at me then reached out her hand to the new Price of Lust, teleporting them to the Second Circle.

Behemoth, or Mammoth, became Mammon, Prince of Greed. Astaroth took him to New Rome for orientation.

That left Leviathan. Satan didn't have a better name than that. Oh, he had Whiner and Crybaby, but they didn't have much dignity to him. Leviathan became the Prince of Envy, appropriate I think, and he left with Abaddon for the Seventh Circle of Hell.

"The rest of you!" Nick shouted. "For now, just spread out across Circles Two through Eight and torment some of the Damned, but show up in my reception room come Monday morning. My new secretary will have your assignments ready for you."

"Yes, my lord!" they cried with one voice. A few of these teleported away, but only a handful. The rest of them sprouted wings and flew off.

"Nicely done, my lord Satan," I said, a small smile on my lips.

"Thanks." Nick yawned. "Well, it's been quite a busy few thousand years, but at last, all the pieces are in place. Let's put this place on a high burn!"

The rebellious devils have all settled in and become good workers, though Leviathan's envy of Satan can be a bit much to take at times. Still, there has been no argument about who runs Hell for over five hundred years.

And yes, Satan is still my boss, but he doesn't rub my face in it. He knows we did all this together and that his victory was my victory too.

Go Team Satan.

There's not much more for me to tell you, except for perhaps my voice, or rather, how I finally found it. Funny how that happened. I was standing on the edge of the bazaar that sits near my office on the Eighth Circle of Hell, when a swarm of worshipping flies overwhelmed me. They flew at my face, into my mouth, up my nose, buzzing all the while. One of the bugs even got lodged in my throat, and to this day I can't seem to cough him out of my windpipe. The flies were so glad to see me that they had the "zzz" sound going at about a hundred and fifty decibels. It was driving me nuts.

"Buzz off, you!" I said testily, but my voice was oddly transformed. It sounded lower to me, and my zee sound came out with a raspy quality. It was interesting, so I tried again. "Zzzoom away or I'll zzzap you!"

I guess I said it a little too loud. Most of them lay dead or stunned at my feet.

"That's perfect!" Nick said.

"Where did you come from?"

"Where else? The Ninth Circle. I wondered if you wanted to go for sushi."

"Sounds good."

Satan looked down at the still black insects who lay at my feet. "It certainly took you long enough."

"Long enough for what?" I said, brushing the dead bugs out of my way.

"To find your voice. Do you realize it's been thousands of years since I first suggested it?"

I shrugged. "Whatever." I did like the voice, though.

An extract from

The League of Unusual Denizens
(A Circles in Hell Novel)

Featuring the return of Steve Minion

Prologue

The universe is full of many wonderful sights – planets, solar systems, galaxies, alternate dimensions – but none are as mind-blowing as the metaphysical realm that houses Heaven, Hell and the spaces in between.

Of course, few beings have had the opportunity to gaze at the realm from a proper perspective. First off, it's quite large, so a little distance is needed to see the whole thing. Second, one must observe it from "outside." And what is outside of Heaven and Hell? Chaos.

Chaos is a funny place. Light and dark sort of smoosh together, this being Chaos and all, the same Chaos out of which the Almighty created the heavens and the earth. But, well, He didn't need *all* of Chaos, at least not at the time. There was plenty left over at the end of all Creation, so the stuff was put in storage. After all, you never know when you'll want to knit a sweater or cobble some shoes or create another galaxy. That kind of thing. Having a little of the old Chaos lying around is a good thing. It's like a cosmic Parts Department.

Oh, you may wonder where our universe resides in relation to Chaos. The Heavenly Realm, which includes its wholly owned subsidiary, Hell, sits between them, both as a buffer and mediator of sorts. This is by necessity. The regular universe is chaotic enough. For example, there's Congress. And Chuck-e-Cheese. We don't need the primordial version of Chaos rendering the universe in which mortals reside any more dysfunctional than it already is. Thankfully, Heaven and Hell are proof against even Chaos.

More or less.

In order to get that rare panoramic view of the Heavenly Realm, you need to be at least fifty miles, minimum, out in Pandemonium. Only then can you get a sense of the shape of Paradiso and Inferno, and the cosmic light switch of Chaos must stay in the "on" position for longer than a moment, rather than constantly switching off and on, as it is wont to do. Doesn't happen very often, a brief period when one can count on a little direct lighting, but it does happen. If a broken clock can be right twice a day, light in Chaos can occasionally be useful for illumination.

So be patient, and eventually you will see the Realm, or at least the outside of it. The insides are another matter, but on the outside, Heaven and Hell look much like ... wait for it ...

A giant carrot.

That's right. A carrot, and a stumpy one at that. At least in shape. Hell corresponds to the orange part, a vast cone. Heaven is the greens, or in this case, the whites. They flow from the top of Hell, up and out. The Whites appear to sprout from the crown of Hell, or rather from Gates Level, the cosmic Demilitarized Zone where St. Peter sorts the dead into damned and saved souls. Heaven is ginormous, much larger than Hell, even though the former is intended to hold a much smaller population than its infernal counterpart.

So, I suppose, the whole thing looks like an infinite carrot, about nine miles of it being Hell, the rest of it being Heaven. When I say infinite, I of course exclude the Chaos in which you're standing. Infinity, as you may know, comes in different sizes. Chaos combined with Heaven, Hell and the rest of the universe is just a bigger infinity.

Don't like the carrot simile? Then how about this? Hell looks like a spinning top, and atop that top is the mother of all flashlights, its diffuse lens sending beams of photons upward and outward for as far as the eye can see.

Farther, actually.

Now, let your vision settle on a spot about where the big, spinning top meets the even larger light beam. There you will notice something very odd. What's that? you ask. A gargantuan eye staring outward into Chaos?

In a way, yes, but to truly understand what you are seeing, you once again need to change your perspective. You must leave Chaos, though you don't need to pass through Heaven or Hell, even provided you had a passport to one of those two places. It is time to enter the Interstices.

The what? you ask. The Interstices. Before leaving Chaos, take another look at the Celestial Realm. Closer examination will reveal that there is an outer membrane enveloping and protecting all of Hell and as much of Heaven as the eye can perceive. Coursing through that membrane are thousands of veins. Well, they aren't really veins but passageways, maintenance tunnels. The Interstices is comprised of this membrane and its tunnels.

Let us now leave Chaos and slip into one of those veins. To minimize our walk, we enter a passageway close to the monstrous eye we were just regarding. The tunnel, not unlike what you might find in a coal mine, is easily walkable. A few dozen yards and we are at our destination: a large door made of stout yew. Open the door – put your shoulder to it, since it's quite heavy – and step inside.

You have entered a cavernous space, paneled in the same black wood that formed the door. In the center of the area, a spiral staircase corkscrews thirty feet into the air. We follow the stairways, treading softly so as not to disturb the single other occupant in the room.

You, as the reader, and I, as the narrator, are the other two, of course.

At the top of the stairs, we encounter a small, blue creature. He appears to be ancient, wizened, though that is only because he died an old man. If he had expired in his youth, we'd be looking at a youngster. What we are really observing is an immortal soul, though not of the human variety.

This is a dweebil, one of a long-dead race from the far corners of our own universe. The dweebils are, or rather, were, a theologically challenged people, theologically challenged because, being eminently practical, having a religion never occurred to them. In that, they seemed to subscribe to the adage, "I'll believe it when I see it." Since they'd never seen a god, they never even considered the existence of one.

When the dweebils died, they found themselves in an awkward situation. Turns out, they had immortal souls, but no place to park them. Heaven, taking pity on the dweebils, invited them to move into the Interstices. In gratitude, the newcomers assumed the responsibility for maintaining the outer boundaries of Heaven and Hell, patching an occasional crack in the membrane separating the two from Chaos.

So, the small blue creature at the top of the stairs is a dweebil, and not just any dweebil, but Lord Doofa himself, archdweebil and ruler of his people. Doofa has not heard our arrival, one, because we aren't really there, except in our imaginations, and two, because his attention is focused elsewhere.

His eye is pressed against an ocular device, a lens that has been fitted into a long cylinder made of rosewood, with brass fittings. That cylinder is in turn fitted into a larger cylinder, and that one into one still larger. And on and on.

This device appears to be a gigantic telescope of the refracting variety, but don't be fooled. It is, instead, a Chaos scope, designed for looking into and across the primordial bedlam from which we have just returned.

I wonder if he saw us out there. Probably not, since we weren't really standing in Chaos. Imagination, remember?

"Broot!" curses the old one, as he takes a final look through the scope. Shaking his head, he makes a note in a large ledger that is draped across his lap. "This won't do at all."

The creature slams the ledger shut, pushing it off his lap, until it falls with a thud on the floor. He grabs at a tin can that is suspended by a string above his chair. Pulling the cord taut, he shouts into it. "Dorla! Come here. I want you!"

I'm sure he doesn't mean it in a carnal way.

In moments, the yew door opens then slams shut. Two feet tap out a rapid rhythm on the stairs. In short order, another blue creature has climbed up to the viewing station.

"What is it, Uncle?" she asks, brushing her hair to one side.

"Trouble, my child. Very big trouble. Something has broken."

She turns to go. "I'll just get my tool belt."

"No," he says ruefully. "We'll need more than that."

"Why, Uncle?" She sweeps her hair to one side again, a gesture that in the language of the dweebils imparts to the word "Uncle" considerably more meaning and honor than if it were spoken without a hair swipe. "What has broken?"

He looks worriedly from the scope to his young assistant. "Chaos itself, I'm afraid."

Made in the USA
Middletown, DE
21 June 2020